NIGHTS OF WINTER

CASCADE OF LIES
BOOK 2

Cora Flynn

Content Notice

This book is intended for mature audiences, recommended for readers 18+ years only. It features scenes of recreational and addictive drug use, drugging, graphic depictions of violence, references to past cyberbullying, confinement, profanities, sexual innuendo, and detailed sexual scenes.

It is not considered a dark romance, but readers may encounter some material they may find sensitive. A full description of content can be found at www.coraflynnauthor.com. Take care of yourself, first and foremost! ❤

Nights of Winter is a direct continuation of the Cascade of Lies Series, and it is highly recommended that you read Days of Winter, book 1, before reading this one.

This is a why choose/reverse harem romance novel. The FMC will end up with more than one love interest and will not have to choose between them to find her HEA.

This novel is written in American English by a Canadian author, and the spelling, terminology and grammar have been edited accordingly.

Nights of Winter has been edited multiple times by multiple people, both personally and professionally, but the imperfection of human beings is a beautiful and inevitable thing. If you notice a typo in any form, please contact me at coraflynnauthor@gmail.com with the subject "Typo Found."

Thank you!

xo

Cora Flynn

Acknowledgments

Thank you, once again, my lovely reader, for deciding that the world of Cascade Falls is worth your precious reading time. I had so much fun writing this next installment in Cascade of Lies. I laughed when Shane laughed; I blushed when Drew blushed; I smirked when Travis smirked; I brooded when Cam brooded; I cried when Winter cried; I cursed Logan a few times, and like these wonderful characters between these pages, I grew too.

This book did not get written without the help and support of so very many people.

My husband, who once again indulged me when I lied to us both by saying, "I promise this one won't take as much time as the last one." I too, live in my own Cascade of Lies.

To the lifelong friends I made at 20Booksto50K Indie Author conference; incredible authors who are forging their own paths; you're an inspiration and a guide to me on this journey. Take a look at Lexie Scott, Mercy Desimone, Elle Sparrow, Sarah Storin, and Lynn Larkin's fantastic work. They are my truest accounta-buddies. A special shout-out to Rebecca Quinn, for just being so damn open and kind.

To my reading team: Shelby, Paula, Brianne, and Carrie. Your insight and input made this book what it is; thus far, my greatest creative creation. Thank you for loving this world and these characters as much as I do. You mean the world to me.

To my editor, Lara. Once again, you've brought out the absolute best in my writing. I look forward to book 10, when we can look back on this one and laugh.

To Artscandare Book Cover Designs, for your breathtaking cover. I can't wait to share your final creation for this series with the world. You are incredible at what you do.

To this fantastic wonderful community. Every single author I have reached out to has willingly shared their knowledge and encouragement. It is the most positive creative environment I have ever known.

And to YOU, my lovely reader. Thank you for supporting these make-believe worlds that are living rent-free in my head and the characters that have become my real-world best friends. I hope their lives touch yours as much as they've touched mine.

XO,

Cora

To all the book boyfriends kept on my shelf,
And the toys kept in my drawer

We have quite the collection now,
but let's add a few more

...

For science.

I was freaking the fuck out.

Five hours; it had been five hours since the fight was supposed to be over. Eight hours since I had last heard from anyone.

As staff of the illegal fight night, Travis and Winter hadn't been allowed to have their phones on them, and as an attendee, Drew had to leave his in the car. I had been banking on not being in contact for a few hours.

What I hadn't been banking on was all three of them missing their check-in at midnight, when the fight was supposed to be over.

I hadn't been banking on none of them answering my gazillion texts and probably more phone calls I had made in the past five hours trying to get through to them.

My stomach was in knots, and my body hummed with the sinking feeling of pure dread.

Something was really, really wrong.

It was almost five in the morning and I hadn't slept a wink. I was a hair's breadth away from an epic adrenaline crash, so I pulled myself off my black leather couch to the small galley kitchen to make another pot of coffee. I probably had pure caffeine for blood right now, but I couldn't risk falling asleep until I had heard from somebody.

Anybody.

I was monitoring the local news on television, but Cascade Falls was a tiny mountain town and didn't have a 24-hour news channel like CNN to keep the locals apprised on everyone's business. We just had the local gossipers for that, and they were pretty damn good at their jobs; secrets didn't keep long in our neck of the woods, even if every single one was steeped in lies.

I couldn't count on them to run their mouths this early in the morning, though.

Pacing my apartment, I swept my dark shoulder-length long hair out of my eyes and up into a ponytail, anxiously waiting for the coffee to brew.

What the fuck could I do?

Everyone I trusted with our mission to find out what was going on with Georgio Carlos and the criminal underworld that had saturated our town was underground, in an illegal building hosting illegal activity, surrounded by not-so-nice men. If what they had done to Drew's dad was any sign, I was more than worried about what they might do to the people I loved if they discovered we were spying on them.

This idea had been stupid. Beyond stupid. We were a bunch of college students and twenty-somethings trying to change our tiny part of the world.

I poured a massive cup of coffee and scooped a few teaspoons of sugar into the mug. Normally I drank it black, but I needed the boost from all sides this morning.

I could show up at Bourbon & Blues to see if anyone was there. It was only a twenty-minute drive and at least it would make me feel like I was doing something.

I didn't give the idea another thought. I grabbed my travel mug and keys and ran out the door. I jumped down the two flights of stairs to the parking lot and hopped into my red Dodge truck as fast as I could without spilling coffee all over me. I hadn't grabbed my jacket, though, and I could already feel the February chill saturating my bones.

It wouldn't matter. A big guy like me stayed hot most of the time, anyway. I would survive.

Anxiously, I tapped my fingers on the steering wheel the entire drive, my thoughts racing to Drew, Winter, and Travis — even Cam, who was supposed to be fighting tonight. The likelihood they all wouldn't be able to answer their phones was zip. Nada. Not conceivably possible.

Half-expecting to see a crater where the club sat, I turned the corner down the side street to the club's main entrance. Either aliens or one of America's many enemies had nuked the little jazz club as a big "fuck you" to Uncle Sam; it was the only logical reason I could think of.

What I saw instead was much worse. So much worse.

The club's entrance and the entire parking lot were cordoned off with yellow police caution tape. I counted five officers from the sheriff's department just in my sight line, moving in and out of the front entrance, the flashing lights from their cars lighting up the dark morning sky.

Fuck. *Fuck.*

Were they all in jail? They had to be. That's why they didn't have their phones and I hadn't heard from anyone — they were all in jail.

FUCK.

Mind racing with this recent development, I turned the truck around as inconspicuously as possible and headed back towards Cascade Falls. There was only one way I could confirm this fairly obvious theory, so I pulled onto the shoulder of the road and pulled out my phone.

I dialed the familiar number and held my breath.

"Shane?" The high-pitched croak of my Aunt Donna's voice came through the line. "Do you have any idea what time it is?"

"I know, I'm sorry, Auntie. I would have waited, but I really need your help right now." I smoothed my palms down my pant legs, trying to keep my rising panic at bay.

That got her attention. "What's happened?" she asked, much more alert. "Are you alright? Is Shiloh okay?"

"We're fine, but I can't get a hold of Winter. She was working at Bourbon & Blues tonight. She's a new server there and didn't call me when she got home. She's been radio silent all night, and I just drove by the club and the police are there. I'm worried something's happened to her."

"Oh, honey," my aunt said breathily, her voice softening. "Winter is probably fine. Maybe she took someone home with her, or her phone is dead. I know you two are close but —"

"No," I interjected, more forcefully than I would have liked. "Something is wrong. Can you please use your contacts at the station to check if anyone's reported anything or if she's even there?"

I collected myself.

"I've got this bad feeling in my gut, Auntie. Her spirit is always with me. Something is wrong."

My aunt sighed, and I could picture her rubbing her eyes in the darkness and grabbing her glasses on her nightstand. "Alright then. It's hard to argue with that. I'll see what I can find out."

I breathed a deep sigh of relief. My aunt, Amelia's sister, worked for the Department of Justice and, thanks to the gossip mill throughout all of her contacts, could work out what was happening far faster than I could.

"Thank you." I put as much appreciation and warmth into those words as I could, despite the cold, empty feeling in my heart. "Thank you, thank you. Let me know as soon as you find anything out."

I hung up the phone and sat silently in my truck. It was approaching seven now, and the sun was poking its head out from its bed on the horizon. I blasted the heat and fidgeted while I waited for the call with answers.

I just hoped those answers didn't come with a hell of a lot more questions.

Ring. Ri—

I didn't let my phone get to the second ring. "Whatdidjafindout?" I said in a rush, desperate for any answers at all.

"Honey, I'm sorry," my aunt said placatingly. "There's no sign of Winter at the department. Try calling her in a couple of hours, okay? I'm sure she's fine."

I nodded slowly, before remembering she couldn't see me.

"Thanks," I croaked with panic clawing me apart from the inside. "I'll keep you posted."

I ended the call and stared at my phone through the dim morning light.

Bourbon & Blues had shut down with the sheriff's department acting like the gatekeepers of death. None of my friends were at the station, and they weren't answering their phones.

Where the fuck were they?

CHAPTER 2

DREW

Winter was catatonic.

She hadn't said a word in hours, folding in on herself when we sealed the dark earth-walled room up tight. None of us had spoken a word for a few hours, waiting in the deadened silence in dread someone would find us.

I couldn't imagine which would be worse — Georgio and his men finding us hiding out in here, or Ralph Sutton and his goons at the Sheriff's department.

We were fucked no matter what.

She shivered, and I rubbed my palms down her arms in an attempt to warm her up. It was cold and damp in the cramped space and I had pulled her into my lap a few hours ago after multiple attempts to get her to talk fell flat. I wished Shane was with us. He would know how to get her out of this state. *He* would know how to comfort her.

Travis sat next to me, one of his hands entwined with hers. I had bitten back a bitter comment when he had come over to comfort her too. She had been honest with me about her feelings for him and hadn't shied away from his touch, but I'd be lying if I said it didn't irk me. I guess I was the jealous type. Who knew?

Cam had seated himself against the door, its ancient wooden slab nestled into the dirt walls. He was the biggest of all of us and reasoned if anyone tried to get in here, he could at least hold them off for a bit, maybe let them think there was nothing in here.

Since we hadn't been able to put the metal storage unit hiding the entrance back in place behind us, I doubted we could remain hidden for long, but I held on to a brief glimmer of hope. If I didn't, I would drown in my own catatonic state.

Logan was pacing a hole in the dirt floor on the farthest side of the room. It wasn't that big, maybe the size of a small bedroom, but in the darkness, I could only make out his faint shadow as it moved, the sound of his treads in the dirt softly scraping away at my senses.

What a ragtag bunch of misfits trying to play T-Ball against the Major League. I grimaced at our stupid decisions leading up to this point. As if we had a chance when going up against the biggest organized crime syndicate on this side of the county. I would laugh at the ridiculousness of it all — if I wasn't so sure I would cry first.

Cam flicked on his lighter in the darkness — I was so grateful he had the foresight to grab his sweater in the chaos, otherwise he would be stuck in here wearing nothing but boxer shorts. That lighter in his pocket, though, was our only source of light. Travis had a pack of gum in his pocket, our only source of sustenance if we could call it that, and I only had my wallet, my car keys, and a pack of tissues in mine.

Logan didn't have anything of use in his pockets; just the set of keys to his Audi and what looked to be an absurdly expensive tie clip. Winter had nothing in her pockets, her pants too tight to hold anything in them.

We were all really shitty Boy Scouts.

Cam flicked the lighter again — he was being careful not to burn too much lighter fluid since we had no idea how long we'd be in here — when I noticed the trail of wetness on Winter's cheeks.

"Hey, baby," I said softly, breaking the silence and pulling her tighter into my arms. "It's okay, baby. We are going to get out of here, I promise."

She turned her head into my chest and sniffled, and I felt Travis shift beside me to get closer to her. It took everything in me not to push him away.

"I'm okay," she whispered, her lips barely moving against my chest. "I haven't had a panic attack in a long time."

I had figured that's what it was but had never seen one in action. Travis knew what to do; she had collapsed on the ground as soon as she had made it inside the room, and he had crouched down beside her once the door was fully sealed, walking her through a deep breathing exercise with her eyes closed.

Cam, Logan, and I had stayed silent; there wasn't much we could say or do in this situation, and an unspoken agreement hung in the air that none of us would make a sound out of fear of getting caught.

When she had calmed down, she had laid down on the ground in the fetal position until I pulled her into my arms.

"You've had these before?" Travis murmured quietly, jostling my arms as he squeezed her fingers.

"Yes," she whispered simply, then she pushed up from the ground we were sitting on to stand and stretch out her back and legs.

"Does anyone know how long we've been in here?" she asked into the darkness. "My watch is analog."

I twisted my wrist to light up my digital Timex screen. We'd been in here for almost five hours.

"3:05," I answered, rising to my feet to stretch as well. The ceiling was low in here and my head almost brushed it as I moved about the tiny cavern. "How long do you think we should be in here before we check it out?"

"This place is most definitely swarming with cops." Cam's deep baritone filled the space, despite how quiet he was trying to be. "I'd say we'll have to be in here a while longer yet, if someone don't find us first."

Of course, he would voice what we were all dreading. Unless by some miracle, Shane showed up and rescued all of us under an Invisibility Cloak, we didn't have a hope in hell of making it out of here without serious consequences.

"Fuck this." Logan's smooth anger cut through the darkness. "We have no food, no water, nothing to piss in; I can't stay in here much longer."

His pacing got more aggressive somehow; I could make out the outline of fidgeting limbs as he moved through the darkness, and he kept holding his side at an awkward angle.

That seemed to snap Winter out of her trance. "Please, Logan, if your entitled ass can see a way out of this mess, by all means, share it with the class." Sarcasm dripped through her overly sweet tone.

"I don't like small spaces, okay?" Logan snapped back; his voice now was almost manic. "I fucking hate dark, small spaces."

"No one invited you to come," Cam said, measured and even. "You followed us. Suck it up, Billionaire Boys Club."

"Fuck you, Chase. Use some of that muscle and dig us a tunnel or something," Logan retorted, his trademark arrogance coming to the surface.

Travis held up his hands. At least, that's what I thought he was doing. "Guys, please. Fighting in here isn't going to get us out any faster. Why don't we go over what we all saw tonight?"

"I don't think we should share anything in present company." Winter's voice was cold as ice. I could imagine her expression — I had seen it directed at Logan more than enough times.

She sat back down beside Travis, and he put his arm around her. She didn't push him away like I had hoped, instead she cuddled closer. I sighed and sat down beside her, taking her hand and interlacing our fingers. I guess I was the other guy for the moment. It would take some time to get used to this.

I didn't hate Travis as much as I initially did when I found out he was making the deliveries to the diner. I still didn't like him or fully trust him, but I was grateful he'd had a plan.

As precarious as our situation was, we wouldn't be in a safe space without him; I didn't want to picture what could have happened to Winter otherwise. Someone could have shot, killed, or arrested her. All terrifying scenarios.

Her safety meant more to me than my own. It was why I was willing to share her, however begrudgingly, with the likes of Travis.

"Logan, what's your business with Georgio? Are you with him or against him?" I asked, finally, sick of this back and forth and wanting to feel like we had control over *something* in this fucked up situation.

"If he and I were good buddies, do you think I would be trapped down here with you guys?" Logan's tone sneered, almost louder than his words. "We're business associates."

"That doesn't answer his question," Cam stated flatly. "Are you and Big G in bed together with those businesses? Is that why you were here tonight? Cozying up to the big man to make billions on your billions?"

"Suck a nut, Chase. It didn't stop you from taking my money, did it? Who's in bed with who when *you're* throwing fights for him?"

That was new information. Logan had paid Cam? I didn't know the guy. The first time I had ever seen him was this evening, but I knew Georgio had him in a vise-grip like he had everyone else in here. Well, Logan's ties were still a mystery.

"I didn't spend a cent of your blood money, you insufferable prick. But you're not gettin' it back neither. When we get out of here, I'm donating it to a homeless shelter or something. Balance out the scales of your three houses."

If we hadn't been locked in a dank room three stories underground, I would have loved to watch Cam continually roast Logan. I would have relished in it.

"Logan," Travis interrupted, bringing back the focus of the conversation. "Can you —" He cut himself off.

We all fell silent at a thumping muffled sound of metal beyond the door of our tiny sanctuary. It sharpened all of my senses, and my heart pounded as adrenaline flooded my veins.

I didn't even breathe as I waited for the inevitability of the door opening to reveal us to whoever was on the other side; the only way we *would* know was if we got shot by Georgio, or handcuffed by the authorities.

Ten minutes passed. Twenty. We continued to hear muffled scraping and the sounds of movement, but nothing as close as the first thunk, and eventually the world outside appeared to go still once again.

Winter broke the silence first. "I saw my dad tonight." Her confession came out in the barest of whispers, but it might as well have been a shout in our silent space.

Darren had been at the fight? That was news, alright. It proved Shane's theory all our fathers were more deeply involved with Georgio than we had thought. If Darren was there, I'd bet Emmett most definitely knew about it.

I grimaced as I thought of Mom in that moment. She had no idea where I was and I was supposed to open the diner today. Hopefully, I'd make it out of here alive to explain myself.

Explain myself, as in come up with a believable excuse. As much as she was fully aware of the Georgio situation, she would likely kill me over this. With Dad still in the hospital, I don't know what she would do if I were gone too.

For her sake, and my own, I needed to make it out alive.

Winter's words hung in the air for a moment longer before Travis spoke up.

"I saw that guy from the grocery store talking with Logan most of the night."

Winter's hand gripped mine to the point of pain, and I felt her stiffen in Travis' arms beside me.

"What business do you have with Carson Baker, Logan?" Her tone was almost timid, like saying his name was like saying 'Voldemort.'

Logan stopped pacing for a moment and plopped down on the ground on the other side of Cam. It was the first time he opted to sit since we had sealed ourselves in here. I heard a small gasp, almost as if he were in pain, as he settled on the hard earth.

"He is also a business associate," he said in a clipped tone, fidgeting with his watch while tapping his fingers on his knees. "Not that it's any of your business, Princess.

What, you're not excited to see him again?" His smirk could be heard, if not seen.

"Fuck you, Logan." There was no venom in her words, just a forlorn sense of sadness, and we all fell quiet again.

I had graduated with Carson Baker. He, Logan, and I had all been in the same homeroom class. If memory served, he and Winter had dated briefly in high school but had a falling out. There had been a big rumor going around the school that she had slept with a few guys, but I hadn't paid much attention. I had been working at the diner five days a week at that point and was captain of the football team. I barely had time to socialize, let alone keep up with gossip.

My stomach rumbled, and I was so damn tired. A deep achiness settled into my bones and I shifted my body to lay my head on Winter's shoulder. If we had no hope of getting out of here soon, I might as well try to get some sleep, if that was even possible.

"Here." Winter turned her body to face my own. "You can put your head in my lap."

She gently palmed my face and pressed a chaste kiss to my lips before guiding me down. I settled into the warmth of her thighs. If I wasn't so tired, and we weren't so trapped, and we didn't have an audience, I'd be tempted to do other things, but a quick nap nestled into her body heat was the best I could ask for in these circumstances.

She stroked my hair and softly trailed her fingers through my beard as I drifted off into a dreamless sleep.

CHAPTER 3

LOGAN

I was bleeding through my suit jacket, and eventually, someone was going to notice. That, and I was itching for a fucking fix like my life depended on it.

I could smell the tangy, coppery scent in the air. I couldn't stay standing anymore, even if the pacing had been helping me manage my craving. The ache in my side was raw where the bullet had grazed my skin. It had been too fucking chaotic to notice before I followed Drew through the crowd.

Everyone else had been running in a blind panic, but Drew and Crew were moving like they knew where they were going. Like the opportunistic asshole I was, I took advantage of their exit plan. If we could even call it that.

I fucking *hated* small dark spaces, but I could survive it with the rest of them here with me. Even if they were all twats.

I couldn't say if this outcome was much better than the one that awaited us on the other side of the dirt. I had to piss like a racehorse, my Armani shirt was ruined, and I was slowly losing my mind with the need for a little taste of the good stuff. I guessed, though, it was better than being dead.

When I got out of here, I was going to snort a gram off of Brittney's ass and fuck her raw, and then I was going to swear off the stuff for good. It was controlling me more than I was controlling it, and nothing controlled Logan Eccles. Not anymore.

But I might as well go out with a bang before never enjoying that sweet precious powder again.

I would never admit this to anyone, but I had fucked up; royally fucked up. My insurance plan had come back to fuck me up the ass with a thorny dildo, and I was fucking paying for it. If I had known —

A foot clipped my side. Letting out a hiss of pain, I brought my hand to my rib as my shirt scraped against the open wound.

"Sorry," Drew mumbled, half asleep with his head buried in Winter's lap. Lucky fucker.

"Watch it, Jughead Jones," I snapped, easing back to rest against the dirt wall.

"I think you mean Pop. Pop owned the Chock'lit Shoppe," Cam said dryly, like he was the fucking savant of comic books.

"Shut up, Chase." I sneered into the darkness. I didn't like the guy and his attitude. I hadn't liked him when I had to be in his shitty little sauna of an apartment offering him cash to fix the fight, and the fucker wasn't growing on me. Not one bit.

I breathed in some dirt and immediately sneezed. The motion ripped through my abdomen and I cried out through gritted teeth. "Fuck!"

Winter's outline sat up straight. "Logan, are you hurt?"

"Does my little songbird want to nurse me back to health?" I leered at her through the darkness, unable to help myself. "Come on over here and kiss me better, Princess. Better yet, sit on my lap."

"Fuck off," Drew and Travis said in unison. That made me grin even more.

So, Winter had a little love triangle going on with these two dickwads. I hadn't seen that coming, but I should have known she'd be a sharing little minx. All rumors had some truth to them; it's how I had such a stranglehold on so many people.

A rustling of movement and suddenly she was kneeling in front of me. If I had known she had a Florence Nightingale kink, I would have spoken up about my injuries hours ago.

"Yes, please," I drawled and licked my lips lasciviously. Maybe she could see me, maybe not, but I could see her sexy shadow and the faint lines of expression on her face. Even in the darkness, she was fucking hot.

"Fuck off, Logan," she snapped. Her hands brushed down my shoulders and traced along my arms. "Quick's better at first aid than I am, but I'm all you have at the moment, so put up and shut up."

I let her place her hands all over me. If I wasn't in so much pain, I would have lingered in the feel of her touch. It had been so long since she had been this willingly close.

She let out a soft gasp when her hand gently grazed over the sticky wet patch of fabric clinging to my side.

"You're bleeding!" she exclaimed with what sounded like genuine concern.

"Yeah, I'm bleeding, Princess. I got shot." I wanted to continue to razz her, but I was getting tired of this charade. With the pain and my nerves buzzing, my heart just wasn't in it.

"And you didn't say anything?" Drew asked incredulously. I could envision his pretty boy, goody two shoes face staring back at me.

"No, Jughead," I spat, shooting a glance in Drew's direction, although he couldn't see me. "I didn't. It's just a graze, and I don't think it matters right now, do you? I've survived worse."

Winter unbuttoned my shirt and peeled back the expensive silk fabric from my skin. I sat back and let her be in control; I loved it when she took what she wanted from me. Or at least I had, until her movements pulled at my stomach hair and tore at the slice in my side. I hissed at the contact — it was fucking painful.

"You've survived worse than a gunshot wound?" she murmured to herself as she reached out to Cam for his lighter so she could see. "What kind of secret life are you living, Logan Eccles?"

"I like to live dangerously," I answered simply, knowing I would never be in a state to respond to that question honestly.

Too many secret lives. Maybe I could fake my death out of this situation. I shook off the thought. I was many things, but I wasn't a coward.

"Unfortunately, there's not much I can do about this." Winter sighed and rearranged my shirt back in place, careful this time not to bump the wound. "I have no water to clean it, nothing to disinfect —— but it's not bleeding anymore that I can tell. You're going to want it looked at as soon as we get out of here, though. You're at a high risk for infection down here."

"I'll cauterize the wound for you," Cam said dryly. I threw the lighter at what I hoped was his head. The tight skin on my side pulled and I winced again. I couldn't make any more sudden moves without paying for it.

"Logan." Winter leaned over me. Despite the thick air, she still smelled like lavender and honey. Her body heat radiated towards me, and my cock stirred in my tailored pants. "What were you doing at the fight tonight?"

"What were *you* doing at the fight tonight, Princess? Working for Georgio now, are you? That's not the upstanding Winter I know and want to fuck. And what about you, Johnson? How did a diner-nobody get an invite to one of the most exclusive underground fights in the States? Travis? Does Georgio have dirt on you like he does on Cam, or are you just in it for the thrills like the good little trailer park boy you are?"

The room was dead silent. That's what I thought.

"You want me to confess my sins while you pretend to be God, is that it, Princess? I'll show you mine if you show me yours. And please, *please* show me yours." I grinned at her in the darkness. "Chase, throw that lighter back over so I can get a good look."

"Fuck off," all three men said, and I laughed obnoxiously. This situation was too fucking funny for words.

"I'm ready to talk when you are." Smugly, I shifted myself back against the wall and settling in for the long haul. "We'll get out of here soon enough. But you're getting nothing out of me until you spill first."

CHAPTER 4

WINTER

Twelve hours. We had been trapped underground for twelve hours. I turned Drew's wrist over to read his watch again. Only ten minutes had passed since I had last checked.

What would be going on up above? Surely the place would be one massive crime scene. We had no idea who had been shooting; our best guess was the feds or a rival of Georgio's, but even in the bunker-like atmosphere, a big event like that couldn't go unnoticed, even if Ralph Sutton was dirty.

In fact, he had been there, a detail I had completely forgotten about until that moment. So was the governor. How did they get out? Did they get out? It must be a total clusterfuck up there.

Which didn't bode well for us. We hadn't heard anything else since the muffled thumps hours earlier from beyond our Hobbit hole door, but we all agreed that it was still too risky to peek our heads out to do an actual risk assessment. We didn't trap ourselves in here for hours only to get ourselves caught because of our own stupidity.

Although, I had been questioning our intelligence since the moment the first shot had been fired.

How the fuck were we getting out of this one?

The room had taken on a collective smell. Five bodies trapped in a poorly ventilated room slicked with sweat, fear, and apparently Logan's blood, were enough to taint the already metallic soil scent that permeated the air.

The gloom in here was truly stifling. The air had a density to it that sat on top of all our chests slowly pressing downward until we suffocated completely.

After Logan's ultimatum, everyone clammed up. I was now laying with my head in Travis' lap and my legs draped over Drew. We huddled together to keep warm.

I had draped Logan's suit jacket across his front to keep him warm, ignoring his lewd invitations for me to drape over him instead. Cam insisted he wasn't cold and offered me his sweater. I refused. The man would not sit in a cellar with just shorts on while I wore two layers of clothing. The sentiment was sweet, though. Ever the southern gentleman.

Despite our surroundings and our very obvious predicament, I felt oddly content. I would be lying to myself if I said I didn't really *really* enjoy being between both men. Travis was stroking circles along my spine, and Drew's heavy hands felt like a comforting blanket across my thighs. If we ever made it out of here, I wanted more of this; on my couch, under a blanket, with no clothes, and when my body didn't feel so damn sore.

The panic attack earlier had ridden through me like a freight train. My limbs still felt heavy and spent, while my brain still felt gauzy and slow. My last panic attack had been when I was eighteen; I had hoped it would be the last one.

I couldn't pinpoint the trigger. It could have been my nerves, or the constant feeling of being watched, or seeing Dad, or the gunshots — I rolled back my thoughts. Dad.

My stomach churned with the thought of my father sitting cozily in a black suit and tie next to a beautiful blonde woman in a deep purple cocktail dress.

I couldn't claim I was close with my parents. How could I be when they barely acted like they wanted to be a part of my life? I never in my wildest dreams would have predicted Dad would be a willing attendee to an illegal boxing match while cheating on my mother.

Gross, gross, gross.

My upstanding citizen, hardworking father had a lot of explaining to do. Except, to confront him, I'd have to admit I had been there, too. I could only hope he never saw me.

Did he make it out? Was he hurt or arrested right now?

God, what about Quick? He would be killing himself with worry and guilt right now. He would take all the blame for this plan going awry, even though none of us in a million years could have predicted this outcome.

Maybe we should have? The Scooby Doo crew didn't know what the fuck we were doing. That much was obvious.

"I think we should check it out." Logan's tenor filled the silence, and it shocked me out of my quiet contemplation. "I can't stay in here for much longer. I need a piss. I'm starving, and if I have to smell you guys much longer, I'd rather be in lockup."

The man had a Ph.D. in assholery.

"I actually think that's a good idea." Travis spoke up behind me, and I turned to peer at him.

"We can't stay down here for much longer," he explained, moving his fingers up to stroke my hair. "Our families are going to be worried; we really don't know if or when someone will find us, and I don't think it's a good idea for Logan to go much longer without getting that wound tended to."

"Thank you, someone is talking sense over here," Logan said triumphantly, but his voice lacked its usual arrogance. Instead, he sounded erratic and tense. Maybe his body was going into shock? I sat up and moved towards him to check his pulse.

It was low; I counted 56 beats per minute. I checked again.

"Do you normally have a low heart rate?" I asked casually, trying to gauge him in the inky black.

He brusquely shrugged me off. "I'm fine, Princess. Like Travis said, I need some medical attention. I can be the one to go."

"Like fuck," Cam drawled from his position at the door. "You're injured and will probably get us all caught. I'll go."

"I actually think it would be better if Drew and I went."

Travis shifted from his position and stood.

"Cam, you're the strongest and could help carry Logan once we find a path out. You can also protect Winter."

"Unless he's protecting me from vicious moles or Logan, I don't see how that's relevant right now," I shot back.

I didn't want them making their decisions based on who needed to protect me, like I was some damsel in distress. Given I had succumbed to a panic attack just hours ago, I probably wasn't going to be very useful; that, I had to admit.

Given none of us had slept in the past twenty-four hours, other than the twenty minute cat nap Drew got in my lap, I couldn't see how *any* of us were going to be very useful, but I didn't enjoy being the one singled out.

"Travis is right. It should be the two of us who go." Drew stood as well, and the two tall men's shadowy outlines loomed over us more ominously than a Dean Koontz novel.

I leaned against the wall next to Logan and sighed. My deep labored breath released as much of the fear from my body as it would allow. Travis *was* right.

He was the unofficial leader tonight. He had led us to temporary safety, thanks to his foresight and quick thinking, and if I had to believe that anyone could do it again, it would be him. He knew the layout of the building and all the exits; we might have a hope in hell, if he would take the risk.

"Okay, what is the plan? I can't let you leave us here without knowing exactly what you're going to do. My nerves won't be able to take it," I joked, but it was a weak one.

"The hallway we came through leads to three more hallways within twenty feet of this room." Travis' words were soothing and patient. "Two of them lead deeper into the bunker, but the third one leads to a small serving stairwell that enters the kitchen at Bourbon & Blues. I don't think it's been used for years by the amount of spider webs and broken steps there are. Drew, you're barely going to fit, but it's our best chance."

"And then what?" I prompted. "You guys see if the coast is clear and then come back for us? What happens if you get caught? How are we going to know?"

Drew removed his watch and handed it to me. The heavy plastic of the Timex was dead weight in my hands.

"If we're not back in eight hours, you'll have to decide what you're going to do." Drew cupped my cheek and brought his face close to mine until my gaze was level with his hazel eyes. "We won't be able to contact you, but we'll sneak back in for you before then, if we're able to make it out."

"Can one of you call Quick as soon as you're topside?" I brought my fingers up to trace the outline of Drew's dirty blonde beard, indulging in the tickle of its short bristles against my fingertips. "He's going to be beside himself."

"Of course," Drew promised. "He's been on my mind, too."

"Here." Logan tossed a key ring towards Travis that he barely caught in midair. "Grab my phone from my car. It's linked to my watch, so you should be able to give us a head's up when you're on your way. I'm parked two blocks away on Aspen Street."

He surprised me by his amicable tone, but then, apparently, he just couldn't help himself.

"Just hurry the fuck up."

Drew rolled his eyes and pulled me into his arms, enveloping me in his warmth. He still smelled faintly of citrus and cinnamon underneath all the scents in the small space and I took comfort in him one last time.

My blond protector tilted my chin up with his thumb and brought his lips to mine for a deep, languid kiss. He took his time, his lips soft and pliant, coaxing me to open up to him.

There was a promise in that kiss; a promise to keep me safe.

Far too soon, he pulled back and let me go. I mourned the protective cocoon he had just wrapped me in. Then Travis stepped in, his large hands tentatively resting on my waist.

He was being cautious. I had told him I wasn't sure if we could ever go back to where we had been before his lies, and he honored that.

None of that mattered now. When push came to shove, I cared about this man, and I needed him to come back to me safely, regardless of our history.

I brought my own, smaller hands to my waist and unwrapped each one of his, bringing them around my body into a loose hug instead.

"Kiss me." The words came out on a soft breath, sounding more like a plea than a command. "Kiss me and tell me you'll get us out of this mess, Travis. I trust you."

In the dim light I could see what saying those words meant to him. A slow, unencumbered grin consumed his features and I couldn't help but return it. Two smiling fools in one somber situation.

The words were the truth. I did trust him. If we got out of here, we could start mending what had broken between us. But there could be no more lies, and I would need the entire story of how he had gotten into bed with Georgio in the first place.

He tightened his arms around me to where it almost hurt and burrowed his head into my surely disgusting hair. I could feel his chest expand as he breathed me in, and felt the pounding of his heart against my chest. Maybe it was my heart pounding. I couldn't be sure.

He kissed the skin on the underside of my ear; it was just a gentle, reverent touch of lips to flesh, but it sent a shiver of desire through me. His lips trailed featherlight kisses up my jaw, and when he finally reached my lips, his kiss turned hard, almost ferocious.

I could feel the release of pain and the force of his own promise in that kiss. His promise was one of hope for a future.

I let him guide the kiss entirely, parting my lips to feel his hot tongue explore me. It was a very inopportune time to feel my panties dampen.

He softened the kiss and then pulled away, placing one last chaste kiss to the tip of my nose.

"We'll be back for you, I promise."

He let go of me and I gingerly sat back down beside Logan. Cam had stood to help Drew with the door while Travis and I had been having our moment.

The faint thud of wood against earth resounded through our protective cave; dirt and dust particles rained down from the loose door frame. Although the door had only opened an inch or two, the room flooded with light. I had to close my eyes at the sudden brightness.

We all stayed silent, listening for any sounds beyond the door into the storage room.

Nothing. Not even the rustling of the ventilation shaft or the skitter of a cockroach.

Faint scents of smoke and what resembled the powdered residue from a bar fog machine came through, but the fresher air of the next room was invigorating.

"Okay," Travis whispered as he turned back to us. "Eight hours, max. We'll see you guys soon. Cam, close the door behind us."

He opened the door just enough to slide through the crack, and he was gone.

Drew gave me one last look, his concerned features finally visible. I gave him a weak smile in return.

"Go. Be my knight in shining armor, Hardy Boy."

He nodded, his facial expression serious and determined. He pushed the door open a little more to make it through. Then the two men disappeared into the great unknown.

CHAPTER 5

TRAVIS

It was eerily quiet throughout the bunker. All the lights were still on and cast an ominous glow. It made me think of the zombie apocalypse movies Devon and I would watch as kids, where the heroes would be creeping through an abandoned hospital only to be attacked by some bloody, headless skeleton creatures when they turned the corner.

My skin prickled with unease with every step down the concrete hall. We had to move on silent feet as quickly as we could. At my back, Drew followed my every footstep. He was light on his feet despite his size. He had the build of an athlete, but I really knew nothing about him other than in the time I had been away from Winter, he had captured her heart.

My stomach curdled at the faint image of her kissing him back with such passion. The buzzing in my veins only calmed when she had let me kiss her that way too. I had no idea what that meant for us, or for Drew. I shook my head. Three stories underground in stealth mode was not the time to be thinking about our apparent love triangle.

We turned the corner where the hallway narrowed into a tight passageway. The door to the stairwell was on my right. I motioned for Drew to stay close.

I stood still and listened, really listened, to the environment around me. It remained silent save for the soft sounds of Drew and I breathing. I would have expected something, any noise, after the chaos of the raid, but the place might as well have been a tomb. It was unsettling.

I turned the door handle slowly, the sound of its creaky hinges filling my ears. I held my breath, waiting for someone to race around the corner pointing a gun at us. When no one came, I eased open the door and entered the tiny corridor, closing it tightly behind Drew as he took up all the room behind me.

The steps were the old wooden ends of rail ties, embedded into caked mud and rotting in many places. Based on their condition, they couldn't have been used for Georgio's purposes, or if they had, just barely. I couldn't believe my luck when I had stumbled across it during my "get myself out of jail" treasure hunt. Thank fuck, I had.

There had only been three wall sconces along the path when I first discovered the stairwell and they weren't on now. I wouldn't risk getting us caught by daring to find a switch, so we'd have to fumble our way in the dark. I was going to get one of those cheap keychain penlights as soon as we were safely a hundred miles away from this place.

Deliberately and carefully, we ascended the stairs. Time was of the essence, but we'd be useless if we broke our necks trying to get out of this temple of doom.

Logan was in withdrawal; I was sure of it. From what, I didn't know, but I had seen Devon go through the symptoms more times than I could count, and if he was bleeding on top of it, I didn't want to leave Winter in there with him any longer than she had to be.

I trusted Cam with my life. He would keep her safe from anybody who would try to hurt her. At the moment, I couldn't be sure which category Logan fell into. He was a major dick, but Winter seemed to hold her own against him. I smiled slightly at that. I liked when her feisty side came out.

I didn't like when she fell apart, and I was helpless to save her. Her panic attack had shown me a completely new side of Winter Wallace; a side I wanted to protect and cradle in my arms until she didn't have a tear left in her.

A sound grabbed my attention when we were about halfway up the stairwell. I froze in place, Drew did the same behind me. My heart-rate skyrocketed when I heard the thump again. It was coming from below us.

Adrenaline flooded my core, and I picked up speed, taking the steps three at a time with little regard for my neck being broken when there was a possibility that I could end up thoroughly dead at the hands of whoever was trying to get in downstairs.

Drew followed my lead and didn't hesitate, his footsteps still impossibly soft as we raced up the last flight.

At the top step, the shadowy outline of the door loomed over us. It led to an old pantry at the back of the Bourbon & Blues kitchen. I took a breath, then gently turned the knob.

The door made a soft crackling sound, but eased open. I quickly stepped in and closed the door behind Drew, motioning for him to wait on the other side of it.

If we had someone following us, we could surprise them when they made it to the top. Two men wouldn't have a huge advantage over someone if they had weapons, but I could hold my own in a fight. I had a feeling Drew could too, if they forced him into it.

Something told me violence wasn't his thing.

We waited for five minutes — ten. When we didn't hear another sound and it felt safe enough to abandon the bogeyman in the closet, I turned my sights on the path ahead. We were nowhere near out of the woods.

I listened again, but still heard nothing. We crept through the doorway and into the main kitchen space. Still nothing. No voices, no music, only the hum of the commercial refrigerators and the whoosh of the overhead ventilation.

One of the staff exits was just beyond the corner. I peered out a galley window in the door and saw ... nothing. Nothing out of the ordinary, anyway.

It was the middle of the day, a gloomy one at that, snowflakes falling across a gray backdrop. The view from this side of the club was just a community park and the half-empty parking lot of a nearby apartment building, beyond the chain-link fence of the alley.

When I slowly pushed open the door, no alarm sounded. No one came running to handcuff us in place. Nothing.

It all seemed far too easy, and yet, I couldn't shake the zombie apocalypse feeling in my gut.

The frigid air hit me in the face like one of Cam's punches. The lightweight dress shirt I wore was now soaked through with layers of sweat, dirt, smoke, and dust, and not nearly warm enough to combat the cold.

If we were out here too long, I'd lose my fingers to frostbite.

I shimmied myself along the brick wall of the alley, and peered around the corner where the front of the club faced the street. Yellow caution tape lined the front walk and the stairs leading up to the entrance, and two squad cars with lights flashing had parked in front of the building, blocking off the street.

Shit.

Not unexpected, but a new shiver of fear coursed through me as I considered the ramifications of getting caught with Winter and Cam still trapped downstairs.

I motioned for Drew to turn back. There was another exit at the rear of the building; we would have to climb a section of chain-link to get through, but there was still no sign of anyone, so if we hurried, we could probably get out unseen.

I was banking on that thought while I quickly scaled the fence as quietly as possible. The chains rattled under my feet, but the surrounding snowfall muffled the sound. The skin nearly ripped off of my hands when it stuck to the freezing metal and I hissed at the contact. A bloody handprint stood out on the railing. We'd have to wash that off before we all got out of here for good.

Once on the other side, I did another assessment. This rear parking lot had three dumpsters and a few abandoned cars. Still no bodies, living or otherwise, to be found.

It was midday on a Sunday in an industrial area of town, so the quiet wasn't unusual; it was just a stark contrast to the night we had experienced before.

Drew landed on his feet beside me.

"Okay." I turned to him and crouched low beside the dumpster that would block us from any outsider's view. "Where are you parked?"

"I'm a few blocks away," Drew admitted, tucking his bare hands underneath his armpits. "I have my keys, though."

"Okay." I nodded. "Let's get to Logan's car first. Once we're a block away, no one is going to notice us. I'll grab his phone and you can go to your car. Grab your phone and call Shane. All of my stuff is still in my locker at Bourbon & Blues, so I won't be able to get my car keys or my phone yet. Neither will Cam or Winter."

Fuck. That was going to complicate things. I could hot-wire mine and Winter's cars, thanks to the fact that they were old and not drivable computer systems, but not having our phones was going to be a challenge.

Once this clusterfuck was over, I needed to check in on Mom.

"It's still pretty quiet around here," I continued, standing quickly to take another look around, a plan forming in my mind.

"I can sneak back in and get back into the stairwell. You'll need to text Logan, so he'll get the message on his watch when I'm on the way down, and they can be ready for me. You and Shane can be waiting to pick us up. Park on Aspen by Logan's car. I can send you a message as soon as we get to the top of the stairs."

"I have Logan's number already, so that'll work. I'll get Shane to grab a few blankets and some food and water," Drew said solemnly, squinting around the dumpster to peer into the gloom. "We'd better get moving or I'm going to lose my fingers."

"Be safe." I nodded to him and crouched low around the dumpster, angling my body to see as much as I could of the parking lot without exposing myself. I took off into the wooded park as soon as I saw the coast was clear, only looking back once to see Drew heading in the opposite direction.

Once the building was out of sight, I slowed my pace and took a deep breath. I was freezing, and the adrenaline that had flooded my veins just minutes before was crashing, but I had to keep going. I could collapse once we were all home and safe.

Logan's Audi was easy to find, its shimmery silver paint job a stark contrast to the dull grays of the winter's day. I clicked the unlock button and slid into the buttery leather seat. The soft material molded to my body while I turned on the car and blasted the heat. I wouldn't be able to save anyone if I had hypothermia.

Of course, his car would be the nicest thing I had ever touched. If I wasn't so cold, I would have rolled my eyes.

I found the phone in the center console, along with a small baggie of white powder.

My instincts had been right. Our millionaire pain in the ass was a cocaine addict.

The sense of urgency to get Winter away from him as soon as possible hit me hard, and I rubbed my fingers together, then turned up the heated seat to get the blood back into my extremities.

Once I felt warm enough to move again, I looked around the car for a jacket or something to keep the cold at bay. A pair of expensive leather gloves with sheep's wool lining had been stuffed into the side door pocket.

Perfect. I'd be keeping these.

I grabbed the phone, put on the gloves, and turned off the car, glancing around the street before stepping out into the arctic chill once again.

It was time to rescue my girl.

CHAPTER 6

CAMERON

I needed a cigarette.

The nicotine itch had worn on me, and I was getting restless.

I flicked the lighter against my palm, partially for warmth, partially to see into the Hobbit hole we were calling our sanctuary. Sanctuary or prison; after fifteen hours holed up in here, I couldn't be sure which.

I was not a small man and the dampness of the earth and the cool air chill had seeped into my bones. Thankfully, Winter still had Drew's jacket to keep her warm, and Logan had his suit jacket. I didn't like the asshole, but I didn't want him to die on my watch either.

Winter had checked his heart rate twice in the last hour and both times, it was below 60. He was twitchy and irritable. Maybe that was just his regular personality. I didn't know, but he seemed pretty smooth and sure of himself when he offered me a boatload of money to win the fight for him.

Billionaire Boys Club probably wasn't used to being uncomfortable.

I flicked the lighter again. The flame cast a bright glow in front of my face and in the shadow beyond, I could see Winter burrow further into the coat, wrapping her arms around her knees.

"Hey, sugar," I said softly, careful to keep my voice low. "Come on over here and I'll keep you warm, okay? No need to shiver alone."

I cringed after saying those words, not intending to proposition her. "I meant nothing by that, sugar. I just want to keep you comfortable, okay?"

I heard the rustling of her standing, then her shadow sat beside me.

"It's okay," she whispered. "I didn't take it that way. You're not Logan."

I could hear the smile in her answer through the darkness, and I smiled back, even if she couldn't really see it.

"Definitely ain't Logan." I said with a quiet laugh. "Why don't you sit in front of me and I can keep you warm that way? Is that okay?"

She hesitated for a second and then shuffled along the dirt floor. I adjusted my position and opened my legs so she could sit between them. I wrapped my arms around her slight frame and pulled her body back tight to mine. She fit into me like a perfect little puzzle piece.

"That better?" I whispered, my lips unintentionally grazing the tip of her ear.

She shuddered slightly, and the primal part of me preened inside my chest. I would be lying if I said I wasn't pleased I had this effect on her.

I was trying real hard to ignore the effect she had on me.

"Better." She sighed and her body relaxed into mine, then she laid her head back onto my shoulder.

I was so much taller than her and my broad frame draped over her like an oversized blanket. The chill was easing in my bones too; another bonus of having her close.

"Oh, fuck off," Logan snarked from his corner of the room. "Is everyone riding the Winter bicycle?"

I saw red at his statement. An intense desire to pound him into the dirt and make him bleed more than he already was rose to the surface.

"Logan." I growled as the deep need to protect this woman forced the words through my teeth. "If you disrespect her again, I'll rip each one of your limbs off, one by one, and stuff them down your throat. Don't make me tell you twice."

"Yeah, sure," the Prince of Prickness muttered darkly, who was evidently smarter than he looked. "And I won't even be getting my money back, either. Asshole."

I grinned into the dark, not dignifying his retort with a response.

My Rising Tide of Rage was disappearing as fast as it had come. I was glad it was fading quickly this time. I had no time to battle my demons while waiting for Travis and Drew to come back.

My muscles were cramping badly from lack of hydration after the exertion of the fight. We had got one and a half rounds in before they had fired the shots. Whoever 'they' were.

What was a routine fight night had turned into one of the biggest shit shows of my life, and that was saying something.

The thirst for bloodlust in the air had vanished as soon as the first crack broke through the noise. I had dropped and rolled immediately on the mat, trying to find Travis through the chaos.

He had planned for a moment like this. If he hadn't, I could be dead right now.

The aching muscles, the intense pressure to piss, and the longing for an ice-cold bottle of purple Gatorade were well worth the discomfort of being alive.

I was confident Travis would get us out. My best friend was resourceful and always did everything in his power to care for the ones he loved. The guy had a savior complex that would need some therapy to work out, but at least it would serve us now.

I hoped.

Winter had gone quiet in my arms, and it took me a minute to realize she had fallen asleep.

How about that?

Another satisfied preen pricked my chest. She had felt comfortable and safe enough with me to fall asleep in my arms. That, or she was so exhausted she didn't have any control over her faculties.

I was going with the first reason.

My fingers absently stroked through her hair as her gentle breathing filled the silence.

I didn't want to utter the words aloud, but the raid had been sent from an angel, if I were to believe everything my momma had. It was nice to pretend sometimes.

I had planned on throwing the fight, just like Georgio told me. It had tempted me, oh, had I ever been tempted to say "fuck you Big G," and win it on my mettle.

I wanted to show that man he didn't own me like he seemed to think he did. Maybe I was the disillusioned one.

I wanted to win, to take Logan's money and spend it on something to help my poorer-than-sin neighborhood, my own sorry version of Robin Hood. Although, I had a feeling he was saving a hell of a lot more by paying me $25K to win.

I had known no one with money, and it made my skin crawl to see how some people had that kind of cash just lying around.

I'd wanted to help Travis' friend too, although seeing them interact tonight was more like 'rival lovers' than friends; that had been an interesting triangle to witness.

I looked down at the pretty angel in my arms and pulled her a little tighter to my chest, craving the warmth and softness of her body.

I shouldn't be holding her like this. She wasn't mine to hold.

She was Travis' girl. Apparently, Drew's too. I didn't want to become a corner of a love square, even if that was something people did.

I was no stranger to unconventional sex. The wild, untamed man in me relished in it, but I liked to play in an environment where I knew the rules. Hell, I liked an environment where I *made* the rules. I didn't know what the hell this was. Or what it could be.

But I sure enjoyed having her tucked into my body and snuggled into my chest like no other man owned her. I was honest enough to admit that.

"You were never going to throw the fight for me, were you?"

Logan's clipped voice broke our peaceful silence, and I mourned its passing.

"I didn't have a choice." I weighed my words carefully. "And if you were offering me money to win, sounds like you're just as owned by him as I am."

That bought me another few moments of quiet.

"What would it take to break his hold on you?" His question was oddly thoughtful, no trace of his usual pompous air.

"I dunno," I answered truthfully. "What price would you pay for the same privilege?"

He fell quiet again, and the three of us melted into the shadows of the dark room, save for shallow breathing and the stink of fear, sweat, and dirt.

By now, it had been sixteen hours.

I said a prayer to high heaven Travis would be back soon.

CHAPTER 7

SHANE

The sound of the phone ringer made me shoot up from the couch. I had set the volume to full blast to make sure I didn't miss a single message or call, just in case anyone finally called me back.

I looked down at my rumpled cotton shirt and felt the crusting drool on the side of my cheek and wrinkled my nose. Despite the two pots of coffee I had chugged in the past fifteen hours, I had fallen asleep.

I blearily fumbled around the couch cushions in search of my phone. I couldn't remember the last time I had set my phone to anything but silent, and the shrill, tinny music assaulted my senses.

What time was it? I looked at my watch and sluggishly wiped my face with my hand.

4:17 pm.

Fuck.

I found the source of noise crammed between my ass and the flattened cushion. I practically jumped off the couch when I saw Drew's face on my screen. My fingers worked far too slowly in pressing the "accept call" button.

"Holy fuck. Are you guys alright? Is Winter alright? What happened? Where are you?" I said in a rush, not waiting for him to give me a greeting.

"Hey, buddy." Drew answered in a tired but patient voice. "Not a lot of time to explain, but can you get to Bourbon & Blues as soon as possible? We're going to need some food, water, and blankets. Just grab whatever you have at home. We don't want to waste any time."

I was immediately alert; the twelve cups of coffee had nothing on the adrenaline now coursing through my veins.

"Done." I replied. Already I was moving to grab the duvet off of my bed and the soft throw blanket Snow had insisted I keep here for our movie nights.

"Thanks, man," Drew said with a sigh. "It's been a long night." I could practically feel his weariness through the line.

"Can I get a little more information, at least? I've been worried sick over here." I reached into my fridge for a few bottles of water, juice, and Gatorade, tossing them into the collapsible cooler bag I used for rugby.

After Aunt Donna had confirmed Winter wasn't at the station, I had wracked the depths of my brains to come up with any likely scenarios for the evening. Knowing what we knew about Georgio, none of them were good.

If they weren't at the sheriff's station, they were being held by someone else, or hiding somewhere.

Travis knew there would be security measures for weapons and cell phones, but surely someone could have bypassed those if they were crafty enough. That thought had nearly killed me with anxiety; I had driven back to Sheldonville and spent a solid hour lurking on the side streets of Bourbon & Blues, peering through the trees of the park and trying to see if anything was amiss.

A useless exercise really, since I had only ever been there once. The place was crawling with the sheriff's department outside, and what the hell would I have been able to do even if I saw something?

I looked into the public archives to see if the schematics of the building were on file. I had access to the digital files through WAQ. Bourbon & Blues was in a historical property from the 1800s once used as a prohibition storage facility for gangs of old. That was one of its 'claims to fame' when the club opened.

Not that I knew it at the time. I was only fifteen, but when I found out Winter had been working there secretly for two years, I researched the shit out of the place.

A bunker showed on the old blueprints, but the revised documents submitted for permits fifty years later showed that part of the building filled with cement and sealed shut.

Falsified documents based on what Travis had told us, so that had been a dead end.

I had desperately needed a joint to calm my nerves, but hadn't risked it in case I got a call. I thanked past me for that decision.

Drew broke through my thoughts while I was grabbing a box of crackers and a handful of protein bars from my cupboard.

"Long story short, there was a raid or attack at the fight, and we found someplace to hide. Travis and I made it out to get reinforcements. Winter, Cam, and Logan are still down there."

I stilled. "You left her down there?! What the fuck, Drew?"

My body flooded with anger and indignation, knowing she was still trapped. And why was Logan with them?

"It was the best decision at the time, man. We needed to make sure we could get out safely without getting caught." His tone wasn't defensive, but it was firm. On a softer note, he added. "I care about her too, you know."

By now, I had everything thrown into my cooler bag. I strapped it to my back, grabbed the blankets under one arm, and took off down the hallway of my apartment building, phone still to my ear.

"I know, man, I'm sorry. If anything ever happened to her ..." My voice trailed off and I swallowed the lump in my throat. I couldn't even consider that possibility. "Hell, if anything ever happened to *you*..."

"I get it," Drew said, and I heard his car engine starting in the background. "We're all okay, but Logan is hurt. Is your first aid kit in the truck? He's going to need it."

"Yup, it's fully stocked too." I was at said truck by now, dumping the contents of my arms into the back cab before jumping in the front seat to start the vehicle.

It was another freezing day, but the roads were clear, so I'd be able to punch it to Bourbon & Blues. I figured I could be there in fifteen minutes if I pushed the old girl.

"I'm on my way. I'll meet you on Aspen in fifteen or less." I clipped on my seatbelt and peeled out of the parking lot.

"Okay, man. See you soon."

I ended the call and sped along the highway, passing the Sunday drivers a bit too aggressively. The past twenty-four hours had felt like a lifetime, and I would not sleep tonight without Winter tucked into my arms. Hell, Drew could join us in one big snuggle-party. I needed the reassurance they were alive, and safe, and mine.

I don't even remember the drive; autopilot saved me from my spiraling thoughts as I pulled onto the quiet side street at the edge of the industrial park of Sheldonville. Drew's Corolla and Logan's Audi were inconspicuously parked a few driveways from each other.

I parked on the opposite side of the road and leapt out of the truck. This neighborhood was extremely quiet; not a single person was present on the street.

Drew got out of his car and I was beyond relieved to see the tall blonde bastard. He definitely looked worse for wear in a wrinkled dark blue dress-shirt and pants, and his dress shoes were dirty and totally impractical for the day's chill, but he was a true sight for sore eyes.

I couldn't help myself. When he was within arm's reach, I pulled him in for the biggest bear hug I could muster. He wasn't a small man, and we were close to the same height, but I was bigger, and I crushed him to me. The swirl of relief to see my friend safe and alive almost brought tears to my eyes, and I pulled back to look at him fully.

"Thank fuck, you're okay."

He smiled, the corners of his hazel eyes crinkling, despite the exhaustion and worry clouding them.

"I'm glad you're here, man." He let go of me and motioned to my truck. "Can we get warm in there while we wait? Travis should already be working his way back down to get them out of there."

I nodded. "Sure, tell me what's been going on while we're waiting."

Once inside, with the heat on full blast, and after Drew had guzzled a bottle of water and devoured a protein bar in two bites, he told me everything.

The shots and smoke bombs. Travis' escape route. The hours inside the cellar room with no idea what was going on. Logan's injury. Winter's panic attack. How they escaped.

Eventually, we went silent, the buzz of edgy anticipation too much to spend any more time talking. Drew had already sent the text to Logan's phone and Travis should already be down in the room. Hopefully, we'd get a text any minute to confirm they were on their way up.

I knew one thing for sure. When Winter was back in my arms, I was never letting her go again.

Then we were going to figure out what the fuck was going on.

CHAPTER 8

WINTER

I awoke enveloped in the muted scent of sandalwood and something distinctively manly, cocooned in body heat and hard muscle.

It was comforting and disorienting; I was so damn exhausted I could have stayed in Cam's safe embrace for the rest of my life, but I couldn't avoid our circumstances any longer. I was grateful to have found a few moments of sleep, though.

I shifted my weight and Cam stirred behind me, his corded biceps tightening their hold around my body. From the sounds of his soft, measured breaths, he had fallen asleep too.

Our hands had entwined in my lap, and his calloused grip held me firmly in place. Somewhere in our dreams, we had clung to each other in every way we could find.

"Hey, Big Guy," I whispered softly, my voice crackling and croaky from lack of use. "I need to check on Logan. Any word from the guys yet?"

"Soon," Cam muttered, his own voice draggy from the stupor of sleep. "Should be here soon."

I gently pushed away from his solid form and unwrapped myself from the safe little haven in the corner of our cave. Immediately, I missed his warmth.

What time was it? I checked the watch Drew had given me, now loosely fastened to my wrist. 3:57 pm. Almost seventeen hours had passed. As if to remind me of the sheer length of time without food and water, my stomach let out an aggressive growl.

When we got out of here, I was eating a whole pizza, gooey with too much cheese and smothered in olives and pepperoni. *And* a cake. I had to stop thinking about food.

"Cam, can you flick the lighter for me?"

I moved in Logan's direction, barely seeing the outline of his body on the ground. He had laid down during the time I had fallen asleep, and I could hear soft snores coming from the other side of the room.

I wanted to make sure the wound on his side wasn't getting worse. He wouldn't have told me if it had; the stubborn bastard wasn't interested in telling us anything tonight, apparently, but I couldn't just let him die.

Perhaps that was a tad dramatic, but who knew after this clusterfuck of a night?

I heard the familiar metallic click behind me and the soft yellow glow at my back gave structure to the vague shadow in front of me. I sat down beside him, careful not to jostle his body and hurt him even more.

"That'd better be you, Princess, and not Donkey Kong." Logan's eyes remained closed, and his voice was strained, a higher pitch than usual, but no less arrogant and bratty.

"I think you mean Mario, Billionaire. Donkey Kong doesn't have a princess," Cam said dryly, although there was a tinge of amusement beneath his tone.

"I meant what I said. 'Crash, Bang, Boom.' You're Donkey Kong, alright. Why don't you crash us out of here?"

"Glad to see you're not losing your charm, Logan," I chided and eased him upright in front of me. I raised my hand to feel his forehead; his skin was clammy, but he wasn't feverish.

"Can I check your pulse again?" I moved my hands to his neck, searching for the pulsing artery beneath my touch.

Cam had moved beside me so I could see better in the glow of his lighter. Logan's rich brown eyes reflected the light of the flame and stared back at me, lacking their usual depth of devious disdain.

"Why are you helping me, little princess? Do you get off on nursing knights in shining armor back to health?" He was attempting his usual brand of asshole humor, but it fell flat since he listlessly sat there while I counted his beats per minute.

Still, I snorted. "I don't think anyone could confuse you for a knight in shining armor, Logan."

Fifty eight beats. How was this man still living? I needed to check it again to be sure.

"But, although you are an expert asshole, I don't want to see you die. Can I check your wound?"

It wasn't the best idea, moving the material to expose it to the air in the cellar once again. With dirt and dust and God knew what else down here, I still selfishly needed to set my mind at ease.

He nodded, so I pushed the suit jacket hanging loosely from his shoulders away and unbuttoned his shirt from the bottom up. The bullet had grazed the soft flesh underneath his ribs and just above his hip bone. He was very lucky—had it been an inch to the left, the bullet would have hit an organ and he would be lying dead upstairs instead of holed up in here with us.

I didn't want Logan Eccles to die. I wouldn't have minded if someone gave him herpes or something, though. Because, karma.

"Cam, can you bring the light down toward his hip?" I asked, as I peeled the sticky fabric from Logan's skin. We had been using the lighter as sparingly as we could until now. Now, we held onto the hope we were getting out as soon as possible.

And if we weren't, it wouldn't be the lighter that would save us.

It was two hours since Travis and Drew had left; maybe three. It was all a distorted haze at the moment. I had faith they'd be here before the eight hours were up. Travis would come for us. Drew wouldn't give up on us.

I gasped when Cam shined the light on Logan's exposed hipbone. The bullet graze was already scabbing over, the lymph fluid had glazed the wound to seal it shut; hopefully with minimal bacteria under there. It was a red and angry mark, but it wasn't infected as far as I could tell.

What I wasn't prepared for the was the large, raised imprint of scar tissue creeping around his exposed hipbone from his back.

The scar looked old, but the injury must have been brutal. It was in the oddly familiar shape of a metal belt buckle. Before he could stop me, I pushed his shirt back further and glimpsed his back. His well-defined muscles and hairless skin couldn't hide the number of similar scars scattered along the edge of his lower back and torso.

I froze in place as realization hit.

I could feel Logan's glare on me before I saw it. He yanked his shirt back over his side with jumpy, erratic movements, and moved to button it up again when I placed a hand over his.

"Who hurt you?" I murmured quietly, the uncomfortable recognition now a secret we shared.

"No one fucking hurt me, Winter." Logan practically spat the words, pushing my hand away and finishing the task of putting his shirt back on. "I have birthmarks. Even the wealthy aren't perfect, even if I seem that way."

His arrogance was back, but his usual self-important smirk didn't meet his eyes. I was seeing the bitter words he was constantly biting us with for the mask it was.

What else was Logan Eccles hiding?

The familiar chime of a message through his Apple watch saved him from more questions. I nearly jumped out of my skin at the sound, its interruption both incredibly relieving and terrifying.

Logan glanced at the screen, and a genuine grin crossed his face.

"Travis was on his way back forty-five minutes ago. He should be here any minute. Thank fuck. I've spent enough time with you fuckers to last a lifetime."

His demeanor completely transformed, as if we didn't just share his uncomfortable truth two seconds before.

"Well, not you, Princess. You can spend as much time with me as you want."

I ignored him and moved to stand, nodding at Cam who had kept the flame from the lighter going. It would likely go out soon too; it kept getting smaller every time the flint lit the gas-soaked wick.

"Help me get him up, please?" I asked Cam, moving to one side to grab one of his arms. Before I could even shift Logan's weight, Cam had lifted the man by his underarms and lifted him upright to standing with minimal effort at all.

It was easy to forget how strong this man was sometimes.

"Get off me, you fucker," Logan protested, but it was half-hearted.

"I'm not arguing with you," Cam said. "Fuck off and let me help you out of here, or we're leavin' your ass behind. I won't be worryin' my pretty little head about it, but Winter might because she seems to have a heart, so put up and shut up."

Logan shut up.

We all stood there in silence, waiting for any sign of our savior on the other side. I needed to know Travis and Drew were safe. I needed to feel their warmth and comfort for myself, wrap my arms around them, and show them how much I cared for each of them.

I couldn't deny my feelings for Travis any longer, and after this hell of a night, I was willing to forgive. Travis was my spark.

I wouldn't let go of my feelings for Drew, either, and I needed him to know just how important he was to me. Drew was my safety.

And Quick. Quick was going to be beside himself. I hoped he still had some of his long, beautiful chestnut brown locks left, because he had probably torn out half of it in worry. I needed to reassure him we were safe and sound.

The wooden slab of a door shifted in the dirt walls around it, and wide slivers of light flooded the cellar.

The wave of relief at the sight of this beautiful, bedraggled man was so strong I fought back the tears that wanted to burst from my eyes.

"I'm going to kiss the shit out of you when we're topside and safe," Travis promised me when he gave my shoulders a light squeeze. He turned to Cam.

"You good to help him? I made it down here without seeing anyone, but I don't want to count on that going up. We'll have to move as quickly as we can."

Cam nodded once, and we were off. Moving as quickly and quietly as we could, we took off down one hallway, down another, and into a creepy dark stairwell, but at least we had the phone flashlight to use as a guide. Then we were in a pantry, sneaking through a kitchen, through a rear staff entrance and, finally, out into the unimaginably freezing air.

We clung to the side of the building as we sidestepped to the chain-link fence that blocked off the rear parking lot. Travis gave me his gloves to climb over it, and then Cam pushed Logan over from one side while Travis grabbed him from the other side.

Travis turned to Cam. "I'm going back in to get our phones and keys from our lockers. I don't know how long this place is going to be shut down and I need mine. What's your code? I'll get yours too."

My heart leapt into my throat. We were too close to freedom to lose him now. "Travis, it's too dangerous. Please, just come with us and we can worry about that later."

"I'll be okay, beautiful. I already scoped it out, but I wanted to get you guys out first. I won't be long. Promise." He leaned in to give me a quick peck on the lips to seal the deal. Then he scaled the fence like a spider monkey and disappeared around the set of dumpsters.

Cam pulled Logan along, and we walked as swiftly and as nonchalantly as we could through the park across the street. I could only imagine what we looked like to innocent passersby.

Quick's familiar old red truck shone like a beacon in the distance. Outward appearances and my exhaustion be damned; I broke into a run. Quick opened his driver side door and got out of the cab, opening his arms wide. I threw mine around his large, hard body and squeezed as tightly as I could.

His familiar scent of pine and leather instantly calmed my nerves, and I clung to him like a koala bear. He lifted me up and twirled me around like in our favorite Fred Astaire movie, and I laughed through the tears streaming down my face.

He buried his face into my hair and tightened his hold on me. His warmth and strength radiated through me like a comforting blanket or the world's best cup of coffee. I melted into his embrace. We were safe. We were safe. He was here, and we were all *safe*.

He lifted his head and tilted my chin up to meet his gaze, still holding me tight to his chest. I could vaguely hear Drew and Cam getting Logan into the passenger seat of his car, despite his protests, but it all dimmed into white noise as I stared into my best friend's slate gray eyes.

"I love you, Snow," he whispered, the pain and trepidation from the past twenty-four hours leeching out of his soul at the words.

"I'm so glad you're safe. I love you," he repeated. Then without warning, he pressed his lips to mine in a brief, expressive kiss.

It wasn't the first time Quick had kissed me. He was a boisterous, emotional, expressive man who was a bear-hugger and a touchy-feely person in all ways. But this kiss was different. It wasn't passionate — *that* would have been weird — but it was oddly ... possessive.

Before I had a single moment to process, Travis' voice broke through the din and I jumped out of Quick's arms to give him the hug and kiss this man deserved.

We were in the middle of the quiet street, filthy and exhausted, and smelly and sore, and I kissed Travis as if the world stood still; because of him and his plan, we were safe.

I kept it brief, but the passion behind our lips and the heat in his eyes when we broke apart caused a deep stirring in my lower belly.

"Thank you," I whispered breathlessly. His kiwi-green eyes were brighter than I had ever seen them against the grim gray backdrop.

Drew stood in my periphery, holding out a water bottle and Quick's bright red duvet out to me. I let go of Travis and gratefully took the water bottle to guzzle as Drew wrapped me into the blanket.

I squeaked when he lifted me off of the ground, wrapped up like a burrito, and kissed the shit out of me. He held nothing back, and I was flustered and dizzy when he put me back down on the pavement.

"Thank you," I repeated to Drew, as he let me go to stand on my own two feet.

"Before the neighbors think we're about to host a street party orgy," Cam intoned behind me, "what's the plan?"

He motioned to Logan sitting in the passenger seat. "I'm gonna take him home. He refuses to go to the hospital, and that'll only bring more questions, anyway. Drew, can you follow me and drive me home after?"

Travis produced three sets of keys and three cell phones from his pants pockets.

"I could get your phones and keys, but they still have the front parking lot blocked off, so Winter, why don't you go with Shane and I'll go with Drew? We can grab our cars later."

"Everyone is welcome to come back to my place when they get cleaned up." Quick said, grabbing more snacks from Drew's car and handing them out. "I think we need to regroup and get up to speed on what happened in there and out here."

"I think we all need to get some sleep, man," Drew said gently. "And we'll all have to go about our regular lives tomorrow. You guys have school. I'm going to have to explain to my mom where the hell I've been for the past two days, and these guys" — he nodded to Cam and Travis — "will have to work."

"Later this week, then." Quick was undeterred. "I'll text you."

We all said our goodbyes, and I pulled my weary body into Quick's truck, still nestled in the feather blanket.

"Stay with me tonight, Snow." He interlaced our fingers over the stick shift and stroked the underside of my palm with his thumb. "This day scared the shit out of me and I just need you close. Please?"

I smiled and closed my eyes as I leaned my head back against the well-worn black leather headrest. Breathing in the comforting scent of motor oil, I squeezed his hand.

"I'll stay with you," I promised, as I drifted off into darkness. "Throw me in the shower and order us a pizza. And tuck me in, okay?"

I didn't hear his response. The rumbling of the truck tires on the highway lulled me into a deep, dreamless sleep.

CHAPTER 9

TRAVIS

If I hadn't known beyond any shadow of a doubt that we had been stuck in an underground bunker just fifteen hours before, I would have sworn the entire experience had been just a terrible dream.

I woke from a mild coma tucked safely in my bed like I had a thousand times before. Dim light peeked through my closed curtains, and the distant rumble of traffic sounded from the highway just beyond the flimsy wooden fence that bordered my trailer park. It could have been any other day of my life.

Or it would have been, if I didn't hear soft snores seeping through the paper-thin walls of the bedroom beside mine. Cam had insisted on staying in our tiny trailer, and I bunked him in Devon's room after changing the sheets and opening a window to air out the cluttered space.

I had been living alone in the trailer for weeks with Mom still in the hospital. It was a little disorienting to share my house again, but neither of us had wanted to be alone last night, even if we never said the words out loud.

Logan had practically kicked Cam out of his car as soon as they got to his condo. I waited patiently as the man searched his car for the bag of cocaine I had hidden in the lining of his trunk's carpet.

I could have thrown it out on him, and I probably should have. The man needed help. I wasn't going to willingly watch him destroy himself, even if he was a grade-A asshole.

I was grateful, though, he hadn't gone off the deep-end while Drew and I searched for an exit route. I had hoped the twenty-four hour period of sobriety might bring him to get clean, but it wasn't my problem.

I had enough problems.

Rolling over, I groaned at the time flashing across my alarm clock.

8:04. Too early to be alive yet.

Luckily, Cam and I worked bartender hours today and wouldn't need to be at the club until mid-afternoon, so I could get some more sleep. I couldn't imagine working as if life was 'business as usual' after the clusterfuck of a weekend.

Realization hit me.

Bourbon & Blues had been shut down the last time we saw it—the last time, as in, last night. In all the chaos and confusion, I hadn't even stopped to consider how it would affect my livelihood.

Would I even have a job after this?

Would I have my held-by-the-balls illegal side-gig after this?

Brief hope flickered through me, followed by agonizing fear, then a flatline of solid indifference.

Another problem for another day. Tomorrow I could reassess my life and start planning a legitimate future, but I probably wouldn't have a shift today. I settled back into the warmth of my covers and threw my arms over my head.

An hour later, after a restless bout of tossing and turning, I reached for my phone and sent off a quick text to Winter.

She had classes today, and if she was feeling the way I was, she wouldn't be having a great morning. I knew I wouldn't want to sit through a lecture feeling like this.

At least, I imagined I wouldn't. I had never sat through the doldrums of a college lecture before, though I hoped to one day. When I got my shit together and had hopes for a real future.

Tomorrow. That was tomorrow's task.

An email came through just as I was putting my phone down. Janet Lindross, Georgio's assistant, addressed it to 'All Staff'.

I opened it curiously, skimming through its contents in disbelief. We were being summoned back to the office for a staff meeting. Today. In just a few hours.

"Cam!?" I hollered through the wall while shifting myself up in bed and banging on it with the palm of my hand. "Wake up, man. Did you get the email?"

My phone pinged immediately with a reply from Winter, followed by another text asking if I got the email from Janet, too.

My mind raced with possibilities. Had the sheriff's department completed their investigation? Did this mean we would open up for business again, or could it be a closing announcement, and tomorrow I could truly start planning my actual future without all of Georgio's baggage and my poor decisions tying me down?

Fuck, how were they going to explain what had happened to the public? Only a fraction of Bourbon & Blues staff worked Georgio's 'other' gigs. What about the sheriff's department?

I got up and got dressed, determined to hash out every conceivable possibility with Cam before we had to get to that meeting.

"Thank you all for meeting with me."

Georgio stood behind his large cherry-wood desk, its lacquer matching the paneling in his luxurious office.

Seeing him in living color when I entered the room with Cam and Winter behind me shocked me, fucking shocked me.

We took our seats toward the back of the room. Cam sat to my left and Winter on my right, her hand holding mine tightly. She had been nervous, but didn't let a single facial muscle show it on her face.

She was tougher than she let on, my beautiful girl.

Georgio looked the same as always; his cream-colored suit jacket perfectly crease-free, matching slacks, and a white-collared shirt paired with an Italian leather set of loafers. Not a single hint of stress, worry, or general discontent was reflected in his neutral expression as the thirty-something employees of Bourbon & Blues joined him in the large room.

Despite its size, the room felt stifling, and I wanted to get out of there as soon as possible.

"Some of you may be wondering what happened this past weekend to close our place of business." Georgio spoke conversationally.

He moved around to the front of his desk and sat on its edge casually, as if we were all there for a trivia night instead of a very impromptu meeting.

"On Saturday night, Bourbon & Blues experienced an attack at our private function which was reported to the authorities. Unfortunately, a man was severely injured. I am sorry that we failed to bring you all up to speed yesterday, but events were still unfolding and the sheriff's department had to investigate. I am told that as of nine a.m. this morning, they are satisfied with their conclusions, and they will allow us to open up once again for business."

My eyebrows must have reached my hairline, and Winter squeezed my hand even tighter. That's what they were going with? An attack? In our small town?

Bourbon & Blues had been closed that Saturday evening for a 'private function', which is how the fights below and the resulting cataclysmic aftermath had flown under the radar of the epic rumor mill, a miracle in and of itself.

This explanation was jarring, but also anticlimactic. Which I supposed was a good thing. Anticlimactic was safe and not suspicious, and we'd all keep our jobs and continue to be trapped in our current shitty situations.

Great.

"The attack was specific in nature and our local authorities do not believe there is any risk to the public. So, we will continue on with our regular opening schedule today."

"If you lost a shift yesterday," Georgio said, continuing over the din of the now muttering crowd, "you will be paid for it on your next paycheck, but I'm afraid that won't be able to make up for the tip income you would have received. Everyone scheduled for yesterday's shift will also receive an additional $100 on their pay as a stipend to potentially make up the difference."

Another appreciative muttering erupted and Georgio smiled graciously as some of the staff thanked him.

The offer was generous of him, but that was Georgio; charming, considerate, calculating, deadly. It was how he could hold people like me and Cam in a vice grip. His help was so generous until the price became too high to pay, yet you still held onto the hope it wouldn't be your last dollar dropping into the slot machine as you asked him for one more favor.

Maybe that was just me.

"That's all to report, I'm afraid." Georgio stood up from the desk and pointed to Janet standing idly in the corner. She held a tablet in one hand and a coffee in the other.

"I wanted the opportunity to explain the situation to you personally, and offer my sincere apology for not having communicated with you sooner. Janet has revised copies of the upcoming schedule, so please take a copy with you on your way out."

Cam, Winter, and I just sat there for a moment while people around us stood up and filed out. The bar would open for business in an hour, and no one wanted to start late, especially with the boss on site.

Winter had to cut her last class to be here this early for the meeting, but she hadn't said a word about it. We were all so surprised to get called in this quickly we had just wanted to know what was going on.

Now we knew. Business as usual.

Logan appeared in the doorway of Georgio's office, and Drew was right behind him, looking confused and frazzled.

An icy chill crept up my spine. This was definitely *not* business as usual.

"Just in time," Georgio said, smiling as he looked up from his desk at the two very different men as they entered the room. He and Janet exchanged a meaningful look and Janet turned to usher the remaining employees out, leaving the three of us with Logan and Drew and closing the door behind her.

Winter squeaked beside me, and I knew we were thinking the same thing. The five of us in a room with Georgio so soon after our escape?

Not a coincidence.

Logan's trademark smirk was fixed in place, and he looked like a million bucks. My heart sank a little in my chest when I realized that meant he must be using again. Fuck addictions and the chokehold they had on otherwise decent, hardworking people.

Well, most were decent. *Some* were assholes.

Drew looked uncomfortable as fuck and kept shooting nervous glances to Winter across the room, but he didn't come over to us or make any attempts to reach out to her. I could guess he was trying to keep his distance from her in Georgio's presence, so the boss wouldn't see she was important to him.

Smart.

"Thank you all for meeting me on such short notice."

Everyone's attention immediately went to the front of the room. Georgio had settled comfortably in the large black leather chair behind his desk, looking far more ominous than he had just minutes before.

"The five of you remained undetected at our gathering on Saturday night."

It was a bold statement. His tone was friendly but firm, and I couldn't tell if we were being praised or chastised. He answered that question quickly.

"I'd like to congratulate you on your quick thinking. You managed to not only hide, but escape the building without getting caught. Yes..." He nodded in Winter's direction, where her eyes had grown as big as dinner plates. "I have cameras throughout *my* business, dear Winter. It was quite impressive to watch."

"Now, it's important to be clear when communicating a message. Please listen to me carefully. I not only have cameras around all areas of my establishment, I have recordings. Very clear recordings. If anyone in this room remembers the events of Saturday differently than the messaging the staff has received here today, these recordings will identify the potential culprits of the unfortunate attack. The poor man involved is on life support, so the charges may even amount to attempted murder.

"I can't predict how the sheriff's department will respond to new evidence, but I'm sure they will want to pursue legal action, at the very least."

You could have heard a pin drop in the room. No one said a word, not even Logan. What could we say? We were all in attendance that night; now we knew officially that we had been on record.

I literally ran money for Georgio and carried an illegal unregistered weapon while doing it. But that wasn't attempted murder.

Cam made his money fighting in rigged fights for cash. Georgio had gotten him out of a bad jam, but it wasn't attempted murder. I winced at the memory of Cam recounting his story one night over beers. Well, not *exactly* attempted murder.

If Logan's look of disgust was any indication, he was already held at Georgio's mercy, but it probably hadn't involved murder, either.

Drew was stuck more than any of us. He could get a significant prison sentence from the agreement he'd inherited. This development would hold his balls a little tighter, but he was fucked either way.

That left Winter.

Fuck, she had signed up for that stupid night to help Drew and Shane. She was loyal and brave and now paying for the favor. She didn't deserve any of this shit.

"If we are all in agreement..." Georgio smiled cheerfully, as if he hadn't just dropped an atomic bomb on our motley group of misfits. "We can continue on, business as usual. Nothing else needs to be done or said."

As if in afterthought, he turned to Winter. "I am sorry you had to miss classes this afternoon to attend this meeting, but I think you'll agree that it was important."

She nodded meekly and said nothing.

Satisfied, Georgio pointed to the door and ushered us out. We all filed out, speechless and dumbfounded. Janet waited on the other side with non-disclosure agreements in hand for us to sign. As if Georgio's threat hadn't been enough to keep us quiet. The woman was efficient.

Winter was frantically texting Shane, her fingers flying across her phone screen despite the tremors wracking her body.

"Let's meet up at Shane's later on this week," I murmured in her ear while we walked down the stairs to our lockers, Drew and Cam following. "We'll be okay."

Winter looked up from her phone, her soft lips pressed into a flat line and her eyes crinkled with barely masked anxiety.

I didn't believe the lies I was spewing, either.

CHAPTER 10

DREW

"Knock, knock," a distinctly female voice said from the doorway of the office.

I looked up to see Winter smiling warily at me, her dark hair frizzing around her face. A smudge of ketchup arced across her creamsicle-colored uniform.

"Hey." I smiled back at her, grateful for the break from the computer screen I had been staring at for the past hour. It had been hard to concentrate on anything to do with the diner over the last few days.

Mom had accepted my very mediocre explanation that I had come down with a twenty-four hour stomach flu, so sick

I couldn't get out of bed. She hadn't even questioned it. She was still swimming in guilt for my circumstances and Dad's hospital stay. Using that to my advantage made my stomach *actually* sick, but I had done it anyway.

Four days had passed since our ordeal and we had yet to get together like Shane wanted. There wasn't time; we all had lives to get back to.

He was knee-deep in his final semester, Winter had to finish her classes for her general business degree, and she was still working two jobs, here and at Bourbon & Blues since she was afraid to quit, and Cam and Travis both had to work to pay for their own lives. We all knew that included working other jobs for Georgio, but now that we were all in the same boat, it was really hard to judge.

The deeper into debt I got in with Georgio, the less I could dislike Travis. I wanted to, I really wanted to, but my resolve had crumbled after running into him at the hospital.

It was hard to hate a man who tried to protect his sick mother and addicted brother. Shane had texted me Travis' entire story two nights ago while trying to convince me to let him into our 'friendship throuple'. The 'Core Four,' he was now calling us.

I shook my head with a smile as I thought of my boisterous friend. Shane was one of a kind, and I loved the hell out of him for it.

It was also hard to hate Travis when I was putting Winter in as much danger by keeping her as an employee and wanting to have her for myself at the same time.

None of us could protect her from this tangle with Georgio. Not anymore.

"Have time for a coffee break?" Winter asked, holding up the vintage glass carafe with one hand and two of the bone-colored ceramic diner mugs in the other. "I even have creamers in my pockets."

"Well, isn't that thoughtful." I stood up from the desk and walked over to her, motioning her inside the room and closing the door to lock it. "I would love a coffee."

I took the carafe and mugs out of her hands and set them on the desk. Then I pulled her into my arms and held her tight to my chest. I breathed in the scents of coffee, salt, lavender, vanilla, and the underlying familiarity of grease that just couldn't be eliminated from the diner, no matter how upscale Carl's cooking could be.

She leaned back and stared up at me. I loved her eyes; swirling light blue irises flecked with bits of green and gold, lined with dark eyelashes. They were tired, mildly puffy and smudged with eyeliner from a long day, but they were damn captivating.

"What are you thinking about?" she asked with a smile in her voice, tilting her head to one side and staring at me curiously.

"I love your eyes," I answered honestly, as I brushed the frizz out of her face.

They crinkled at the corners and she stood on her tiptoes to brush her lips against my own. It was a very brief and gentle touch of warmth, but heat seared through me all the same. This woman was *mine.*

Well. Ours.

"I love *your* eyes. They're the kindest eyes I've ever seen, my Hardy Boy." She gave me a squeeze before making her way over to the desk to make our coffee.

Her Hardy Boy. I didn't love the nickname, but I had to admit it fit. Frank and Joe were likable, dependable guys who always caught the bad guy. I considered myself a likable, dependable guy, but I wished I could channel some of their mystery-solving capabilities.

Winter turned around and grinned at me as she pulled out her 'creamers.' She held up a mickey of Bailey's Irish

Cream in one hand and a small bottle of Grand Marnier in the other.

"Pick your poison," she quipped, pouring the Bailey's into what I assumed was her mug. "Life's been a bit too testing around here. Enjoy a drink with me."

She winked as she waited for my response. "It's okay," she mock whispered, her hand in front of her face like she was telling me a secret. "I know the boss."

I laughed. The lightness of the action felt foreign after the heaviness of the last week. Last *weeks*. Months.

Walking over to the desk, I wrapped my hand around the Grand Marnier bottle, unscrewing the lid and pouring out a healthy measure into my mug. I topped it off with coffee, then held it out to clink with hers.

"Cheers," I said before knocking back a healthy gulp of the steaming drink. Orange-anything was my weakness.

I sank back down into the well-worn office chair and tugged her hand to pull her into my lap.

"So, are we celebrating anything in particular?" I mused as I stroked circles across the starchy uniform shirt on her back.

"Does life need an occasion to be celebrated?" She smiled, playfully bopping me on the nose. "I don't know about you, but I'm happy to *be* alive right now, regardless of our circumstances."

She fiddled with the silver arrow ring on her thumb. "It was pretty scary there for a while," she admitted, softly.

"I know, baby. I was scared too."

I placed my coffee back down on the desk and pulled her tighter to me, wrapping my arms around her waist and tucking her head underneath my chin.

We sat in silence for a few minutes, not moving an inch, our breaths slow and even while the chaos of the diner continued to carry on outside the locked door. Her fingers absently stroked intricate patterns across my chest, and despite my best intentions, my cock stiffened in my jeans. It felt like ages had passed since we'd been alone together.

I shifted in the seat, trying to be discreet about my growing hard on. Winter lazily raked her hand down my abdomen before stroking one finger down the seam of the zipper of my jeans.

So much for hiding it.

I shuddered at the contact, zings of aching need shooting through me.

"Being the boss must be hard," she whispered seductively, tilting her head up to peer up at me through those dark eyelashes. "Is there something I can help you with? Maybe take some pressure off?"

The air in the room shifted from languid to lustful as she palmed my dick through the thick fabric, working me gently but thoroughly.

My cock was so swollen it bordered on painful.

"You're going to have to stop doing that," I rasped, placing my hand over hers and tugging it gently back up to my chest. "My dick won't be able to take it."

"I think your dick can take me just fine." She grinned wickedly, licking her lips and pushing off from me to stand in front of the chair. "Or have you forgotten?"

I scoffed, my eyes widening as she swiveled the chair to the side and lowered herself to her knees in front of me. My voice came out low on a tremor of anticipation. "I don't think I could ever forget."

I sat there dumbly while she unbuttoned my jeans and pulled the zipper down to expose my boxers. She lightly stroked the soft cotton and moved her hand through the folded opening to palm my dick, skin on skin.

I nearly jumped out of the chair at the contact.

She released me from the boxers, my throbbing length standing tall and proud out of the hole in the fabric. With her tucked behind the desk and my pants still on, no one could tell what was going on beneath it.

Not that it mattered with the door locked. Maybe I had subconsciously hoped for this.

I looked down at my dick leaking pre-cum and desperate to be touched, before looking at her. I watched with reverence as she put her mouth over my tip, suckling the drop into her mouth gently, then she opened wide to swallow all of me.

My balls tingled with pleasure as she bobbed up and down, her hot tongue laving the seam underneath before closing tight and sucking me hard like I was a Popsicle.

Fuck. Me.

She alternated between licks, sucks, and strokes of her tongue, then she took me deep and swallowed around me. My whole body trembled, and I thrust my hands into her hair, holding her there while she did it again and again.

I couldn't concentrate on anything, could barely see past the vision of her sucking me off in the middle of the office that held so many bitter-sweet memories.

This—this would be a good one.

"Baby, I'm going to cum," I gasped out the warning, ready to pull out of her mouth before I completely lost it.

Her mouth closed on me even tighter and she thrust me back into her throat, humming along the underside of my cock.

A deep, guttural groan rose from my chest as the hot jets of my cum filled her. She didn't stop for a second, her lips holding tight around me and swallowing everything I had to give her. Gradually, she slowed her movements and I gently popped out of her mouth.

Her hair had fallen out of her ponytail, the mascara around her eyes had gone smudged and watery; her lips were swollen and cheeks flushed.

She was breathtakingly beautiful.

I tucked myself away and zipped up my jeans, then I cupped her cheek in my palm and pulled her up to kiss me, tasting myself on her tongue. It was a slow, leisurely kiss.

"I don't know what I did to deserve that, but thank you," I breathed when we broke apart, as I looked into my favorite eyes of my favorite girl.

"You've been carrying the weight of the world on your shoulders," she said seriously, before her eyes sparkled with mischief. "I just wanted to help lighten the load."

"Did you just make a cum joke?" I asked incredulously. Grinning, I poked her ribs with my index fingers until she collapsed into a fit of giggles in my lap.

A banging on the door broke us out of the moment, and I stiffened in the chair.

We hadn't been hiding our relationship — if this thing had an actual title yet. I wasn't entirely sure. But we hadn't been publicly affectionate at the diner yet either.

"Drew!?" The shrill voice of my mother leaked through the steel, and I leapt from my chair, grabbing Winter by the elbow at the last second before she hit the concrete floor.

"Sorry!" I winced, grimacing apologetically at her while I quickly tucked in my shirt and adjusted my pants. Mom had never caught me in bed with a girl and I didn't want to start now.

Reaching for Winter's hand, I squeezed it before letting go and moving to unlock the door.

Mom stood in the hallway, her blond hair askew and her brown eyes swollen from crying. She was clutching her purse with white-knuckled hands, barely seeing me through her tears.

"Mom, what's wrong?" I immediately wrapped my arms around her and pulled her close, my mind racing with the many possibilities.

Were the kids okay? Did Georgio threaten her?

Winter subtly ducked her head to sneak out the door behind me. I was grateful for both the privacy and her understanding. The light and playful mood in the office just minutes before was now thick and somber.

"It's your father," Mom sobbed into my shoulder. "He's awake."

"Easy, Dad," I lightly scolded as he tried to push himself up from his hospital bed. "Let me help you with that."

I moved the mountain of flimsy pillows my siblings had stacked in the corner of the room to prop him up to a seated position.

Mom and the kids had left a few hours ago. Dawn and Rosie had crawled into the bed with Dad and held his hands the entire time they'd been here. Tom and Charlie both regaled him with stories of everything that had happened to them since Christmas — presents, skinned knees, and all.

We all had a good family cry when the doctor confirmed Dad could get out of here in a few days. I couldn't believe he had been in a coma for six weeks.

I had wanted to bring the kids home, so Mom could have some time with Dad, but she insisted I stay with him for a little while. I suspected this was her way of trying to mend our fence for us since we hadn't been in a good place before the accident, and I didn't have the heart to tell her no, despite my reservations.

Still, I was so grateful he was awake. Awake and alive.

We'd been sitting in quiet company for the past three hours, watching reruns of *M*A*S*H* on the ancient TV.

Dad shifted in his bed and waved me over to sit beside him. I moved from the cramped seat near the fading beige wall and gingerly sat at the edge of the bed, not wanting to jostle his frail frame.

He smiled appreciatively at me and reached for my hand. We had never shied away from affection in my family, but Joe probably showed it to me least of all.

His limp, cool skin felt foreign in mine.

"Son," he began, shifting uncomfortably in the bed with a scowl. "I need to apologize to you."

"Dad, it's okay, now's not really the —"

"Now is the perfect time. I never thought I would have the chance to say these words to you, and I want to say them now."

In spite of his weary state, he managed to give me a stern look, one I had seen a thousand times in the past few years, so my lips remained shut.

"I'm sorry," he said in a whisper. The words were so low I leaned in to hear him better.

"I'm sorry I pushed you into this business, thinking it was the best thing I could do for you. I can see how wrong I was now. I never expected Georgio to hold this over me for as long as he has, and I never would have wanted this arrangement for you. I certainly never expected this kind of blowback." His calm face molded into an ugly glare. "I would have never risked you like this had I known."

I kept the onslaught of retorts from escaping my mouth. His actions *had* put me at risk; they had put the whole family at risk.

Now, though, wasn't the time to talk about that.

"I'm glad you told me you don't want this life," Dad admitted, staring at our joined hands where they rested on the flannel hospital blanket. "I wished it had come out another way, but it makes my decision on this one a lot easier."

He drew in a shaky breath, then said, "Camden has been wanting to buy the business for a long time. I suspect it's a business arrangement with Georgio. Hell, this retaliation could be the next step in making me give the diner up, I don't know. But I've decided I'm going to let him."

"Dad," I protested, surprised and taken aback by the announcement. "You don't need to do that, you —"

"Yes, I do. You don't want the business, and I don't want this for you anymore. Not when you could get hurt, or anyone else in this family could be at risk. I'm just glad it was me who took the knife that night." An agonizing look of sadness flitted across his features and he squeezed my hand.

"But, everything you've worked for ... Dad, are you sure?"

I couldn't tell him I wanted the diner; I didn't. I couldn't tell him he was wrong about Georgio, because he wasn't, especially after our recent encounter. But the diner had been Dad's dream, one that literally almost killed him, and there was a deep melancholy in his words despite his stoic expression.

"I'm sure. I was contemplating this move before all of *this*." He gestured to his abdomen with a shake of his head. "I plan to meet with Camden next week to discuss the specifics, then we can work out an exit plan. If you still want to work here, I can throw that in as one requirement, if you like."

"I'll have to think about it," I said slowly, completely unsure at that moment what I would want to do.

I never before had the option to consider a future without the diner. Would I stay? Would Winter stay? Or could we cut and run, get out of this mess of a town and escape somewhere?

The thought filled me with hope until reality hit. Winter wouldn't leave without Shane, and Shane had a future here. I wouldn't want to leave without him, either.

"Please do," Joe responded, breaking me out of my thoughts. "And know that whatever you decide, I'll respect it."

His grip tightened on my hands and I looked up to see his red-rimmed eyes spilling tears down his cheeks.

"I'm so sorry, Drew. I hope one day you'll forgive me."

A weak smile crossed my face and I leaned over to brush my lips across his forehead. We settled into silence, and I stayed in his room until he drifted back to sleep.

CHAPTER 11

LOGAN

"Two months until D-Day!" Hillary announced in a voice far too cheerful for the mini hangover I was nursing.

"Fuck off, Hill," I growled halfheartedly, taking a long drink from my water bottle. I leaned against the granite kitchen counter to catch my breath. I had just run ten miles on the treadmill to rid myself of the whiskey demon riding my ass this morning, but it hadn't worked.

"I guess I'm the only one excited, huh?" she teased. Then she blew me a kiss from across the room.

"You're only excited because you're about to become a very rich woman," I retorted. "And I'm about to get fucked."

"I'm already a very rich woman." She quirked an eyebrow at me and grinned. "I'm just about to get richer."

She grabbed a wine spritzer from our fridge and cracked the top.

"And you mean to tell me you were only marrying me for my money? I'm shocked!" She winked and settled into our expensive white leather couch in the open-concept living room.

I surprised myself with a laugh that escaped despite my pounding head and her presence in my space. Ever since the will reading, we had come to an understanding; this farce of a relationship was over. We would no longer pretend it was what either of us had ever wanted.

If only Frederick Fucknuts had read the will a few years sooner, we could have saved ourselves a lot of grief and told our fathers to fuck off a hell of a lot quicker.

I was getting fucked up the ass, but Stanley was too, and that almost made it worth it.

"Do you need me to help you make any more bullshit decisions? Is there some calligraphy emergency I should offer input on? I want to make sure our day is as perfect as it can be for you, *honey*," I retorted sarcastically and sat my ass down on the couch beside her.

It was her turn to laugh. It was real, not the fake Barbie laughs she had always given in the past. This version of her was way more tolerable.

"Nope. Same bogus invitation list, same sham of a wedding," she declared, grabbing a financial magazine from the coffee table and flipping through it. "I have more important things to worry about now. Like how I'm going to invest my millions."

She grinned at me again, but then sighed at my sour expression.

"I know this is hard. This whole situation sucks. I will not screw you over, Logan. Not with our history or with what Stanley did to y —"

"Don't." I held up a hand to stop her. "Stanley's a twat who deserves everything coming to him. You only know anything because of our *situation*." I said, tossing the word choice back at her. "I'm not taking a pity payout, and for your sake, I wouldn't say anything to anyone. You know what he's capable of."

I let the threat hang in the air, and she took another drink of her spritzer, not bothering to respond.

Fine by me. My fucked-up relationship with Stanley and our sordid past was the last thing I was going to talk about with anyone. The tingling heat of my scars hadn't stopped since Winter had made it her business to see them, and I fucking hated it.

I'd had feelings for her once, back when I could still feel. Sixteen-year-old Logan hadn't been the miserable bastard I was now, and he had been naïve enough to be *hopeful* about things. I had been walking on a fucking cloud after taking her out on that first date.

Stanley had given me one of his best beatings that night; a lesson in temperance, the miserable fuck told me, as if he were a fucking religious man and not Satan himself. I was to marry Hillary. To be seen with anyone otherwise was damaging our 'alliance' with the Lanes.

Two of the scars Winter had seen were from that 'spiritual awakening.' Lesson fucking learned.

"Oh," Hillary interrupted my thoughts and handed me a white envelope from the magazine she was still flipping through. "This came for you today."

I looked at the Bourbon & Blues return address and frowned. What the fuck?

I ripped open the envelope and skimmed the letter, turning purple as I read through the bullshit proposal.

Jumping up from the couch, I grabbed my coat, my keys, and my phone by the door.

I was going to kill that fucker.

Twenty minutes later, I made my way up the familiar stairs to Georgio's office, pissed off and ready to tear him a new one. It took all I had in me to fight my violent urges and stay in control.

After the little stunt he pulled the other day in his office with the ragtag group of fuck-wits, I wasn't in the mood for the formal letter in my mail, officially 'requesting' the sale of my Front Street property *as agreed.*

Like fuck, we agreed. The fight I had made the bet on hadn't even finished, thanks to the 'attack' or whatever other bullshit he wanted to call it, and I wasn't letting him bully me into handing over one of my most lucrative investments.

I knocked on the door and stormed in. His sex-kitten secretary looked up at me with doe-eyed surprise.

"Mr. Eccles, what are you —" she squeaked, pushing back her chair at the smaller desk next to Georgio's.

"He's expecting me," I snapped, pacing the room in a barely concealed rage. "Let him know I'm here."

She scurried out the door like the little mouse she was. I stalked over to the liquor cabinet and poured myself a whiskey from the crystal decanter on the shelf.

I took a long swig, followed by a deep breath. Better. I sat down in the large wingback chair in the corner and waited.

My side throbbed where the suture strips were pulling, but I was otherwise physically fine. I'd had the hit I needed in the morning, and I was feeling good. Good and angry.

Georgio strolled in with an amused smirk on his face.

"I was wondering when you got my note, Logan. Come to discuss the terms of our arrangement?"

I closed my eyes to keep from seeing red and willed myself to stay calm. With the news in Hillary's inheritance, I couldn't count on my relationship with Camden's daughter to keep me safe.

I wasn't untouchable here.

"Our arrangement is void," I stated through clenched teeth. "Your fighter did not win *or* lose, the so-called 'attack' interrupted it. That *arrangement*," I sneered, "is no longer valid."

"Ahhh, yes." Maddening, Georgio smiled, moving to the liquor shelf to pour his own drink. "But you forget that you still owe me money, no? A lot of money."

"I am still well within the terms of our agreement. Hillary and I will be married in two months and —"

"I've recently become aware of some of the new, unanticipated inclusions to that inheritance," Georgio interrupted smoothly, acting as if I had said nothing at all. "It looks like you might not be coming into the money you thought. I am simply being proactive in protecting *my* investments."

Fuck Camden. That was the only way Georgio could know the money would no longer be mine.

He sipped his drink and smiled like a shark. "Unless you have another $180K lying around that I'm not aware of?"

"That's my problem, isn't it?" I retorted, gulping down the last of the whiskey and relishing its burn. "I have two more months before that debt is owed, and if *you're* forgetting the terms, why don't you ask your little secretary pet to confirm them?"

I bared my teeth at the little woman who had just entered the room to stand next to the ingratiating wannabe mafia don.

"I don't need Janet to tell me what I already know." Georgio waved a hand dismissively, and she skittered out the door to wherever she had come from. "You're right, you have two months. But be prepared, Logan. If the debt is not paid in full, I will seize some of your assets. You don't want to cross me. Now get out."

He motioned to the door and turned his back on me as he walked towards his big-dick-energy desk.

"Frequent my establishments, but don't come up here again."

I stalked angrily down the stairs toward the bar and barged into Angelo, Georgio's number two man, at the end of the hallway.

"You know, boss man won't keep putting up with your crap, you entitled twit," Angelo snapped, pushing me back on my feet. "Let's not have to teach you a lesson too, hmm?"

With a self-satisfied smirk, the overbearing oaf moved out of my way. Instead of knocking back an Old Fashioned at the bar like I had been planning, I made a beeline for the front entrance.

Fuck him. Fuck him, and fuck Georgio, and fuck everyone in this fucking town. I needed to get out from under Georgio's thumb. Fast. He wasn't making another dime out of me from any of his available substances.

If that forced me to quit cold turkey, so be it. It was fucking with my heart, anyway.

I left the building to cross the next thing off of my to-do list. Georgio wouldn't own me anymore.

"That was one ballsy risk you took," M said with a snarky grin as I walked into the abandoned gazebo at Kirby Park.

"Can we start meeting in warmer fucking places?" I shot back as I shoved my hands into my jacket pockets. "This cloak and dagger shit is getting old."

"Sure thing, *partner.* I'll meet you at Georgio's next time. You can buy me a drink and we can have a good old conversation about your double life as a rat to the feds."

"Funny," I grumbled sarcastically into the dead night air. This needed to be an in-and-out conversation. I wasn't arrogant enough to think I wasn't on Georgio's radar, and I had no interest in dying today.

"As I was saying" — M folded his arms and leaned against the rickety wooden railing — "that was ballsy, dropping the hint about the underground fight and attending yourself."

"I didn't have much of a choice," I sneered. "How the fuck did you fuck that one up? Wasn't that a 'fish in a barrel' scenario?"

Actual fucking fish in a barrel. There had been over two hundred people there that night, and two exit points. Other than Travis' quick thinking — I could admit that he saved my ass — the feds should have been able to get Georgio alive and kicking.

M grimaced. "Georgio has more pull than we realized. We know he rubs elbows with some powerful people, but we didn't understand how powerful until that night. I'd love to know how you got out without a mark on that pretty little face of yours."

He smirked at me, raising an eyebrow and pointing a finger gun at my head.

Prick.

"If I'm so expendable, what the fuck are we meeting for?" I shot back, already sick of this conversation and my balls freezing off.

"We need to up the ante," M said matter-of-factly, standing abruptly and walking quickly toward me. He lowered his voice to barely a whisper.

"If Georgio has this kind of pull, we need a rock-solid case with irrefutable evidence. The fight ring is small potatoes. I can't pin the drugs on this guy. His distribution channels are a minefield and while this whole town may talk, that's all it is; talk. We're going to snag him with the white-collar crime. The embezzlement angle, the insider-trading angle that you still haven't delivered on."

I shot him a dark look, fighting the urge to punch him in his smug face.

"Get me proof, Logan, and all your sins will be erased." M stepped back from me, pointing his ridiculous, pretentious finger gun at me again and grinning. "I'll be in touch."

I watched the prick leave down the steps and waited the obligatory five minutes before heading back to my car.

I was twitchy as fuck, desperate for some delicious sweet South American goodness to take the edge off and center me again. I had a little left in my glove compartment from last week's visit, but once that was gone, that would be it. Logan Eccles was taking back control.

With Georgio and M closely watching my movements, I was a prisoner of my own making. But when Plan A and Plan B didn't work, there was always a Plan C. And my Plan C was Carson Baker.

I sent him a quick text.

Logan Eccles: We're going to need to move up our timeline.

Carson Baker: I'm game. Just tell me the when and where.

I reached for the dash and drew out the small baggie. One taste, one treat, and then we'd plot the bastard's end.

CHAPTER 12

CAMERON

*D*aisy Knight has been found.

Douglas Fraser's voicemail shocked me from my senses when I got out of the hole in the ground and back on solid footing. It was the last thing I had expected to hear.

Immediately I was taken back to the last night I had genuine hope of finding the woman who had given me life. A night that ended in me being trapped in little Cascade Falls with a debt over my head.

People knew about Georgio's upscale bar in Sheldonville and his construction firm in Cascade Falls and his connections to Carlisle, but I doubted many knew about the dive bar he owned in Kensington; the last place Daisy was reportedly seen.

According to Doug, Daisy had worked there three years ago, going by the name 'Crystal.' I had only been in the county a few weeks when Doug found her after just two days of searching. I couldn't believe Lady Luck was paying me a visit after the hell of the months before.

I got to the bar later in the evening than I had hoped, but I figured it was as good a time as any, with the alcohol loosening lips. Too much so, it seemed.

I had been sipping a beer and listening to the locals get rowdier by the minute, waiting for the best time to pry some information out of the old bartender, when a man my size hauled off and slapped his girlfriend across the face. She fell off her stool with blood streaming from her pretty little pixie nose. Before I knew it, the man was under me, beaten within an inch of his life, a gash from a broken beer bottle opening up the flesh of his cheek.

I couldn't explain the blackout. I had always held the rage inside me, contained it as best I could, but that night there had been nothing in me to keep the monster chained. I let the cops cuff me and bring me to the station where I sat in a concrete cell for two days before Georgio's lawyer showed up in a $2,000 suit with an offer too good to be true.

It was.

The next thing I knew, though, my bail had been posted and I was out of prison. I had no record to speak of and a job offer from Georgio for a hell of a lot better pay, benefits, and one large string attached.

What I didn't know then was that I'd become the man's prized pony, paraded around at every opportunity until he made the decision I'd be better off as glue.

I rubbed my hands down my face, flooded with shame and hate at the memories. Shame over my actions and hate over the fact that I was triggered every time I witnessed a woman in pain.

Could we have actually found Daisy this time? Not a memory wasting away in a crappy hole in the wall, but a real live woman who may want to meet her long-lost son?

I felt a constant push and pull between desperate to find her and terrified of what I'd actually find. Momma would tell me to 'buck up.' Pop—Pop would tell me some fable ending in a valuable life lesson, taught by the actions of a rabbit and a turtle or something. I smiled at that memory, love for Pop shining through the holes in my heart.

I had left a return voicemail for Doug, asking what the next steps were. I guessed for now, I would have to wait and see.

I pulled off my t-shirt and dropped to the floor of my humid apartment, pushing my body through my usual warm up, adding an extra fifty push-ups to turn my arms into jelly, then I rolled over to do ab crunches. I was waiting for the other shoe to drop and needed to be physically prepared.

It had crushed Travis when Georgio made his 'grand reveal,' but not me. Nothing in life is free, and our escape had been too easy to be anything but another well-executed trap.

What I didn't understand was why a man with so much power needed to hold any over us? From what I could gather, none of us were anything special.

Travis was kind and charming trailer park trash; I loved him like a brother and would die for the man, but why would Georgio continue to help him when Travis was just an ordinary broke guy?

Logan was an entitled asshat with money, but Georgio didn't need money. Drew was locked in with his family connection, which was a pretty shitty deal, and Winter got caught up in the mess out of her loyalty to her friend. Why did Georgio need any of them to be compliant?

I was beyond baffled. And worried.

My phone ringing broke my flow, and I collapsed on my carpet after my two hundredth sit-up. The sweat rolled off my pecs and onto the floor as I grabbed my phone from the couch.

A brief flicker of hope bloomed in my chest that it was Doug. It wasn't.

"Hello?"

"Cameron Chase?"

My spine stiffened at the unfamiliar voice on the line. Unfamiliar people didn't call me. They didn't have this number.

"Yeah?" I responded gruffly.

"This is Drake."

Drake, as in Drake Malone? Georgio's "business associate" who coordinated fighters on the fight nights? I could picture the aging MC gang leader with his many pieces of tacky jewelry and face tattoos.

"Okay," I answered impatiently, not wanting to waste time with cryptic conversations. "What do you want?"

"Georgio isn't gonna be able to host fight nights for a little while, and there's a group of us who wanna start 'em back up. I want you to come to fight for me."

Hell no. It was bad enough I had gotten into bed with Big G in the first place, let alone another man branded in blood.

"Does Georgio know about this?" I asked curiously, careful not to give anything away. Drake could most definitely not be trusted. For all I knew, this was a test from Big G himself.

"Pfft," the man scoffed, like I was a joker. "I'm not afraid of Georgio. It's high time that man was brought to his knees."

"Sure," I said amicably, turning on the Southern charm for a second and channeling Travis. "But I ain't gonna be the one to do it. Find yourself another fighter."

"I'll pay you double what Georgio is," Drake said succinctly. "Consider it. We're gonna host them at the old race tracks in my territory in Kensington. First one is in two weeks. You can call me back anytime."

What was with everyone in the universe thinking they could buy me off? I didn't think my vibe was screaming 'desperate.'

"I won't be calling you back," I promised neutrally. "But thanks."

I ended the call before he could say another word and remained seated on the carpet for a few minutes. The beaded sweat had now dried to my skin and even the damp heat from the laundromat below couldn't remove the chill creeping up from the base of my spine.

I should probably just skip town. I was getting too deep into a world I had no business being in. Nothing really tethered me here. Daisy — or Crystal, whoever she went by now — probably hadn't given me an extra thought in years. Travis could still text me if I was a million miles away. They needed good construction workers in Canada, too.

I pushed myself up off the floor and grabbed a bottle of water from the fridge. Cracking its seal, I took a long drink. I *could* leave, but I didn't want to. Big G aside, and that was a *big* aside, I liked it here. There was a nugget of hope in the back of my mind that I could build a home here, if I could only find Daisy and get out from under Georgio's thumb.

I looked at the clock and sighed. Work started in a few hours, and I had errands to run. I'd have to contemplate my life choices later.

Maybe Doug would call me with more good news and maybe even a few answers.

Maybe.

I was walking around the corner of the main entrance of Bourbon & Blues to the side hallway when voices caught my attention.

I turned to the sound and saw two outlines further down the hall. The tall, familiar shape of a man had a woman boxed into the corner of a decorative alcove, muttering softly into her ear. The closer I got, the more I could hear. His angry whispers carried through the empty space.

"I mean it, Winter. If you say a word to anyone, I'll make sure you regret it."

I froze. Logan had Winter trapped between him and a bay window. I could see more of her shapely outline when I got closer, her auburn hair almost black in the dim light. I had moved forward to pull him away from her when her response stopped me.

"Logan, why would I ever tell anyone? That you've been beaten so badly you had scars all over y—"

"Shut up!" Logan moved to place his pretty boy hands over her mouth and I snapped. I barreled forward, grabbed him by the shoulders, and yanked him backward so hard he fell on his ass on the damask carpet.

Asshat handled, I reached for Winter's hand and gently brushed my hands over her arms and torso, checking for any injuries. What had happened before I got there? I cursed myself internally for not being this woman's shadow.

"You okay?" I stopped my frisking and looked into her eyes, dark reflective pools peering back at me.

"I am. You didn't have to do that, big guy. I'm not afraid of Logan. But I appreciate the rescue." She pushed up on her toes, giving me a peck on the cheek. Lavender and vanilla overtook my senses.

"What the fuck, Chase!" Logan snarled as he pushed himself off of the floor, crowding my space. The man's self-preservation skills were clearly lacking when it came to me. He had surprised me in my apartment, but he was no match for my talents in the ring or on the street, and he needed to know better.

I sucker punched him in the kidney, knocking the wind out of him and maybe some sense into him. Then I pushed him back into the alcove to recover. The building rage slowly ebbed as I enjoyed watching the many faces of pain flash through his features.

"Don't lay your hands on her again, Pretty Boy. Consider her under my protection." I turned away from him and reached for Winter's hand, feeling her palm small and cool in mine.

I led the way to the staff lockers. The room was still empty; a safe spot to chat halfway through an evening shift.

"Do you mind tellin' me what that was about?" I asked gently, still holding her hand as I led us to sit on the bench in the center of the room.

"I told him I wouldn't, so I won't."

Winter tucked an errant hair behind her ear, a determined expression hardening her smile.

"But I think he's desperate, Cam. I've known Logan a long time, and I've never seen him like this. Something is up with him. I don't think he's okay."

"Billionaire Boys Club ain't your problem." I smoothed my hands over her shoulders and held her with my gaze. "I meant what I said; I'll protect you where I can, but I'm not always gonna be there."

She stuck out her chin defiantly and my cock roused against the stiff fabric of my jeans. I liked this mix of soft and hard in her. Soft enough to genuinely care about an asshole who didn't deserve the over-inflated gold-flecked air he breathed, but hard enough to push back against me when I wanted her safe.

"I'm not a delicate violet, you know. I wouldn't have been stuck there for a second longer if I hadn't wanted to get more out of him." She looked pointedly at me as if I had robbed her of that opportunity. "But thank you all the same."

That smile again; no teeth, just a teasing smirk of pouty lips and mischief.

I was having trouble keeping my distance from this woman.

I cleared my throat. "Right, well. Glad we cleared that up." I stood, towering over her until I extended my hand to pull her up. She took it, and I enjoyed the soft, brief touch until she let it go.

"I'd better get back to work. Travis is going to wonder where I disappeared to." She smoothed down her black pants and re-tied her long hair in a ponytail.

That statement splashed cold water onto my thoughts and my crotch. Winter was Travis girl. I didn't understand that relationship dynamic, but I knew I didn't fit into it.

"Right," I repeated. "I've got to roll up another keg. I'll see you around, little violet."

Her eyes shone with amusement, a genuine smile lighting up her face with full teeth. "Don't be a stranger, Big Guy."

We parted ways, and I was left wanting from her presence once more.

CHAPTER 13

WINTER

Drew and I snuggled on my couch, watching the movie I had put on as we waited for Quick to show up with some news. Apparently, he had found something interesting when searching his dad's home office and wanted us to see it for ourselves.

Travis and Cam hadn't been available since they both had to work, so I made the two of us some popcorn and settled in to watch *Love & Other Drugs*.

Knowing we'd have work to do when Quick arrived, I was doing my best to behave myself while the cutest boy next door held me in his arms. My resolve was deteriorating with every new sex scene, and I willed the man to show up immediately before I pounced on Drew and rode him like a cowgirl.

When Quick hadn't shown up by the end credits, I checked my phone.

Quick LongJohn Silver: Got held up. Digging up some good dirt! Talk tomorrow.

Quick LongJohn Silver: Give Drew a kiss for me. 😊

I laughed at the cheeky asshole and turned to Drew, who easily read the message over my shoulder.

He leaned in and pressed a light kiss to my lips. "I've been wanting to kiss you all night." He pulled back and tucked me tighter to him, his hand settling on my hip and grazing the warm skin underneath the hemline of my shirt. "I'm not going to lie. That movie was the worst pick when I can't have you tonight."

Quick bailing could have a happy ending, after all.

I looked up at Drew's serious face lit up by the glow of the television screen. "Who says you can't have me tonight, Hardy Boy? If we can't solve any mysteries, I can think of a few productive activities to pass the time."

I stood, interlaced our fingers, and pulled his big frame up from the deep sofa. I walked us into my bedroom and spun around, pushing his ex-quarterback body onto my cozy double bed.

He obliged, a twinkle of amusement in his eye as I pulled off my sweater and threw it to the floor, unclasping my bra and exposing my breasts to the cool bedroom air. My nipples hardened into points.

I would not be wasting any time when I had waited so long to have him again.

His eyes roamed my body appreciatively as he reached down and pulled his Henley off one-handed in that sexy move only hot guys can accomplish. I straddled him, locking my arms around his neck, relishing in the warmth of his skin.

"Looks like we have some time on our hands. Whatever shall we do with it all?"

A genuine chuckle escaped his beautifully pink mouth, and he lightly nipped my bottom lip.

"Well, there was a lot in that movie I'd be willing to try." He stopped talking and brushed a lock of hair behind my ear. "I've only really mastered missionary."

"You mean, you and Sadie never even —" I cut myself off. His sexcapades leading up to this moment with me were none of my business, but of course I was curious.

Not everyone had Miranda as a mother, Winter.

I expected Drew was more of a monogamy man since he and Sadie had been together for literally forever, until he graduated university, but I figured they would have used that time together to experiment with *everything*.

He smiled sheepishly and rubbed his large palm across the back of his neck.

"Er-no," he admitted. "Sadie wasn't exactly adventurous in the bedroom, and other than her, I've only had a few one-night stands since we broke up. She was my first. There's not a lot of experience to speak of other than with her."

He turned pink at his confession, the color slowly creeping up his neck and chin and settling into the tops of his rounded cheeks and the tips of his ears.

My heart instantly fluttered, an excited hummingbird inside my chest. Could this dream of a man get any cuter?

The ache between my legs deepened as I considered I would be the first woman he got to experiment with. My inner she-demon preened. He'd have the memory of his first sexual playtime with me for the rest of his life.

I didn't think I was anyone's first anything, other than Quick's — I shut that distracting train of thought down almost immediately. I only wanted to focus on this tall, dirty blond-haired, hazel-eyed, cinnamon-smelling, sinfully sexy man in front of me.

My eyes traced along the lines of his defined chest muscles and molded abs, with the soft blond treasure trail of hair following his belly button to beneath the waistband of his jeans.

Fuck, he's hot.

"Drew," I exclaimed, "What are you embarrassed about? That just means this is going to be even more fun."

I grinned wickedly at him and wiggled my eyebrows. "I know that not everyone had Super-Miranda as a mom, and my experience was definitely different from most teenagers. But the biggest thing she taught me above the physical was that anything sexual is best when shared with someone you trust and respect."

I paused and gave him a soft smile, curling an strand of hair around my finger. Then I softened my tone. "I'd love to share some of these firsts with you — if you want to."

His shy smile morphed into a salacious grin, and his body shifted like a languid cat as he rolled us over to lie on the bed, his weight on top of me.

"If I want to, Winter? You've been in my fucking dreams for months. I've fucked myself in the shower twenty times since our little quickie in the storeroom, thinking about how you felt around me, and I didn't even get to see this gorgeous body in the dark. Yes, I fucking want to."

He growled the last few words as he ground his erection into me, perfectly aligned to rub against my clit. My body electrified with the friction, and my panties immediately flooded.

I reached down, unbuttoned his jeans, and he raised his hips to tug them down his legs. He ripped off my leggings and panties in one pull. Then his hands trailed up my thighs until they gripped my hips, and he ground against me again. My wetness soaked the front of his boxers.

"Fuck," he groaned. "I won't last long like this." He took a deep, calming breath and rested his body on his forearms, hovering over me.

I grinned, tilting my head up and nipping his pouty bottom lip. "We have all night, baby," I cooed, my voice sultry and low, giving away exactly how much I wanted this. "I don't want to walk tomorrow. Show me what you can do to make me scream."

He took my mouth in a demanding kiss, plundering me with his tongue like I was the oxygen he needed to survive.

In the same moment, he plunged two fingers inside of me, flicking the tips of his fingers. Zings of pleasure shot through my body, surprising me.

My back arched, and I pressed my breasts tighter into him when he massaged one of them, his thumb stroking along the peak of my nipple, deepening the pleasure. I cried out, an orgasm building far sooner than I expected. The warm tingling sensation built within my core, my walls tightening as I pulsed around him.

Without warning, he added a third finger and rubbed the heel of his hand over my clit. I shattered, muffling my scream of ecstasy in the crook of his neck as I broke our kiss for the first time.

My body convulsed with euphoria and my muscles relaxed into a liquid pile on the sheets.

Coming down from my post-orgasm high, I murmured lazily, "I don't think you need to worry about any inexperience." I drew his hand up and pressed my lips to the tips. "You are a god with those hands."

Drew chuckled and a deviously sexy smile stretched across his lips.

"Can you handle more of me?" he teased before moving to kiss the side of my jaw. His lips burned a trail down to my ear, caressing my earlobe with his tongue.

"Fuck yes," I barely breathed the words. Drew sat up quickly and reached for his pants for what I assumed was a condom.

"Wait." His gaze shot to mine. "You said you were clean, right?"

He nodded slowly, then comprehension flicked across his face.

"I hate the feel of condoms, Drew." I confessed, making a face of disgust. "Necessary evil and all, but I told you I have an IUD, and it wouldn't be our first time ..." I trailed off, letting the request hang in the air.

Once again, memories of the storeroom poked through my lust-filled haze. I knew how good he felt bareback; some of the best sex of my life had been riding him hard in the dark space with my back pressed against large commercial-sized cans of stewed tomatoes.

More wetness gushed between my thighs at the mental picture. I needed him *now*.

His eyes widened in surprise, and he swallowed hard, nodding. He yanked his boxers down and off, and his thick cock bounced against the taut skin of his abdomen. The head glistened with pre-cum, and I relished the thought of him coming in me.

Suddenly, he pulled my hips toward him and thrust inside me, driving as deeply as he could at that angle. My body shuddered hard at the intrusion, but I wrapped my legs around his waist as he continued to pound inside of me at a punishing pace. I tilted my hips so he could get even deeper, and his pubic bone deliciously rubbed against my clit, the friction making me moan.

He captured the sound in a passionate kiss, his tongue dancing with mine, tasting every part of my mouth as he drove me into oblivion. My second release was even stronger than the first. My pussy walls clenched him so tightly he let out an animalistic growl before he shouted his own release, his hot cum flooding me and marking me as his.

The sound of his coming undone drew out my orgasm and minutes went by as we panted heavily in each other's arms, not moving an inch.

Eventually, he withdrew and settled in on his side next to me in the bed. His long fingers interlaced with mine and he kissed the knuckle of each finger on my right hand, lips brushing my skin reverently.

"I'm just going to say it," Drew mused as he stroked the back of my hand with his thumb. "That was the best sex of my life."

I grinned, my body fully sated and relaxed by his touch. "It was incredible." I agreed, my own fingertips tracing the faint hairline across his chest. "How long do you think it would take you to go again?"

He stared at me, mouth agape, but then smiled widely and stroked his cock to life. "For you? Minutes." I watched as his words turned to reality as his softening member grew to its impressive size once again, hard and proud and ready for me.

"You said you wanted to try more with me, right?" I raised a quizzical eyebrow as he nodded. "Do you trust me to do something … dirtier?"

He burst out laughing. Clearly, my question took him by surprise, but I continued to look at him with questioning eyes. When he recognized I was serious, his face sobered up.

"Winter, I'll try anything with you. If it was anything like that," — he gestured toward our naked bodies — "I don't think I'll ever leave your room."

I tilted my head in thought. "What have you always wanted to try?"

He flushed deeper than the red tinging his satisfied face and rubbed his palms over the stubble of his jaw.

"I've always been curious about ... anal." He whispered the word and I quivered at the cutest display of vulnerability I'd ever seen from a man. My heart pulsed, and so did my pussy. I was going to give him a night to remember.

I smirked conspiratorially and rolled over to lie on my stomach. "Done. I *love* ass play."

His jaw opened and closed like a baby guppy. I rose on my hands and knees in front of him. He hesitated for a moment before crawling behind me, cock erect and ready.

"I assume you've watched some anal porn?" I looked back at him through my thick eyelashes and his pink cheeks were back on full display.

"Er-yeah," he croaked out, trying to cover his awkwardness with a strained cough.

I couldn't hold back a school-girl giggle; his shyness was so adorable and far different from what I was used to with sexual exploration with hot, self-assured men. This experience, me directing the fucking in this way, was new for me too, and I was loving it.

"Good." I smiled sweetly at him. "But instead of lube tonight, you're going to use our cum. Slick up your cock, Johnson."

He scooped up the mixture of both of our arousal dripping down the insides of my thighs, then rubbed the makeshift lube all over himself.

It was so fucking *hot*.

He paused, awaiting my next instructions.

"Okay, now you're going to need to prep me." I pushed back into him so that my ass was in the air, back arched like a cat.

"Like most porn, it's dead wrong on its depiction of anal sex. You can't just go in guns a-blazing without properly lubing up or stretching out. It's actually really dangerous to do it that way."

I looked at his large stiff cock pointedly with a raised eyebrow. "You could really hurt me with that thing."

His cheeks bloomed into twin dark roses, but he managed to give me a wink and positioned his naked specimen of a body directly behind me.

I grabbed his hand and sucked on his two fingers; the combination of our flavors wove together on my tongue. I spread a thick layer of lubricating saliva across them and popped them out of my mouth.

"Scissor me with these." My voice dropped an octave and came out in breathy anticipation.

He didn't hesitate. His thick fingers gently thrust into my ass and opened up, stretching me and sending sparks across my vision. He never stopped while his other hand pushed two fingers into my swollen cunt, the rhythm deliciously setting my insides on fire.

"Fuck," I cried out in pleasure. "Drew!"

His name on my lips must have unleashed the animal within, because he increased his speed until my body could barely stand the pressure, the fullness, the—

I screamed when his fingers came out of my ass and the blunt head of cock pushed into me; the tip of him was just barely buried in the tight ring of muscle. I turned my head to watch his eyes flutter closed, his full lips parted in bliss.

I pushed my body back into him, pressing him deeper into me. The groan he uttered was pure sin, and my pussy clenched around his fingers in response.

"Please move, baby," I whimpered. My wetness soaked his hand and dripped onto the sheets. "Take all of me. Use me. Come for me."

His control snapped. In one fluid thrust, he was fully seated inside of me. I had never seen such a look of awe and wonder on his face as when he pushed into me, like us sharing this moment was a religious experience for him. Maybe it was.

I heard a muffled sound in the kitchen and it distracted my attention for a moment before Drew started moving, really moving. His cock made me so full I could hardly breathe.

"Oh, fuck, Winter, you feel—so—incredible—so —"

He stroked my G spot, and the sensations of him being fully inside of me everywhere he could caused me to catapult off the edge, my orgasm pulling a ragged cry from my throat as I fisted the surrounding blankets. My vision darkened and my head spun as Drew wrung every last drop of pleasure from my spent body.

I wished I could have recorded the sound of Drew's cry as his cum filled me; his guttural groan was so satisfying I could probably come to it on its own.

I collapsed onto the bed and his heavy body gently landed on top of me. He pulled out and shifted to the side so we lay facing each other once again, naked and fully sated.

The look on his face was so exposed, so pure, it caught me by surprise. My heart stuttered in my chest at the peace in his eyes, the relaxed muscles of his jaw. Drew had never looked this ... happy.

I made him this happy.

"That was" — he pulled me closer to him and wrapped me in his arms — "incredible. You just topped my best experience on the same night. I'm never going to be the same."

He tucked my head under his chin and lightly stroked my hair.

"Stay the night?" I mumbled into his chest, not wanting his warmth or his comfort to leave me.

"Sure, baby. I don't have to be at the diner until noon."

Right. Joe was coming home tomorrow, and Drew was picking him up in the morning. In my lust-colored haze, I had temporarily forgotten.

"Drew, you don't have to stay, you've got a lot on your plate and —"

He didn't let me finish, placing a single, sex-scented finger to my lips. "This is the only place I want to be right now."

We stayed in each other's arms for a few more minutes before getting up to shower. We kept our hands off of each other to soap up enough to get clean, and Drew went to the kitchen to grab some peanut butter toast as a bedtime snack.

My phone was buzzing on my bed when I finally came back into the bedroom after the very lengthy process of drying my hair. It was my least favorite grooming activity, but it had to be done. Sacrifices for beauty. More like sacrifices to not have to ruin another hairbrush with knots that would make a sailor proud.

I picked it up absently, not paying any attention to the call screen as Drew came into the room. He looked divine in just a towel wrapped around his waist and a large plate piled high with peanut-buttery goodness.

"Hello," I answered, finally registering that probably only serial killers would call me at 10:45 on a Tuesday. I made a move to hang up when my father's voice came through the line.

"Hey stranger!" he said cheerily, like calling me at this time of night was completely normal and appropriate. "How's my girl?"

My entire body froze, my mind bringing me back to that terrible night when I saw my father in a whole different light. What could he possibly want?

"Um, fine, Dad. Is something wrong?"

I anxiously picked at the sweatshirt I had thrown on. I hadn't seen my parents since before Christmas, after they had told me I was going to have to spend Christmas with the Quicksilvers or alone.

They had reached out to tell me they had gotten home safe from Switzerland, but they hadn't invited me over or attempted to make any plans with me in almost two months.

Same shit, different year.

"Of course, honey. I've just missed you is all. I know you were upset about Christmas, but your mother and I would love to see you soon to hear all about your holidays. Can we make dinner together soon?"

My heart softened a bit, despite the gnawing unease of having to pretend that I didn't know my dad's dark secret. Technically, I only knew he *had* a dark secret, and that it involved Georgio's fights and a mysterious blond woman, but that made the feeling worse. My imagination was getting the better of me with all of the possible scenarios.

"Sure, Dad. I'm headed to bed now though, okay? I have school in the morning." I motioned to Drew to sit on the bed with me and I snagged a piece of gooey toast from the plate.

"Absolutely. Text your mother, would you, sweetheart? She misses you."

If she missed me, she could take the time to send me a message herself. I bit back the retort, even though it was harder to swallow than the toast I was about to eat.

"Sure, Dad. Talk soon."

I hung up the phone, took a very unladylike bite of our snack, and cuddled into Drew's side. Tomorrow had problems, *many* problems to solve, but tonight?

Tonight had been perfect.

CHAPTER 14

SHANE

I felt like banging my head against the wall to knock some sense into me.

My eyes were burning like I had rubbed them with the roughest form of sandpaper. I had been staring at the computer screen for hours, scouring the flash drive of stolen files from Dad's office. A twinge of guilt hit my stomach every time I considered the betrayal, but I had convinced myself it was for the greater good.

Winter could have died at that fight night. Drew too. Hell, I was really starting to like Travis. I wouldn't risk anything happening to them again.

I was realistic enough to admit that my super-power capabilities had limitations. I couldn't shoot a gun, at least not yet, and I didn't know martial arts like Cam or have Travis' charm to get my foot out of my mouth in tough situations.

If this were a James Bond movie, I could chase the bad guy down the snowy slopes of a Swiss mountainside like a badass, but I doubted Georgio was hitting Spruce Acres up anytime soon.

My superpower was data analysis. Truly the most pathetic of all the super-powers, but I had hoped I could be useful to The Core Four — and Cam. I didn't know where he fit into our mix, but he was going to have to cram in somewhere. Considering he was the biggest of all of us, Winter would probably be the one doing the cramming. That thought brought an uncomfortable twitch in my jeans.

I shook it off. Now was not the time. When my eyes glazed to the point I couldn't tell if a number was a "1" or a "4", I stopped. It was time for a nap and a break.

I needed to drop by my parents this afternoon anyway to see Mom. I owed her a dinner date.

After a two hour siesta, I packed up my stuff to head home for the evening, my heart lightening at the thought of seeing Shiloh and eating Mom's cooking. It had only been a week, but it felt like forever after the events that had taken years off of my life. I was in the mood for some good family comfort.

Winter and Drew were working today, and Travis and I hadn't actually spent any time together outside of being with Winter. I was going to change that soon. It was time to build this budding friendship into bromance status, and I was this perfect person for the job.

I locked up the apartment and made the trek to my parent's place in silence, mulling over my lack of progress. Maybe Dad didn't have any incriminating files at all. Maybe it was Darren who was involved with all the corporate cloak and dagger stuff.

I doubted it. Our fathers were thick as thieves and always had been. It would be more unbelievable to me that one of them had committed crimes without the other knowing it, than it would be to believe they had committed crimes at all.

"Hi, honey," Mom greeted me as I let myself into my happy place. She walked down the hall toward me as I took my shoes off by the front door. She was limping badly again, I noticed. I wondered if she had been using her cane?

"Hey, Mom." I swept her up into my arms and gave her a light kiss on the cheek. "I've missed you."

"You've missed my cooking," she said with a laugh, her gray eyes that matched mine crinkling at their corners. "I know how well you and Winter cook."

I let out a loud laugh. No one could deny my terrible cooking skills. I grinned at her and put her gently back on her feet, careful not to jostle her bad leg.

"Is Dad home? I had a few questions for him about a project before dinner."

"He's at the office right now, but you can leave him a note in the study. I don't think he'll be back until late this evening." Mom started back down the hall toward the kitchen, calling after me as she went. "Dinner will be in twenty minutes if you want to get that done now. Shiloh brought a friend who wants to play board games tonight."

Right. Shiloh had a new boyfriend I had yet to be introduced to. Tonight was going to be fun.

But first things first. Dad's study.

When I entered the room, I tried to see it from an outsider's perspective. Like Jacques Clouseau or another classic detective. What would they look for?

This room had been a comfort to me for my entire life. Some of my earliest memories were of Dad sitting at the large oak desk behind massive computer monitors — they were much thinner now — reviewing designs and mapping out complicated calculations. I would sit in the armchair on the weekends and do my homework while he worked on various work projects and we listened to eighties rock music blasting from the overhead speakers. Fond memories.

I sat now in the older striped chair to look at the room from another angle. It was facing Dad's bookshelves, five floor-to-ceiling shelves of textbooks, journal articles, classic literature, and even a limited edition set of the Harry Potter series. I scanned the shelves with more scrutiny. Maybe Dad's secrets weren't on his computer. He was smarter than that.

I stood and moved closer to the shelves, running my hands over the books on the top shelf. You had to be tall to even see the top row of books, which was no problem for Dad and me, but would be a problem for someone shorter. Maybe he hid something up here?

I grasped the shelf's ledge, but I only grabbed collections of dust. The books were wedged tightly within the frames, and it was unlikely anything could be tucked within them unless Dad had a book with a hollowed-out center like they did in the movies. Somehow, I felt that was a stretch.

I continued along all the other shelves, skimming the titles and assessing if any of them looked out of place.

When I got to the second row from the bottom, my eyes landed on a high school yearbook. Dad had grown up in the area, but I had never seen a record of his high school years before.

Despite my mission, curiosity won out. I grabbed the book and browsed through the pages, laughing at the fashion and the hair. I flipped through to the back, seeking Dad's graduation photo, where I knew the real comic gold would be. I went farther than I meant to and was about to flip back to the "Q's" when something caught my eye.

Some*one* caught my eye. Darren Wallace's picture stared back at me with Winter's eyes. It wouldn't have been weird to see except I had always been told that Darren and Dad met in university not high school. I didn't even know he had grown up here. Winter didn't have any grandparents and both of her parents were only children, and I had always thought the Wallaces moved here because Dad had endorsed Cascade Falls as a great suburb town outside of Carlisle when they were opening up Wallace Anderson Quicksilver.

Had it been a misunderstanding? Did I get the story wrong?

I thumbed through the pages with fresh eyes, critically skimming all the graduating pages. My heart stopped at Georgio Carlos's picture. The man had barely changed his looks since he was eighteen, except for a more dangerous edge and a small amount of gray hair and smile lines.

The face of Eileen Gibbons was on the next page, and Drew's blast-from-the-past twin, Joe Johnson, was a few pages after that.

They all grew up together? How did we not know this?

My heart skipped a beat when I skimmed past the "Z" names into the extracurricular photos, only to see a large page dedicated to one photo with a bunch of handwritten signatures written on it in black marker.

Darren and Dad stood front and center, dressed in leather jackets and aviator-style sunglasses, enormous smiles on their faces with an arm over each other's shoulders.

Next to Dad was Camden Lane, an equal smile on his face, decked out in a football letterman jacket, and a pretty blond girl by his side I didn't recognize. Georgio stood tall next to Darren, his arm wrapped around a beaming Eileen. Stanley Eccles bracketed the other side next to blondie. I looked at the photo closely. The blondie looked familiar, but I couldn't place her.

Holy shit. They didn't just know each other. They were *friends*. Good friends, by the looks of things. *Best* friends. The only one missing was Joe.

Underneath the photo, the caption read *The Shambala Society*, and listed everyone's names. Not that I needed them — I had known everyone but the blonde, and her name, 'Brenda Simpson,' wasn't anyone I recognized.

The handwritten signatures were from everyone in the photo with wishes of good luck for the future and a Latin phrase I didn't know: Vincit qui patitur.

What had happened to this "society?" Camden and Dad were like oil and water — I had witnessed it in enough board rooms to know that firsthand. Camden and Stanley were filthy rich business executives. Georgio was a mobster, Eileen a money launderer. Where did our fathers fit into this equation?

My heart sunk. In no way good, I knew.

I snapped a photo of the picture as evidence to show Winter later and closed the book to put it back on the shelf.

I was sliding it back into its position when I hit some resistance and pulled it out again. A silver piece of metal flashed in the light laying innocently on the wood.

A micro flash drive. My pulse raced at the possibilities. A hidden flash drive on the shelf that held their other secrets? Not a coincidence. Not at all.

I grabbed my laptop bag, knowing I had minutes before Mom came looking for me, and opened my laptop to copy the files as quickly as I could.

It took five minutes of nail-biting agony to get the 137 files transferred over. I quickly unplugged, put everything back to as close to how I found it, and left the study of secrets behind.

I should have known the files were encrypted. If Dad took all the precautions to hide the drive, of course, he would add a layer of espionage protection.

I was back in my living room that evening after having eaten my body weight in spaghetti carbonara and interrogating Shiloh's new guy during Monopoly. My guts churned throughout the dinner, but I had done my best to stay focused. Mom deserved the attention.

Now, I was back at my spy job. I had a mountain of project work from my co-op to finish and I was supposed to be meeting up with Drew and Winter tonight, but I wasn't ready to report anything yet. We needed that information.

I knew who could get it. Or at least try. But did I really want to go down that road again?

Blaise Borden had the skills and the know-how to hack the files. I knew he did. How willing was I to open up that wound and welcome him through the door?

I saw him at work — at least I saw him when Eccles came in to discuss the larger projects and I saw him in a few of my classes, where we did the awkward nod of acknowledgment like bros and went on our merry way. We did nothing that required me to be in a room alone with him. I didn't know if I could handle it.

I took out my phone to text him and then shoved it back in my jeans pocket. Nope.

After wrestling with my relationship demons for the better part of an hour, I got up the courage to text him.

SQ: Hey.

Great. Easy start. Two minutes later:

B-Lover: Hey?

Fuck, I needed to change his name on my phone.

SQ: This is weird, but I've got a major favor to ask you.

Yeah, I wasn't going to dick around. It was bad enough I had to cross this bridge, and I needed to know what was on that little stick from hell.

Blaise Old-News Borden: ... Okay. Is this an in-person thing?

SQ: Yeah. Can we meet tomorrow? Johnson's? I'll buy you lunch.

Blaise Old-News Borden: I'll just take a coffee. 2?

SQ: Yeah. 2 is great. See you then.

This recent development was making me twitchy. The conversation was opening up a wound I thought was healed. Guess I still had some work to do — too bad Mandy wasn't an option anymore. That was definitely for the best, but my heart and dick could have used the distraction tonight.

Fuck it. I was going to Winter's. It wasn't too late; they'd probably still be around. I sent her off a quick text and shot off the couch, filled with an anxious energy I needed to burn off.

I got there twenty minutes later and let myself into the building with the key Winter had given me the day she'd moved in and walked up the stairs with pep in my step. This had been a good decision. Snow and Drew would want the new details, and then we could order pizza and watch a good movie on TV. Or Seinfeld reruns.

I gave a courtesy knock before unlocking her front door with my other key. The room was dark and the small television in her living room was still on, a rom-com running on mute in the background.

I was about to call out when a deep guttural groan, followed by a breathy moan, came from Winter's bedroom. I snapped to attention.

Duh, Shane.

We may have been a friendship throuple, but Winter and Drew were a couple now — if you could call that love nest a 'couple' thing.

You weren't there, they were alone, of course they would use that opportunity to ...

I should leave.

Curiosity was going to be the death of me today because I couldn't force my feet to move in the opposite direction. Instead, I quietly moved forward into the space towards her room, a room I had slept in far more times than I could count, in her bed, in her arms.

It did not prepare me for what I'd see. Drew's sexy-as-hell naked white ass glared at me from my stance in the hallway as he pounded into Winter from behind. I had a slight side profile view, and could see exactly what hole his cock was entering, with my Snow's breasts bouncing beneath the strengths of his thrusts. Fuck, I wished I could see their faces.

My cock had hardened to granite in my jeans as I watched the live porn in front of me.

I shouldn't be here.

I turned as quietly as I could and made my way through the apartment, closing her front door softly and locking it behind me.

Why did I do that? And why did I suddenly have the intense need to join them?

CHAPTER 15

TRAVIS

Today was a good day.

Mom was doing better and could come home soon. Devon had called from rehab and was feeling great; he planned on coming home in a few days too.

I kept telling my heart to not get its hopes up, but it always did when Devon called to enthusiastically describe his 'new man' status. I supposed if I didn't have hope he could change, I wouldn't keep dropping thousands of dollars I didn't have to get him the help he needed. Maybe this time we'd win the recovery lotto.

Work had been nerve-wracking, but consistent. Since that soul crushing meeting in Georgio's office, nothing was out of the ordinary at work. We set up, we cleaned, we made drinks, and the next night we did it all over again. There wasn't a single whisper about an upcoming fight night. It was as if Georgio was intentionally lying low until the heat died down.

Not that there had been any heat, really. Nothing in the news other than the first incident; no suspicious presence of investigators or police. Our daily routine was so normal it was off-putting, like I was caught in a professional version of the *Stepford Wives*. I didn't know if I was the wife or the husband in this situation.

The money runs were still mine to do every two weeks, and that put me constantly on high alert; I didn't want to keep carrying the gun, but I didn't see any other choice, especially since all our lives had been at risk just two weeks before. I dropped the money off, ducked my head, and left quickly, determined to blot out that part of my weeks with much better memories.

The good news coming in from all sides today would help with that. The best part about today was I had an actual date with Winter, our first since we had broken up and we'd kind of, sort of gotten back together again. We had never really confirmed a relationship status, but I took the fact she had agreed to go skiing with me today as a good sign.

Not that I was a good skier. She was definitely going to kick my ass, but that was going to be half the fun. I looked forward to seeing my beautiful girl in action, flying down the hill at 40 miles an hour with that stunning fucking smile on her face.

I was meeting her at the hill, already waiting in the parking lot with my older third-hand pair of skis and boots, ready to crush this day and get her back into my arms for good.

Her adorable green Volkswagen pulled in beside my ratty old Daytona minutes later and she got out of the car. She was already dressed in her forest green one-piece ski suit, looking like a vintage postcard for hot models on the hill.

She flashed me a warm smile. "Is it bad to say I have some first date jitters?" she joked and grabbed my hands with her mittened ones, swinging them slightly between us. "I really want this to work, Travis, but I can admit I've got some reservations."

I squeezed her hands gently and raised an eyebrow. This was a necessary conversation and we might as well get it over with. No time like the present.

"I can say the same, beautiful. You cut and run on me pretty quickly." I held up a hand as a sign of peace when her mouth opened in protest.

"I don't blame you for that. I lied to you. That part is true. But now that you know *why* I lied, can you understand my position? How badly I didn't want to fuck this up with you?"

I leaned against the trunk of my car and pulled her into my arms, looking down into her bright blue eyes with all the sincerity I could muster. No charm, no manipulation, just the raw, vulnerable emotion of a man who had it bad for the woman standing in front of him.

"I need to know that if we say that this is on, that we're going to make a go of this, Drew and whoever else is in the equation notwithstanding," — I had my suspicions who — "then you can't run away from me again. I'm going to fuck up, you're going to fuck up, but we need to make a commitment to each other that we're not just going to run away when things get hard."

"That's not exactly fair, Travis." Winter pulled back from me and frowned, the sharp crease of her brows darkening her eyes. "You didn't just fuck up, and things didn't just get hard, they —"

"I agree. I lied, and I never should have lied, and from this point onward, you will get nothing but the truth from me. Every dirty, dangerous, and dark detail. I hope you'll share the same with me. But I need to know you're in this, Winter. I can't have you without having *all* of you. You're going to break my heart, otherwise."

It was a risky admission, but it was the truth. I couldn't go down this road with her again without having her heart in return. Even if it took me years to get it.

Her gaze dropped to her mittens in front of me, and I held my breath as the long pause turned into an excruciating silence.

Her eyes finally met mine again, and a saucy smirk traced her lips.

"I agree to the terms you've presented. Are we going to sign a contract, or will you take me at my word?"

My incredulity at her casual delivery must have shown on my face. She bit her lip, an apology crossing her features.

"I'm sorry, I'm an asshole." She blew out a breath. "Yes, Travis. I want this. I want you. If you're willing to share me with Drew, I want you."

I couldn't help the broad grin making its way across my cheeks. I smiled so hard my face hurt. I lifted her up and spun her around; she squealed in surprise. When I set her down beside her car, I pressed a gentle kiss to the tip of her nose.

"You've just made me a very happy man." I winked and brushed a finger down the line of her lips. "Let's get your gear so I can watch you kick my ass down the hill."

It was one of the silliest Hallmark-worthy dates I had ever been on.

We held hands and cuddled going up the gondola. We shared spiked hot chocolate at the top of the hill at the little snack shack. She did indeed kick my ass going down the hill, and I nearly skied into a tree three times. Meanwhile, she was doing front flips off some of the smaller jumps and landing with ease, putting my masculinity to shame for a second before I swallowed that asshole ego and cheered her on. I had known Quick was a former pro, but Winter was better than I had given her credit.

She was a little daredevil, and her whoops and hollers down the slope made me feel like a giddy little kid again. The gleam in her eyes and the sexy way she winked at me before doing something particularly dangerous was enough to harden my cock under my many layers of clothing. After a few hours, the restrictive clothes and sexual tension were getting painful.

We stripped out of our suits in the parking lot and packed up the cars with our well-used gear. It was dark now, and the mountain was lit up with large flood lights for night skiing. I loved watching the specks of black shadows whiz down the hill against the snowy backdrop. I had fun today and had I grown up with money, I would have taken up the sport for real. Maybe it wasn't too late.

I was about to kiss Winter goodnight when she folded her arms and stuck out her jaw in challenge. "Were you serious about the dirty, dark truths and all of that?"

I nodded my head slowly. "Every dirty truth," I confirmed. "What's up?"

"I'd like to go back to your place."

I gulped, not at all expecting that request and regretting my previous response. I didn't want to take Winter back to my place. I didn't want her to see my tiny-ass trailer with its retro-seventies wallpaper and rust-colored shag carpet, or my tiny bedroom with its paper-thin walls. I had never felt outright shame for my circumstances before, but the flush of heat crawling up my neck was pretty close.

"Fuck, Winter. I don't want you to see my place."

"Why not?" She cocked an eyebrow. "That's where you grew up, isn't it? It's your home, isn't it? Why wouldn't I want to see the home of the man I'm now officially dating again? No secrets, remember?"

I sighed, letting out a long breath through pursed lips. My lip ring chafed against my skin.

"I'm poor, Winter. I grew up poor, and I'm still poor. There is nothing to see. Can we just go back to your place and watch a movie or something?" I held onto the shred of hope that we really wouldn't have to go back to my place to prove my promise to her. Somehow, I knew that would not be the case.

"I want to see your place, Travis. Please invite me over."

This was a test, and I needed to pass. My shoulders slumped in defeat and I nodded to my car. "Get in. I can drive you back to your car later. I'm only 15 minutes from here."

We both climbed into my dejected Dodge and I barely said a word as we drove toward the crappy trailer park on the outskirts of Sheldonville.

When we pulled up to the building, I tried to look at it through her eyes. The dark brown vinyl shutters were cracking at their edges, and the beige-painted wooden window sills were rotting underneath. It looked tired, but it had been well kept over the years, thanks mostly to Devon because I had been too busy working. I was grateful for it at that moment.

"Home, sweet home," I murmured and blew out a breath through my teeth, grimacing. I opened the car door and got out, and headed to unlock the scratched metal screen door acting as the gateway to my childhood.

Broken promises. Good intentions. Inner demons. Love.

This trailer housed it all. I even felt a sense of comfort here with her standing by my side when I entered the cramped space, its ceiling only sitting a few inches above my head.

"This is it," I said. She closed the door behind us. I swept my arms out wide around me. The doorway entered into our small kitchen with its beige Formica countertops and the pine plank cupboards. It looked tiny with the two of us in it.

I nodded my head toward the adjacent living room; our flowery couches from the eighties were covered in cozy blankets and decorative pillows from back when Mom could still crochet. The only modern item was the 50" flat screen television mounted to the wall, my Christmas gift to Devon one year from a Black Friday sale.

Winter smiled, a genuine, soft smile that gently crinkled her eyes at the corners. "I like it." She grabbed for my hand and interlaced our fingers. "It's warm and cozy. Like a family who loves each other lives here."

That... wasn't the response I had been expecting.

Instantly, I relaxed. Winter came from money, but she was the least pretentious person I had ever met. My childhood home would not be the reason she'd turn away from me.

Lies would. I would not go down that road again.

I needed to kiss her. I took her face in my palms and brushed my lips against hers. The urge to have her flooded through me like a dam of lust had opened up between us.

She leaned into me and pushed me back against the kitchen table, her palms braced against my chest. The kiss deepened as our tongues and teeth battled for dominance in a frenzy, raising the temperature in the room by 300 degrees.

She reached down to grab my belt and unbuckled it, dragging my jeans down my thighs. I kicked them under the table while pulling the hem of her shirt up and over her head. The lacy bra underneath was a deep wine color and the sight of her in it made all the blood flow straight to my cock.

I pulled her leggings down and off, trailing kisses up her neck as she pulled off my ski sweater and the t-shirt underneath. She roamed her hands all over my chest, tugging on my nipple ring and tracing the tattoos along my arms.

Her matching panties were the last straw; my fingers delved into the fabric, trailing the pads of my fingertips along her slit. She was so wet and …

Fuck. She had a tampon in.

Heat flooded up my spine. Ever since our first date, I'd had a fantasy about this. Nothing was going to stop me from taking her right now.

I spun her around, pulling her back to my front, and leaned her against the kitchen table. Pulling my hand out of her underwear, I gently caressed her hip bones, burying my face in her hair.

"Are you past the first date jitters yet, beautiful? Can I fuck you raw inside your hot, wet pussy? Let me feel all of your juices drip down my cock, painting me red?"

She whimpered when I nipped her earlobe and nibbled along the shadow of her jaw. I pulled down her panties and spread apart her legs, reaching for the cotton string between her thighs and yanking it out, tossing it aside, and opening her up for me.

I palmed my cock, harder than it had ever been before in my life, and lined up, notching my tip at her entrance. Her warmth was too tempting to hold out any longer, and I thrust into her in one deep motion. The glide of my piercing along her lubricated walls made us both groan.

My cock pulsed at the feeling of her wrapped around me; hot and wet and deliciously sweet.

So. Fucking. Good.

"Fuck, you feel so good, beautiful. This will never stop me from fucking you again. You wait until Drew gets a taste. We'll have to take turns fucking you all week. Maybe we'll just save time and fuck you together."

I'd meant it — I'd share my beautiful girl with Drew if that's what she wanted. I was going to make her need it so badly she begged us for it.

From the gush of wetness coating my cock and the vise her pussy held me in, it would not be a hard sell.

The image of her between the two of us, moaning our names and her luscious curves bouncing as she took all the cock she could handle, blasted a supersonic wave of pleasure through me, and it took all of my self-control not to come on the spot.

Fuck her body, and what it did to mine. I had waited so fucking long to have her back in my arms again. I had craved her kisses, her hot mouth all over me, her pussy wrapped around my cock like she owned it.

She did own it. She owned me.

I brought my hands up and squeezed her breasts, the perfect size to fit into my palms. She mewled in pleasure, and I kneaded the swollen flesh, brushing my thumbs over her taut nipples over and over while I continued to pound into her at a punishing pace.

This wasn't a tender moment; it was raw and dirty, full of pent-up longing and aggression and pain. Our pain was culminating into the pinnacle of pleasure. I knew once she came for me and me for her, we could finally heal.

I reached my hand down to her swollen bundle of nerves. I stroked her clit, teasingly at first, until she whimpered and clamped down on my cock even tighter.

I grinned against her neck, scraping my teeth over the sensitive flesh as I increased the pressure, rubbing her hard and fast while thrusting as deep as I could inside her. I wanted to live inside her skin.

In seconds, her back arched and she let out a deep, throaty cry that would put any porn I had ever watched to shame.

Fuck me, I could live for that sound.

I rode her hard through her orgasm, drawing it out by slowly scraping my piercing up and down the sensitive nerves of her pussy walls before I couldn't hold out my own any longer.

My balls tightened and the familiar tingling sensation shot up my spine as my cum filled her core.

I held her to me for a moment, my arms wrapped around her waist with her ass tucked neatly into my hips. We were sweaty and sticky, covered in cum and blood, and the rich, meaty scent of sex hung in the surrounding air.

It was fucking perfect.

I was going to be doing that again. And again. And again. How had I not considered this could be a thing before?

I gently pulled out of her, turning her around for a deep, lingering kiss. I told her I loved her in that kiss; that the months apart had killed me, that I didn't want to be in a world without her in it; that she was mine, whatever it took, sharing or not.

In case she didn't get the message, I said the words out loud.

"I love you, Winter. I have for a while now. Can you find it in your heart to let me?"

Before she could respond, the metal door rattled behind us. I hadn't bothered to lock it — why would I? No one was living here but me.

Devon's booming voice entered the small room. I quickly pushed Winter behind me and leaned over the couch to grab one of the small pillows to at least cover my dick. Hopefully, Mom wouldn't miss this one.

"Hey, big brother."

My miniature lookalike flashed an impish, curious grin at me and the dark-haired beauty over my shoulder.

"Miss me?"

CHAPTER 16

WINTER

"So, remind me why we are doing this again?" I asked Hillary as I browsed through the rack of pricey cashmere sweaters at Phinmore's, the most upscale boutique in Cascade Falls. I looked down at my very casual attire and instantly felt out of place.

"We've been over this, Winter." Hillary sighed in what sounded like exasperation. "I need girlfriends. You need girlfriends. We are trying out this" — she grabbed three dresses from the rack next to me and added them to her already full arms — "girlfriend 'thing'."

Under my breath, I muttered, "I have friends," even as a more recent conversation with Quick came to mind where he argued I only had him and Raven.

Fair enough. I could use another friend or two. But Hillary? I wouldn't have pictured a friendship with Hillary Lane in a million years, but today's outing had been good so far. Great, even.

I was floored when she had dropped by the diner last week and asked me to come with her to do a bit of pre-wedding shopping, but I had been insanely curious to see what a day in Hillary's presence looked like.

Pretty predictable, really. She picked me up in her luxurious Jaguar, and then we grabbed very expensive coffee and croissants from Madigan's, the nicest café this side of Carlisle, before proceeding to "Riches Row"—the snootiest set of shops in town. Logan owned many of these buildings. Maybe she got a discount?

I gulped at the price tag of yet another thing in this place I couldn't afford and turned to look at her.

"I don't think I can buy a single thing in this place, Hillary. I can't even afford the socks." I waved my hands for emphasis toward the display of multicolored merino wool socks behind us. "I appreciate you extending the hand of friendship, but this really isn't my scene."

"Winter." Hillary sighed again, and I wondered what I was doing or saying that required so much patience. It was going to take a lot of effort to be this woman's friend.

"Of course, this place is too expensive for you."

I raised an eyebrow at the callous delivery, but to her credit, she stood strong.

"We're here for appearances only. Stanley owns a few of these businesses, and I am *expected* to put some cash into them every few months with my purchases. The charade is going to be over soon enough, but until then, I have to continue this stupid arrangement." She curled her lips in disgust.

I had never before seen the raw hatred filling her features, and it intrigued me. She must have known about Stanley's treatment of Logan — she had alluded to it in our last gut-spilling session at the diner. I just hadn't picked up on the clues — but what else was there?

"And besides," she continued airily, pointing to an attendant and then at the pile of clothes now resting on the adjacent display table. "None of these clothes are for me. They're for you."

The attendant hurried over to collect the burgeoning collection and brought it back to the rear fitting room. It took me a moment to gather my wits.

"Ummm, no," I said with shock. "That's not happening, Hillary. Generous, sure, but I'm not accepting your friendship bribes. We can just be friends, okay? I don't need things or clothes or —"

She held up a hand to stop me. "Winter, sweets. This is a fantastic opportunity for me to fulfill my familial duty." She spat the word. "And stick it to Stan by buying nothing that will be seen by the debutantes and political people and everyone I could give two shits about during our wedding celebrations, okay? You" — she pointed two fingers at me and grinned conspiratorially — "are my solution."

She batted her eyes at me and I couldn't help but grin back.

"And, sweets, you could use the help." She pointedly roamed her eyes from the top of my head to my toes while I casually gave her the middle finger in return. To my surprise, she threw back her head and laughed.

"You know how many people would do that to my face? To my back, sure, but not my face. It's why I want you as my friend, Winter."

I blushed a bit at the praise, despite myself. Appreciative glances from men I was used to. Casual connections I had in spades. But someone who wanted to actively spend time with me, just because? That was ... nice.

I leveled with her. "It would make me incredibly uncomfortable to accept any of this, Hillary. I'm used to making it on my own, and this is..." I did not really know how to finish that sentence.

"Isn't your birthday next week?" she asked absently as she pulled a navy suede skirt off another rack beside me. "Consider this an early birthday present. I'm buying the clothes anyway, Winter, and instead of me burning them in a field somewhere, you'll actually get to wear some beautiful things for no reason. I call that a win, don't you?"

My brows rose in surprise. "How did you know it was my birthday?"

She looked up from the second pile of clothing in her arms with an amused expression. "I'm very good at my job. And it's my job to know things. I don't bake, so you won't get a cake from me, but you will" — she broke into another smile as she held a soft yellow silk shirt up against my torso — "get a great outfit. Or ten. You probably *need* ten."

The attendant hovered on my periphery, no doubt waiting for the next pile of clothes to carry away. How much money did this woman *make*, anyway? She was only a few years older than me. I suddenly felt tiny with all I had accomplished in my life, compared to Hillary with her Ivy League education and family wealth.

Not that I had ever *wanted* any of those things, but Hillary's presence was commanding and powerful, and mine was just... wimpy? She was the blooming rose, and I was the baby's breath nestled next to it.

I froze in my feelings of inadequacy in that moment. I was great at locking up toxic feelings tight in my internal jar so they could never be released to the world. I was fantastic at forcing the lid closed, but not right now. Not this time.

I stood in the courtroom, the room all too familiar to me now, with its wood paneling and stuffy air. It smelled like carpet cleaner and buried sins in here. Icicles dripped down my spine, my palms cold and clammy even shoved into my pockets. I could feel the burn of their gazes on me. They weren't supposed to be here; it was a closed case, but somehow, someone greased a palm or two. His money and the power it gave him made me want to vomit. There were no buckets nearby. I had already checked. I had already puked, so there was nothing left in me to exorcise. My demons weren't from within, anyway. They were in this courtroom.

I swallowed the bile creeping up the back of my throat and turned around, meeting his stare. He smiled darkly at me with bright blue eyes, eyes I had once thought were beautiful. Now they just looked cold and heartless, a true reflection of who he was at his core. I shivered at their intensity. He was intent on ruining me. I just wished I knew what I had done to deserve this. I was...

"Winter!"

I startled, just realizing I now sat on the floor with my hands wrapped around my knees and gasping for air, like I was suddenly breathing through a pinhead.

Hillary was leaning over me, a concerned frown on her otherwise lineless face, and the hovering attendant was trying to hand me a glass of water.

It took me a minute to understand what had happened. Fuck me. Not another panic attack. I was getting to the point where I couldn't trust myself in public.

"You want to tell me what triggered that?" Hillary asked, surprisingly gently, as she put the glass of water in my trembling hands and urged me to drink.

"Triggered what?" I asked lamely, still holding my body in on itself. Hillary and I weren't besties. We were barely even friends. Now wasn't the time to open that well-sealed jar.

In true Hillary fashion, she rolled her eyes dramatically, and it was enough to make me crack a small smile. The woman was relentless.

"I know a panic attack when I see one, Winter. Believe it or not, I've had to help L—" She shook her head. "Never mind, it's not important. Drink, please," she demanded. So I obliged, bringing the cold water to my lips.

The feeling of wrung-out exhaustion blanketed me and I had the sudden urge to take a nap. The panic hangover was way worse than the alcohol kind. Give me a gallon of martinis any day over this nonsense.

"I'm fine," I insisted somewhat weakly as I struggled to my feet. I had been sitting in a pile of clothing that probably cost more than my monthly rent. I needed to get out of this place.

"Jeremy, wrap up what I've already picked out and have it delivered to our place," Hillary directed over her shoulder as she guided me by the elbow to the entrance of the boutique.

"I live two blocks over. We're going to get you settled at my place."

Fuck it, I was too tired to argue. She never let go of me as she guided me down the two streets and into the stairwell of a modern condo building above a busy shopping district. Another set of buildings Logan owned, I mused absently, though everything passed by me in a haze.

Within what felt like seconds, she had unlocked a black door with a fancy electronic key fob and led me into a stark white modern room with floor to ceiling glass windows overlooking the street.

Even in my fugue state, I could sense the luxury. Hillary finally let go of my arm and I drifted onto the huge white leather couch in the center of the room, the leather so supple it felt like butter. I laid down my head, touched my cheek to its soft surface, and closed my eyes.

"Bad, huh?"

I cracked an eyelid. Hillary was sitting down across from me on a glass coffee table with ornate golden arches for legs. She handed me an ice-cold bottle of water, and I was immediately grateful for her kindness. Hillary owed me nothing, yet she was trying to take care of me. That meant something.

"Thank you," I murmured and closed my eyes again, drifting off into the softest cow-hide cloud I had ever felt.

I sat up with a start a few minutes later — at least; it felt like minutes. My body was flushed, and I felt a little ring of drool dried to the side of my cheek. What the—

"I never expected to see you in my living room, Princess."

Oh, dear God, no.

I blearily looked up from my blissful bed of softness and stared into the honey-brown irises of Logan Eccles.

They actually had incredible depth when you had the chance to really look into them. Almost amber, thick layers of chestnut lashes framed them, bringing out flecks of gold. If only they shone with kindness instead of douche-baggery all the time.

He looked tired; his skin was paler than a sheet and dark purple circles rimmed those mesmerizing eyes. He watched me intently, but not with his usual lascivious stare. I smelled the muted tones of bergamot and bark — frankincense. Leave it to Logan to wear one of the most expensive scents in the world.

Things had been weird between us since Fight Gate. Maybe I had my own savior complex, because ever since I saw the remnants of those scars ...

He smirked, the expression so familiar and irritating it was enough to snap me out of my apparently psychotic stupor and smarten up.

"And you never will again." I attempted a glare and stood abruptly, but the quick motion made me lightheaded and I swayed on my feet. Logan's hand immediately wrapped around my back to steady me.

"If you can't stand up straight, maybe I'll just have to tuck you into my bed for the night." The insufferable man winked at me suggestively, but the action seemed to lack its usual bite.

"Logan, fuck off," Hillary called from somewhere behind me. I turned around to see her stirring something on the stove in the open-concept kitchen. I hadn't even noticed it when we came in.

"As I was saying before you rudely interrupted me..." She stared pointedly at Logan. "Winter had a panic attack, so I took her back here to recuperate. Leave her alone."

Logan stiffened beside me, his arm still wrapped around my back. He was warm, hot even, and I wished I could say the contact repulsed me, but ...

"You had a panic attack? Why do you have panic attacks?" His eyes narrowed, and he said it almost like it was an accusation, like I brought the attacks myself.

Yeah, okay buddy, stop touching me now.

Now, the contact repulsed me. That felt more natural. I pulled his arm away from me and stepped away from the couch altogether, the crawling feeling of claustrophobia all over me.

Funny, we get stuck in an underground bunker for almost a day and I didn't feel this smothered and exposed, but this close to Logan?

Yeah, I needed to go.

I reached for my jacket over the back of the couch that I hadn't even realized I had taken off — had I taken it off? — and flashed a peace sign to Hillary.

"Thank you for the shopping date, and thanks for" — I waved my hand in the air at her and then me, and then the space that was her and Logan's very luxurious apartment — "this. I've gotta go."

I rushed to the door and turned the lever before I felt her hand on my back.

"Seriously, are you okay? You could stay for supper; I'm making Aunt Rosie's gumbo. Logan won't eat my cooking, anyway." She stuck her tongue out and crossed her eyes, and I laughed despite myself.

"I didn't even know you could cook. I'll take a rain check."

She smiled, a genuinely open smile, and gave my arm a squeeze.

"Yes, you will," she said matter-of-factly. "We both need girlfriends, remember? I'll call you an Uber."

I left the condo with a milder hangover than before. I spent most of the drive to my apartment slowly unraveling the ball of yarn that was my brain. Thankfully, the Uber driver let me sit in the backseat in complete silence.

What the hell had happened today?

CHAPTER 17

WINTER

Hillary had sent over every piece of clothing in that freaking store. Cashmere and silk and lace surrounded me and … I didn't know what that material was, actually.

Surveying the pile of garment bags all over my bed, I grimaced. It was too much; I absolutely couldn't accept it. She wanted to be friends, okay; we could be friends, but I—

"Stop scowling like that, Snow." Quick interrupted my thoughts. He laid out on the other side of the double bed with his long legs crossed and arms tucked behind his head. "You just hit the *Sex and the City* jackpot. There's no way you're going to give these back."

I tossed a hanger at his head, but he deftly caught it in the air. Stupid panther-like reflexes. "Can you be straight for a second and *not* know any of these brands and how much they cost?"

Quick grinned widely, and his playful joy stopped me in my tracks for a second. A beautiful herringbone braid was slung over one shoulder, and he was wearing his signature single feather earring. It was Sunday afternoon, so he had dressed in an old rugby sweatshirt and gray sweats. When had he gotten so—

"Rude. A straight man of high *caliber,*" he said the word with a fake British accent. I giggled. "...would absolutely know Vera Wang and Versace. It is *you* who lack the refined taste of us higher mortals." His gray eyes glimmered with mischief, and while his guard was down, I leaped at the opportunity by throwing myself at him.

At least, I thought I had. He expected my attack, apparently, because he snatched me out of the air mid-launch and spun me around, wrapping his massive arms around my chest and pinning me against him.

"Ah, ah, little Snow," Quick taunted, his breath feathering over my ear. "Let's keep this nice and civil, shall we?"

His body heat and leather and pine scent took over for a second and a calm settled over me. Quick was familiar, he was family, he was home. My nerves over the continued panic attacks and the gifts from Hillary I was really uncomfortable receiving dissipated and I snuggled into his body.

We sat there in comfortable silence for a few moments before he nuzzled me off of him into the space beside him — the space covered in garment bags with pointy hangers.

"Ow!" A pointed metal wire had definitely stabbed my ass.

"Fuck, Quick! I'm bleeding."

I shot up from the bed and stiffly walked to the bathroom across the hall. I definitely had a hole in my ass cheek.

My asshole so-called "best friend" erupted into booming laughter behind me. I could practically feel him saunter up to the bathroom door. I pulled my sweats down to see the upper portion of the cheek, which absolutely had a dribble of blood coming out of it.

"That's quite the battle wound, Snow." Quick shook his head solemnly. "They'll be sharing your story for generations to come."

I threw the bar of soap at his head. I was thrilled when it made contact, but that only made the insufferable man laugh harder.

"You suck," I grumbled as I reached into the vanity drawer for a Band-Aid. I'd live. I'd just have to make sure the boys didn't squeeze too hard the next time I saw them.

The boys. Men. My men.

A shiver ran through me as I recounted the past two weeks and the many enjoyable activities I had shared with both Drew and Travis. Was it wrong to want them equally? I didn't think so. Not when we were all on the same page and the two men could now talk to each other civilly when in each other's company. Maybe one day they'd become friends.

Travis' words rolled over and over in my head.

"Maybe we'll just save time and fuck you together."

I snapped out of my dirty thoughts and caught Quick watching me with an incomprehensible expression. I glanced at my reflection and saw the red flush creeping up my cheeks.

Yeah, not a lot of mystery what I had been daydreaming about.

He cleared his throat and motioned to the bedroom. "Alright, Florence, now that you've tended your wounded, let's get these clothes put away. We need to talk about birthday plans."

I groaned. "I don't want to do either of those things."

Still, I shoved past him as he continued to lean in my doorway, his tall frame taking up all the space, as usual.

"You know, I think 22 is the perfect year to start liking your birthday. Especially with two boyfriends to buy you presents."

He suggestively wiggled his eyebrows and grinned like the Grinch in the old animated movie. It was borderline evil, that grin.

"I hate you today," I muttered halfheartedly and moved to rack up all the clothes I would never feel okay about wearing. I paused at the beautiful emerald green velvet dress I could see myself rocking during a set at Bourbon & Blues.

Okay, maybe I would wear *this* one.

Quick startled me by taking the hanger right out of my hands and pulling me to him in a hug. "Your parents don't have to dictate the rest of your life, Snow. Spend it with the people who do give you the time of day, okay? It's not just us anymore."

Right. My parents.

My parents who had made it to three out of eighteen birthdays while I lived at home. There was always a card and a gift that Nanny Jacobs would hand me gently while making me birthday pancakes, and a pleasant phone call from wherever they were in the world.

Wah, wah, poor me.

Some people had actual problems in the world. My abandonment issues with my parents were paltry by comparison. Despite that, my birthday wasn't one I loved celebrating. There had been too many broken promises to make the day seem celebratory.

"Okay." I sighed with resignation. "What are you making me do this year?"

"Welp." He let go of me to hang some bags on the bed. "I was thinking Après for some dinner, drinks, and dancing. I want to see Drew and Travis make you a sandwich on the dance floor."

His goofy grin was infectious, and I couldn't stop myself from laughing.

"That's assuming they'll both want to be in the same room with each other all night," I said matter-of-factly, pushing through another pile of clothes. *How many outfits did this woman buy?*

"I don't think you'll have any issues with that, Snow. They both want to be in your life, and I think our 'buried alive' situation made them come to some sort of truce."

I shrugged nonchalantly. I wanted both of them in my life, too. I was becoming too attached to them already, and I didn't know how to feel about that. Travis had even said he loved me. I hadn't told anyone in the world I loved them except for Quick and my parents. Did I even know what love actually felt like?

I knew what it felt like for the man in front of me, but that was different. Quick just loved me unconditionally, and I him. There were no expectations or requirements, we just … were. I couldn't imagine sharing that kind of love with more than one person. Was it even possible?

"I don't know where your head went just now, but can we complete your birthday planning, please?"

I turned to face him, hands on my hips. "I'll do whatever you want to do, Quick, as usual. Let's do Après. We go there all the time anyway. It just means everybody has to buy my pepperoni."

"Everybody gets to *give* you their pepperoni, more like." Quick winked and settled on my cleared bed, all the clothes finally tucked into my tiny closet. There wasn't an inch of room left.

I had to laugh at that one. I had walked right into it.

"Well, it is my birthday ..." I let that thought trail off and smirked, tossing my hair over my shoulder dramatically before grabbing the remote off the dresser and settling in beside him.

"Who will we invite?" Quick wrapped his arm around my shoulders and interlaced our fingers while I flicked through Netflix for something mindless to watch. I had an assignment to finish and a shift at Bourbon & Blues tonight, but all I wanted to do right now was veg out with my platonic soulmate.

"I don't care," I said absently as I selected a terrible reality show about people dating without seeing each other.

"I vote for the Buried Alive crew, minus Logan."

"Is that what we're called now?" I shot him an amused look. He grinned down at me and kissed the top of my head.

"Yup. So much cooler than the Mystery Machine. Speaking of, I have some stuff to share with you and your ménage. I'm calling a team meeting this week."

"Alright." We had been avoiding discussing much about the depths of deception in this town this past week, and I had been grateful for the reprieve, though I knew we couldn't avoid it forever. Some pretty fucked up shit was going on in this town, and with Dad involved...

I refused to think about that right now.

Leaning over my bedside table, I turned off my lamp. I grabbed the cozy faux fur throw blanket at the end of the bed and pulled it over us, ready for a TV escape.

"Now shut up. I want to watch this."

"Thank you all for coming."

It was probably the most serious I had seen my best friend in a long time. Well, a long time since before he'd had his meltdown when we were trapped, and I couldn't blame him there.

Quick had finally gathered all the 'Buried Alive' gang in his apartment.

I didn't know if someone had directly invited Cam, or if Travis had dragged him along, but the large, muscly mystery of a man sat casually on Quick's couch next to my handsome charmer.

I squeezed into the tight space on the other side of Travis, between him and Drew. Drew's arm rested on the couch cushion behind my head, and Travis stroked patterns on the inside of my thigh.

There was no place else I would rather be at that moment.

Quick stood in front of us, his whiteboard mounted somehow to the monstrous television on his wall.

It was comical, really, but very him. No matching notepads and pens this time, but the man may have missed his calling as a teacher. The number of teenagers lusting after him would definitely get in the way, though.

"Travis and Cam, I'm not sure there is much here that'll help you guys, but this will at least keep us all in the loop until I know more."

He paused dramatically for effect — fucking guy — and then an unusually apprehensive expression crossed his features.

"I'm not sure how to say this, or even what this means, so — here." He thrust a large navy yearbook onto the coffee table and flipped open to a club photo page.

It took me a minute to understand what he was trying to show us until I noticed the smiling faces of our fathers staring back at me. Our fathers, and Logan's father, and Hillary's father, and Drew's mom and ... Georgio.

Holy fuck.

"When was this taken?" I asked dumbly, knowing full well it was from high school.

So many questions swirled around my already full brain. Dad had grown up here? Why had he told me he and Emmett were best friends from university?

Why was my father fucking lying to me about *everything?* My chest tightened and my breath caught in my throat. I gritted my teeth. I would *not* let my body have a panic attack over this. My nervous system needed to get its shit together, and fast.

Travis took the book from my hands and held it between him and Cam to get a better look.

"I'm sorry guys, I only recognize Georgio. I'm guessing from the names, though, that they're your parents?" He handed the book back to me, and I handed it back to Quick faster than a hot potato. I didn't want to see more evidence of my parent's betrayal, even if I had no sweet clue what this evidence meant exactly.

"Some of them are, yeah." Quick set the yearbook down and began writing on the whiteboard. "Drew's mom, our dads" — he pointed a thumb in my direction — "Logan's dad, Hillary's dad, and Georgio."

Cam whistled, the deep and low sound piercing through the beat of contemplative silence. "That's fucked up."

"Yeah," Drew said. "I knew Mom and Georgio had dated in high school, but this is next level. I don't know what to make of this."

He shifted his arm behind me and wrapped it tightly around my shoulders, bringing me in to kiss my temple.

It was as if he could sense my impending doom and was trying his best to calm me. Travis had wrapped my hand in his and squeezed gently. These men — I was so lucky.

"Neither do I," Quick admitted, having just written everyone's name on the board in front of us. "But the mystery woman — Brenda Simpson — her name sounded really familiar, so I looked her up. She was the woman who hit mom; she died in that accident."

I gasped, the shock tearing through my lungs and speeding up my heart. When Amelia almost died in the car accident when we were little kids, it had devastated me. She had been my second mom, even then. She had been T-boned at a busy intersection in Carlisle and left temporarily paralyzed. They had blamed the accident on a drunk driver who had died on impact.

Amelia may have lived, but her entire life had changed forever in the single moment a butterfly took to flap its wings. Quick got his looks from Emmett, but his athleticism came from his mom. She had been a marathon runner. But six years after the accident, she could still barely walk. My chest spasmed at the deep well of grief opening up inside me. I cursed this stupid town for bringing up this painful memory, but most of all, for my best friend, who was standing tall and stoic despite the fissures of pain in his eyes.

"And I found something else."

Quick held up a small silver flash drive the size of a Q-tip top. "They hid this beneath it on the shelf. All the files are encrypted, so I've hired a little help." He blew out an irritated breath and looked up at the ceiling. "Blaise is going to hack the files for me. He may have already. I've been waiting for his call."

Oh, poor Quick. This would not be good for him, not at all. They may have been on-again, off-again, but Blaise was Quick's mental weakness and could bring him to his knees faster than a rugby tackle. Combined with the painful memories of Amelia's accident ...

"Is that wise?" I spoke up, finally getting my system back under my control. "Quick, I know you—"

"Yes," he interrupted and stared me down, almost in challenge. "I trust him, and he can also put an ear to the ground if he hears anything over at Eccles. We need help here, guys. We know absolutely fuck-all, and apparently, everyone and their dog in this town are involved. I feel like I'm in some fucked up episode of the *Truman Show.*"

I unraveled my body from both of the men encasing me and stood. Moving to Quick, I wrapped my arms around him. "I know this is hard," I murmured, squeezing him as tightly as I could. "Blaise was a good idea. I just don't want to see you get hurt."

I stared into those beautiful slate eyes almost the color of a full moon and tried to convey all the love and support through our connection instead of having to say the words out loud. He hugged me tightly, so I knew he got the message, and then gently he let me go.

I settled onto the coffee table, facing the remainder of our team for the rest of the evening as we theorized what this all might mean.

A secret society? An elitist club? Friends who had a falling out? No one had a clue, but we'd be waiting on Blaise's hacking skills with bated breath. We'd figure out what to do once we had more information and keep our ears to the ground while trying to stay out of trouble. Since four of five of us were indebted to Georgio, I doubted we would be very successful.

One thing was for sure; I could not avoid my parents forever.

CHAPTER 18

DREW

"Nice shot!" Shane praised.

My shot smoothly hit the striped 18-ball into the side pocket as Shane stood beside the pool table. I only had the 8-ball left, and the game would be mine.

I grinned back at him and grabbed the chalk cube for my cue to set up for my next shot. "Not bad for not playing for a few years."

Shane smirked and leaned back against the bar top, taking a sip of his coke and watching me intently. It was our first game, and it had been neck and neck since the first shot. If I didn't sink this one, he would likely win it. I set up for the last ball.

If I had learned anything about Shane in the past few months, it was that he had a competitive streak as long as my arm. He didn't hate to lose like other athletes I knew, but he *loved* to win.

Winter and Travis were working tonight, and I had needed an excuse to get out of the diner. Shane had been more than willing to get me out of my head, and I was grateful for the brief reprieve.

Dad had officially drawn up the papers to sell the diner to Camden, and they had an appointment for signing next week. I hadn't known whether to take Dad seriously about selling the diner when he first brought it up; he had only been out of his coma for a day, and it was a dramatic, impulsive life choice for the likes of Joe Johnson.

He was still waiting for me to decide if I wanted to stay working there, and I still didn't have an answer. The diner was a home to me; its crumbling interior and grease-scented air were as familiar as breathing. As much as I had wanted to walk away in a rage just a few months before, now I had no idea what to do.

Where would I go? What would I do? I had some savings tucked away I could live off of in the meantime to figure it out, but that seemed like a waste. Everyone around me had things to do and finish before they could make any life choices, and even that seemed like an impossibility. I needed to have a very open conversation with Dad about what it would mean for me and our current relationship with Georgio if I walked away. Would there be repercussions? Would I actually be free?

It seemed a little too good to be true.

"Looks like it's my shot," Shane crowed, nearly spilling his Coke as the 8-ball missed the pocket by an eighth of an inch. It had been an easy shot. My thoughts had killed the game for me.

"We'll blame that shitty attempt on Winter." Shane patted my back with a knowing smile. "Is that where your head was just now?"

I laughed, but didn't deny it, grabbing my Coke and guzzling it down. I wasn't ready to talk about my insecurities about my future right now.

"How is the double-dating life, anyway?" Shane asked as he lined up his final shot. "Is it all it's cracked up to be?"

"Doesn't Winter spill all the details?" I was almost sure the two of them would share every thought that came into their heads.

"Yes!" Shane shouted to a nearly empty pool hall on the quiet Tuesday night, startling the two old men working the slot machines on the other side of the room, as he sunk the 8-ball and won the game. He pumped his fist in the air with a deep "woot woot" in celebration of his victory.

I shook my head and laughed at my friend, as endearing as he was obnoxious.

"Sorry." He grinned sheepishly and racked the balls for another game. "And not really, man. I can see how happy she is. I can see how hard it is for her to be this vulnerable. But she doesn't talk about your favorite sex positions or anything like that." He winked conspiratorially. "I'm going to pretend I'm not insanely curious."

A flush crept up my neck at the image of Winter naked in front of me as I pounded into her ass for the first time — not just *our* first time, *my* first time. The feeling of her wrapped around me, the hottest, tightest friction I had ever felt, had made me come the hardest ever. My cock stiffened in my jeans at the memory.

I scratched the back of my neck uncomfortably and willed my dick to go limp before Shane caught a glimpse. He had seen me naked more than once in the football locker room, but that wasn't even remotely comparable to watching an erection unfold in real time at the thought of his best friend.

I looked over at the pool table and saw him staring at me with a funny expression on his face. Okay, so he had definitely seen my cock inflate like a balloon animal.

Great.

"Um, it's not as bad as I thought, actually." I clumsily fumbled through the words, desperately trying to move the conversation along. "I thought I'd be really jealous, and I didn't like Travis at all." I coughed awkwardly, because that was the understatement of the year. "But she doesn't make me feel like I'm second or less than." I shrugged my shoulders. "She's honest and direct, and she's … special."

Shane had come over in the time I was talking and stood in front of me, a wall of plaid flannel and muscle. He put a large hand on my shoulder and stared directly into my eyes, his expression more serious than I had ever seen it.

"She is special," he agreed solemnly. "I can't remember the last time she dated anyone, let alone two men. You need to know that this is a huge deal for her. Sex is one thing," he stated pointedly, "but this — this is something new. I know you'll be good to her, but I also think you're good *for* her."

His eyes never leaving mine, he continued. "I love that woman more than anything in the world."

In that moment, I noticed Shane had pretty eyes. Pretty was probably the wrong word when referencing a friend's eyes, but they were — like the color of snow at dusk.

Shane's voice broke my reverie. "And I love you too, man. I'm glad you found each other."

He brought me in for a tight 'bro' hug, and I allowed myself to hug him back. It was one trait I loved about Shane; whatever he felt, he felt with abandon, not giving a shit what other people thought, and he didn't apologize for it. I was lucky to have him in my life.

My heart swelled with that appreciation. In all the time we had spent together, we had never talked about Winter specifically. It felt good to acknowledge the woman we shared, even if it was in very different ways.

The back of my neck heated as, unbidden, a vision of Winter laying naked between the two of us took over my brain, her face scrunched up in pleasure just like it had been when we spent the night together.

An electric shock crackled up my spine as I forced that thought way — *way* out of my mind. Where had that even come from?

"Love you too, man."

I patted him on the back and gently pushed him away. Turning to hide my now totally stiff cock, I reached for my pool cue. It was this mess of emotions of my life being turned upside down, I rationalized. I was just all over the place.

Since Shane won the last game, he broke for this game. We hit a few balls in comfortable silence, with only the sounds of the distant music from the slot machines and the cracks of the resin as each ball slid safely into its intended pocket.

Two men came out of the attached doorway that led into the Après club area. I recognized Logan and Carson Baker speaking in hushed tones, their heads together in deep conversation as they headed toward us.

"That fucker," Shane growled. His tone was enraged in a way I had never heard before. "What the fuck is he doing here?"

He set his pool cue against the bar and lumbered over to the two men, who had stopped next to the farthest pool table, their heads still bowed.

"What the fuck are you doing here, Carson?" Shane stood tall and crossed his arms over his chest, radiating pure fury. Our boisterous friend was always smiling; it was intimidating to see him this angry.

And, if I was being honest with myself, it was also hot.

This day was fucking confusing.

Carson and I had been in the same graduating class in high school, but I hadn't really known him. He was from a very well-to-do family, far outside of my diner-poor circles and I thought he had moved to New York once he'd left Cascade Falls.

He'd attended private schools until eleventh grade and rumor had it, he had gotten kicked out of too many of them, so his parents threw up their hands and put him in public school instead. Logan was an entitled asshole, but any interaction I'd had with Carson proved him to be far more of a dick. What had he done to Shane?

Carson gave Shane a cool-eyed appraisal and smiled. It was a practiced, politician-type smile, and my dislike for him increased by a thousand. "Nice to see you again, Shane. How's Winter doing? I've missed her."

The way he said those words insinuated something far deeper, and I instantly stood to attention, my hackles raised. I moved closer to them but still watched from a distance. We were the only ones here aside from the gamblers, and they were far too interested in the minuscule chance at winning their fortune to pay much attention to us.

"Winter is great. Thanks for asking." Shane widened his stance, the muscles of his jaw ticking. "I thought we had gotten rid of you for good."

Logan watched the conversation with amused interest, but he lacked his usual air of entitlement. He was pale, even in the dim light of the pool hall, and his face looked gaunt. Sick, maybe?

Carson, meanwhile, looked like a hungry shark. "Five years, that was the deal, wasn't it? It's been five years, Quicksilver. I'm here on business." He nodded his head to Logan, though his gaze never left Shane's. "Not," he added with a malicious smile, "that that is any business of yours."

He arrogantly pushed past Shane and Logan followed behind, smirking at us halfheartedly as they headed toward the rear entrance.

"Give Winter a kiss for me!" Carson called back just as he walked out the door, laughing loudly. The sound stopped entirely once the door closed.

I had moved to stand by Shane's side; Anger vibrated off of him in violent pulses as he stared off into the distance.

"Hey," I said quietly, tugging on his arm to pull him out of his trance. "Mind telling me what that was about?"

He scowled and shook out his ponytail, nervously running his hands through his dark hair over and over. "It's not my story to tell," he admitted with a sigh, walking back over to our pool table and putting the balls away. "But I hope she'll tell you soon."

He left that cryptic thought hanging in the air and grabbed his jacket from the coat hook on the wall. "Sorry to bail, man, but I'm not in the mood for this anymore."

I nodded, moving to grab my jacket to head out with him. "It's okay. I'm sorry that ruined your night."

He flashed a strained but genuine smile at me as we walked out the door toward our cars. "It was a great night. Nice to hang out, man. I'll text you later."

I sat in my car for the longest time, staring blankly into the space between the windshield and the air in front of it.

Winter had a secret that involved a bigger asshole than Logan, I had no job prospects unless I wanted to stay in a familiar but illegal situation that I had no control over, and despite being head over heels for the woman in my life, apparently a pool night with Shane had me questioning my sexuality.

Fuck my life.

CHAPTER 19

CAMERON

"Wait—you're a political science major?" Winter's eyebrows hit her hairline as her pretty little mouth gaped at me, a smile dancing on her lips.

"Well, I was," I answered, taking a sip of the beer Travis just handed to me. "I guess you could say I'm a poli sci graduate now." I paused before adding, "It's a master's degree."

"What!? How old are you?"

"26. I only graduated the year before I came here."

She threw a handful of popcorn at me and grinned. Those blue eyes kept reeling me in like a fish in a pond sparking up like dynamite. "You never told me that at the hot springs!"

"You didn't ask," I said truthfully as I fiddled with one tiny edge of the bottle's label. "I told you I worked construction."

"Yeah, construction!" Winter repeated, pointing a teasing finger at me. I wanted to bite it. "I didn't think you were dumb, but now I know you're smart. *Really* smart."

"I wouldn't know about that. Smart would mean I was doing something with it."

Travis returned from the kitchen with a plate of nachos and settled on the couch beside me. Winter sat in the chair across from us. It was my first time in her apartment, and I liked it. Feminine and wild, just like the little violet. Momma would love her plants, although Winter seemed to keep all of hers alive. Momma never had that gift.

"Why aren't you doing something with it?" Winter quirked an eyebrow and leaned over the table to grab a few nachos, filling her mouth for a few seconds to stall the driving questions.

I'd be lying if I said I didn't enjoy her attention. I didn't like attention generally, but Winter was different. She had a way of seeing through the bars of my cage and seeing the man inside. I was beginning to see just how dangerous that was.

"I haven't found my family yet." I said simply. "If I even do. Once I know one way or the other, then I can decide what to do with the rest of my life."

Once I get the courage to go meet her. Doug Fraser sent me the location and her usual schedule before that crap disaster at Bourbon & Blues. She wasn't working at a dive bar this time around, but for a crappy insurance brokerage in Carlisle, a rougher neighborhood.

I knew, because I had pumped myself up enough to drive the two hours there, only to sit in the parking lot outside the dingy office building for another two hours. I stared at the shadow of a woman in the window, imagining what it would be like to reunite with someone who had to give me up. I couldn't bring myself to leave the safety of Pop's Chevelle, so I turned around and made the disappointing drive home.

The fear embedded beneath my skin from the last time I had tried to find her — the last time when I didn't find her, but instead found Georgio's men, and this entirely new path of dangerous living had opened up to me. I couldn't find it in my soul to risk it.

The holes in my heart were only widening into chasms, and I needed the familiar edge of violence to fill them.

Georgio's current ban on fight nights was the shovel making the holes even deeper. Surprisingly, I longed for the release, the opportunity to clear away the demons in my head.

What I had once viewed as a burden was now something far clearer to me; a form of freedom to cleanse the self-loathing and anger without harming those I cared for. The temptation to call Drake was growing by the day. At least Drake was a devil I knew how to dance with.

And it would be on my terms, of my own free will.

My eyes snapped up to Winter's, whose eyes had softened into doe-eyed pools.

"I'm sorry, Cam. Is there anything we can do?" She leaned over and placed a gentle hand on my knee, the kindness in that gesture radiating through me.

Travis just sat beside me, silently sipping his beer. He knew this story, and he was letting me tell it. I loved this man and respected the hell out of him for giving me this space.

There was something she could do. But did I want her to do it? Perhaps I didn't want to admit that it could help.

"My PI has found a woman he believes to be my birth mother." I stated slowly, working my way up to the ask. "She's working for a shitty insurance company in Carlisle."

Winter gasped with excitement, her hair falling in front of her face as she leaned forward. "That's amazing!"

"It is," I agreed slowly, peeling the label clean off the bottle and crumpling the wet material between my large fingers. "But the last time I tried to find her, Georgio got his hands on me. I'm struggling to get up the courage to go."

What I didn't say was 'what if she doesn't know me?' 'What if she doesn't want me?'

I couldn't be left again.

"Would it help if someone came with you?" Winter placed both palms on my knees, earnestly searching my eyes for the answer as she gently stroked the sides of my thighs with her thumbs. Her touch was a comfort I never knew possible.

But I couldn't be thinking these thoughts. Not while she was Travis' girl.

I shifted in my seat, suddenly too aware of my surroundings and the people I was baring my raw pain to. I didn't like this feeling of vulnerability, but I was sick to death of being alone.

"It would." I stared deep into those blue windows to her soul, letting every ounce of pain show through. She never blinked, peering back into me with a depth and intuition I had never seen from her before. We were linked in the moment through our shared secrets without daring to say what those secrets were.

"Okay. Would you like it to be Travis? Or maybe ..." She trailed off, and I knew what she wanted to ask.

"I'd like you to come with me, little violet."

"Then you'll have me with you, Big Guy."

My entire soul breathed a sigh of relief. She squeezed my thighs one last time with a soothing smile before removing her hands. I hadn't even registered she was still touching me, but my body immediately missed the warmth when they left as she stood to leave for the kitchen.

I turned to Travis, scanning his face for any sign of discomfort or jealousy. This man was one of the most open and understanding I had ever met, save for Winter's best friend. I would do nothing to harm him or our friendship, no matter how much Winter's magnetic pull was drawing me in.

"Are you comfortable with that?" I asked quietly while Winter wasn't in the room. I didn't ask if he was okay with it — Winter's choices were her own, but I needed his blessing for the sake of our own friendship.

Travis' poker face was a well-trained mask, but I could usually see through its facade. He cocked his head to the side, assessing me with a bland expression, before nodding once, seemingly satisfied.

"You feel something for her," he said with no sort of anger or accusation.

"She brings me a sense of calm," I answered honestly, not knowing one way or the other what these feelings could possibly be.

Travis grinned widely, then stretched his long arms out, and placed them behind his head. "She has the opposite effect on me. I could run a marathon when I'm with her."

I chuckled at that, knowing it was true. Travis' lost his normally cool head when it came to Winter and was head over heels. He deserved the happiness she brought him.

"Listen, man." Travis' eyes darted back to the kitchen before lowering his voice. "I love her. No secret to anyone. I love you, also not a secret. I think you fulfill something for her too. You two can figure that out, or not. I'm not going to stop you. But I would like to know what's going on at the high level view, so I can know what to expect, yeah?

"Drew and I are getting along fine. It's a bit weird to navigate, but it's also okay too. Not nearly as rough as I thought and —"

I held up a hand to stop him there. "I'm not trying to date her, Travis. Your dynamic ain't something I can picture for myself. I like spending time with her and I just wanna make sure you and I won't risk our friendship."

Travis smirked knowingly, like he knew something I didn't. Maybe he did. "Yeah, okay, man. It won't risk our friendship; I can promise you that. Do southern boys pinkie swear?"

He held up a ridiculous ringed pinkie finger and waved it in my face. I shoved it away, laughing. Just then, Winter walked back into her cozy little room.

Okay, then. Winter, meet Daisy. Daisy, meet Winter.

Two hours had gone by in a flash. We'd decided to go the next day, since Winter had the day off from both Bourbon & Blues and the diner. We were going to spend the morning on our mission, and I would drop her off at Shane's to finish her assignments that afternoon.

Their relationship was foreign to me, but it had its appeal. I had friends back home, enough friends to keep me busy when I wanted to be, but few enough I could have my space and keep it when I needed it. Friends I hadn't bothered keeping in touch with.

When Momma and Pop died in the river, I washed the rest of my life away along with them. Grief was funny that way.

Shane and Winter were two halves of something bigger than themselves. They moved along each other's path without thought and tended to each other's needs without question.

Shane brought life to any room he entered. I liked him from the first moment I had met him in Après last fall. He had a way of making everyone in the room feel seen, and Winter saw him. It was a unique love, and I envied them for it.

I trusted Shane with my life. And now, I trusted Shane with *her* life too. He was there when we all got out of Georgio's jail, and he insisted on trying to solve our problems, even though Georgio had never once threatened him or involved him in any of this mess.

He was one hell of a guy.

Winter and I had spent the hour listening to music and speaking through sporadic bouts of comfortable quiet. She seemed to sense when I wasn't up for talking, although it was always easier to speak to her.

As we got closer, my nerves sparked. The aching burn of restless energy riled at the base of my spine, and I was itching to strip my bare knuckles raw on a punching bag or another man's face.

I chain-smoked out the window the final fifteen minutes of the drive; the nicotine soothed my insatiable hunger for answers.

"This is it?" Winter asked cautiously as I parked my Chevelle in a near-empty parking lot by the same beige building I had cased a few weeks ago.

"Yup," I said succinctly, tamping down on the demons within me begging for release.

She must have felt the waves of tension rolling off me, because she shifted her body to face me, sitting on her knees to level our gazes. I had almost a foot of height on her, and it was even more noticeable in the tight cab of the vintage car.

"Hey, Big Guy. Look at me." She placed her palms on my cheeks and peered into my eyes. "This is your chance to find answers. We don't need to get our hopes up, but we need to pull on our big-girl panties and be brave enough to walk in there and give it the old college try, okay? You can do this."

I drew in a deep breath, filled my lungs until the point of pain, and released it as slowly as I could. Her version of a pep talk and the new air gave me the boost I needed to open the door and step out.

"How do you want to play this?" she asked quietly as we walked to toward the door. I had already told her I would like her to come in with me, but we hadn't discussed the specifics.

"She can make her own assumptions." This was hard enough without trying to explain honestly who Winter might be to my potential mother. "Let me take the lead."

Winter dipped her head in acknowledgment and followed behind me as we walked into the dim space.

Offices were depressing spaces to work in general. This one was where dreams went to die.

Low cement board ceiling tile, cheap thin carpet, fading paint, and the stale scent of cigarette smoke, worse than the smell that saturated Doug's suits, lingered in the air. The woman working the desk had her head bowed over a stack of manila folders that looked older than I was.

"May I help you?" she asked politely, though she never looked our way, too deep into the pile to properly acknowledge us.

"Hello." I turned on the smooth voice I had honed while working for political offices. "I'm looking for Daisy Knight?"

The woman's head whipped up fast enough to sever it. Immediately, I recognized her face. It was my face.

Her caramel skin had richer coloring than mine, and her eyes were a rich chocolate brown. But there was no mistaking the similarity in our cheekbones, lip shape, and jawline. If this woman wasn't my mother, I was a pig who flew.

She shook her head vehemently and stood abruptly. "I'm sorry, there's no one by that name here."

I frowned and searched the desk for some sort of nameplate to confirm. My eyes fell on a steel rectangular plaque on the corner of the desk that read "Darlene Knightly."

"Are you sure?" I asked, even as my heart clenched so tightly in my chest, I thought it might shatter. "She's a family member, and she was last seen at this location. I was hoping to —"

"You need to leave," Daisy-Darlene hissed, her voice low. "There is no one by that name here." Her eyes darted to the hallway to her left before resting on Winter, who was now standing beside me, having slipped her hand in mine.

She pointed to the door behind us. "Please. Leave now. I don't want any trouble."

I memorized the image of this woman in front of me, so clearly my birthright, but not at all interested in the man before her. I could feel my walls forming, the bricks being layered by cement and firmly mortared in place.

"We're going," I said. Firmly, I squeezed Winter's hand and turned on my heel, walking toward one of the dirtiest glass door I had ever laid eyes on. "Thank you for your time."

My heart had lined with stone by the time we got back into the car. I put the car in drive and peeled out of the parking lot, burning rubber tire marks into the pavement.

Winter only let go of my hand long enough to get in on the passenger side and clip in her seatbelt. She reached for me again and I interlaced our fingers, locking them tightly to my own.

The beautiful woman sitting beside me didn't say a word. She didn't offer false words of comfort or pretend platitudes; there was nothing to say. She let me squeeze all the blood from her extremities and brood the entire drive home.

When I dropped her off at Shane's apartment building, Winter leaned in to kiss me on the cheek. It was a brief peck of kindness, but I appreciated the peace the motion brought me.

"I'm here when you want to talk about it," she said as she grabbed her backpack from the backseat and stepped out.

Never. I'd never want to talk about it.

I gave her a pained smile and a wave before leaving the parking lot without a backward glance. My skin crawled with the need to unleash.

It looked like I was going to be giving Drake a call after all.

CHAPTER 20

WINTER

"I'm coming!" I hollered for the third time as I fumbled my way through the mess of my apartment and hurried to the front door.

It was my birthday, and the rarity of being able to sleep in on a Saturday without a diner shift — thanks to Drew's scheduling kindness — had been interrupted by someone banging on my door at 8:00 in the morning.

If Quick was on the other side being a cheerful asshole, I was going to kill him.

I didn't even pause to look out the peephole to see who I was going to murder today, I yanked open the door to my father standing in the grungy hallway, looking awkward and out of place in his expensive clothing and tastefully styled hair.

Darren Wallace was a handsome man, not yet 55. His salt-and-pepper hair was natural and full, and his lean frame was still trim from a rigorous workout routine. Blue-green eyes stared back at me.

"Hey, hon! Happy birthday! How's my girl?" He opened his arms wide for a hug and stepped through my doorway, as if this were a regular occurrence and not only the third time in as many years he had visited my apartment.

I settled into his hug, as familiar as it was strange. Our relationship had never been that of a traditional father and daughter. Nanny Jacobs had taught me how to ride a bike and change a car tire. Dad had made it to my graduation and had taken me to get my license when I was sixteen — just not on my birthday because he had a work event that year. One of many events over many years. I loved him for the man he was, but he wasn't the testament of a doting father.

Of course, he had attended a highly illegal fight night with a beautiful blonde woman I didn't know. I couldn't forget that bitter pill, either.

"I'm fine, Dad. What are you doing here?"

I stepped back from him and folded my arms across my chest, suddenly self-conscious in my skimpy pajamas. I grabbed Drew's hoodie off the end of my couch and pulled it over me, wrapping his cinnamon and citrus scent around me in a comforting embrace.

Dad scrunched up his face at me and laughed. "It's my daughter's birthday?"

He settled himself on my couch and looked around my small, bohemian-themed apartment discerningly before returning his gaze to me. "I'd like to take you out for breakfast, unless you have plans?"

"My plans were to sleep in." I yawned deeply, regretting my reading binge until two in the morning now that my sleep had been interrupted. "But sure, let's do breakfast. Give me five minutes."

I didn't want to do breakfast with my father. The very thought was giving me sweating palms and heart palpitations as I considered Shane's year book reveal and the fact Dad very well could have seen me at the fight night too. Was that why he was here?

"Sounds great, honey. I'll wait here."

He took another appraising view of the small living room; two mugs of half-full lukewarm tea were leaving brown rings on my white coffee table; a Mars Bar wrapper and a half-eaten bag of Skittles with a few rogue candies littered the remainder of the couch cushions. I scurried back to the bedroom to get changed before I could see his mouth curl in distaste.

Yes, I was a slob, but I didn't need another reminder of one of my many shortcomings in my parents' eyes.

I threw on a pair of warm red leggings and an oversized gray sweatshirt, braiding my hair loosely over one shoulder. That would have to be good enough.

Dad had never taken me out on my birthday. Ever. Sure, a few weeks after the fact, when he and Mom's schedules lined up enough so we could all share a meal together somewhere, but never actually on my birthday and never unannounced. I couldn't help being suspicious about this development.

"I'm ready," I announced as I re-entered the living room to see Dad typing on his phone. I took out my winter jacket from the small closet by the door and grabbed my keys.

"Where are we going? Can it not be the diner? I was trying to avoid that place today."

Dad shoved his phone into his pants pocket and stood, walking out the door behind me as I turned to lock up. I could see the amusement in his eyes and tried to relax. This would be fine. Surely, I could keep my ears open and my mouth shut over a meal to pry some information from him.

"I was going to take you to Madigan's," he commented casually as we strode down the dim hall.

"Oh!" I smiled brightly, remembering the croissant I had eaten with Hillary that had rocked my world. "That's great. Hillary and I were there last week."

"Since when are you friends with Hillary Lane?" Dad looked at me with scrutinizing eyes, and I realized in that moment that keeping things to myself may be harder than I thought.

"It's recent," I admitted, downplaying the fact that the richest heiress in the county had taken an interest in my friendship. "We bonded over some mutual frustrations."

"Huh," Dad muttered, more to me than himself as we climbed into his pearlescent white Land Rover.

The silence was semi-comfortable as we drove. Dad and I never talked a lot, preferring in the past to listen to music and enjoy quiet company. I watched him from the corner of my eye, trying to get a pulse from his unreadable exterior.

He had grown up here, but had pretended otherwise my entire life. He had been friends with Georgio and obviously still had a connection with him. Were they still friends? What involvement did they have in each other's business? I should ask.

"How's working going? Are you guys still working on that big tender?"

Surprise flashed across his face, then vanished as quickly as it had come.

"Yeah, we are, honey. It's due next week. It'll be the biggest contract we've ever gotten if it's awarded. This bridge will rival some of the largest mountain span bridges in Asia. It'll be an engineering masterpiece."

Dad was so passionate about WAQ and their projects; he always had been. Despite the ache in my heart from being left by the wayside, I was envious of the joy it brought him. Nothing fueled me the way my parent's careers did; nothing except maybe singing at Bourbon & Blues, and that was now tainted in so many ways.

"How does that all work?" I asked carefully, trying to appear intrigued but not desperate.

"We're working with the government on the design against two other firms out of state. Technically, we don't have the final approval yet, but when we do, it will be the largest project we've ever taken on, and the most profitable. It will put the company in the position to go public and make many people a lot of money."

When, not if. Interesting.

He paused, seeming to consider his words for a moment. "Not that that is what Emmett and I care about, but our silent partners will."

Silent partner, as in Brendan Anderson, their third partner, who provided funding and not much else. He was the Anderson in Wallace Anderson Quicksilver. I had never met the man and Dad rarely spoke about him.

"How does that work when you're partnering with Eccles?" I asked thoughtfully, trying to wrap my head around it. We studied corporate structure in school. I couldn't understand how the two companies could work together if only one got the tender.

"Technically, we hired Eccles as a design consultant, and the contract is under our name. They're already publicly traded, and Stan and Camden want to buy shares in our company when we go public. They're bigger, but we've got a larger reach with our overseas operations that make for a strong business case. Why the sudden interest?"

"Corporate structure class," I answered quickly, realizing it was the perfect excuse for the line of questioning. This business degree may be useful to me after all.

We had arrived at the pretty little café. A beautiful androgynous server seated us in a private nook in the corner, the turquoise blue and silver accents providing a peaceful backdrop for this unexpected birthday date.

"22 years old, honey," Dad mused as he smiled at me from across the small round table. "Where did the time go?"

The question triggered a raw anger in me that spiked my blood unexpectedly. "The time was there, Dad. You just weren't around for most of it."

I should probably regret the words, but I didn't. Twenty-two years, and only four birthdays with my parents in that time. Where was Mom, anyway? I hadn't received a text this morning from her either.

A pleasant drive and breakfast did not make up for the indifference I usually received from the people who gave me life. I picked up the menu to do something with my hands, feeling awkward and exposed at the outburst.

Dad grimaced, a hint of color on his cheeks. "I admit we haven't been the world's best parents."

"You haven't been terrible parents, Dad." I sighed, raising my eyes from the menu and staring into his matching blue ones. "You've been absentee parents."

And lying parents.

He rubbed the back of his neck, the pale pink flush now broaching the tips of his ears. "I know. I want to do better."

"And Mom?" I prompted, raising a questioning eyebrow.

"Your mother too," he confirmed, but his tone held less conviction. "We'd like you to bring your boyfriend over for supper soon."

I startled, totally blindsided by the comment and invitation. How did he—

Quick. Of course, Quick would let something slip.

"Actually, Dad, it's *boyfriends*." I bit my lip before deciding to own it. I was dating multiple men seriously and wouldn't apologize for it. "Drew and Travis."

"You're dating Joe and Eileen's son?" Dad blinked hard and squinted at me. "Since when?"

"A while now," I said smoothly. "And I met Travis at the diner too."

"I—uh." Dad shifted uncomfortably in his seat, and I enjoyed the tension in his jaw just a little too much. "Okay, then. I guess we'll have your *boyfriends*," — he emphasized the 's' aggressively through his teeth — "over for supper."

"Sure," I agreed amicably, not believing for a second I would see them anytime soon. They'd get sidetracked with a project, or a work trip, and we'd catch up again in May.

We ate breakfast with familiar companionship, with nothing else really being said.

On the drive home, I asked one last question, hoping my father would choose to tell me the truth, instead of burying us both in more dishonesty.

"Dad, if you and Mom were ever having problems ... you would tell me, right?"

He glanced over and laughed, but to my ears, it seemed a bit forced. "Your mother and I are fine, honey. Why do you ask?"

"I dunno." I picked at a non-existent piece of lint on my coat and spoke into my lap. "You guys are all I have; I don't want to be left alone for real, I guess."

Dad reached for my hand and I looked up to see the face of concern only fathers wore; calm and kind, yet agitated.

"We're fine, honey. Never better, in fact. We just haven't seen much of each other lately. We'll have that dinner sooner than later."

Never better, but attending an illegal fight with a beautiful woman. Not that I expected that answer, but I had been hoping for some slip of the tongue.

The only thing clear to me after this morning is that my parents' newfound interest in me was highly suspicious and Dad was still lying.

Why?

"This is awesome!" I shouted to Quick over the assaulting noise of the dance club now in full force.

We had only stood in the freezing cold line for three minutes before Ted, the bouncer, let us into Après via the VIP line. Quick had pulled some strings, and while I really didn't want a big fuss made over me for this day, I would definitely take special treatment to avoid risking frost bite. It was hard to dress sexy in February and avoid an emergency room visit in Cascade Falls.

By the looks of the guys' faces when I took off my coat inside, I had succeeded. I had settled on a red long sleeve body-contouring dress that hit me mid-thigh with striped cutouts throughout the torso, and paired that with black thigh-high boots. I'd also styled my hair in a high ponytail. Thick rings of black eyeliner rimmed my baby-blues and a poppy-red lip stain finished the look. I dressed with success in mind; success in getting laid, that is.

And I had choices tonight, incredibly attractive and undeniably sexy choices.

Travis looked sinful in a pair of tight blue jeans and a white t-shirt — a change from his usual black attire — and he had swapped out his black lip ring for a silver bar. His hair was tousled to one side and messy black strands hung over one sparkling kiwi-green eye. The corded muscles and colorful artwork of his forearms popped, and I wondered in that moment if a girl could orgasm off looks alone.

Drew wore his usual white Henley and dark jeans and gelled his hair back from his face, highlighting his stunning hazel eyes. He had trimmed his beard and his full lips taunted me with thoughts of his kisses. The man was handsome personified, and he had no idea.

Cam surprised me. Quick and I often joked about how model-like gorgeous he was, which in reality was no joke at all, but tonight — tonight he could have been the main feature of a GQ ad. The light blue button-up he had chosen was the exact color of his piercing eyes, and the fitted tan khaki pants he wore showed *exactly* what he was packing under there.

I gulped when looking at him. I had two breathtakingly handsome boyfriends; there was no reason why the look of Cam tonight should make my panties wet. I would be a liar if I said he wasn't a contributing factor, though.

Even Quick, admittedly gorgeous every day of the week, had stepped up his game, wearing a delicate black wool form-fitting sweater and black pants; his jet-black hair parted in the middle down to his shoulders, and a silver eagle pendant dangled from his neck. The whole look made the pewter in his eyes practically shimmer.

It was my birthday, and a harem of the hottest men in town surrounded me. Poor me.

Drew, Travis, and Cam had taken their seats in the booth and were waiting for us. Quick had decided since I was a "smoke-show sex-bomb" — his words, not mine — that it would be quicker if I went up to the bar to order our drinks instead of waiting for the server.

So far, that theory was not proving correct, but at least our order was in.

Quick moved closer and put his arm around my shoulder, brushing his lips against my ear so I could hear him.

"I'm glad you're enjoying yourself, my little Snowflake," he teased, then booped me on the nose and placed a gentle kiss on my cheek. "I just want you to have fun tonight, okay? No limits, no rules."

I startled at the phrase; it was one we hadn't repeated to each other since prom night in high school. "No limits, no rules" had meant something entirely different that night. Or had it? My brows furrowed at the potential insinuation, but I had no time to think about it because he moved to grab three of our drinks from the bartender and motioned for me to take the others.

I took Drew's beer and Travis' elaborate birthday cocktail request for me and carefully navigated the treacherous path back to our booth. I lost Quick in the sea of people ahead, but I wasn't concerned. My only fear was spilling the specialty $17 cocktail—*what in the world was in this thing, anyway?*

I was stuck behind a massive wall of a human being and used the brief opportunity to snag a sip of the hazy pink liquid through the purple party straw. The delightful zing of cherry flavor that burst across my tongue made me smile. Of course, Travis remembered it was my favorite flavor.

A firm hand latched onto my arm and I wrenched away from it instinctively, spilling some of the delicious pink elixir on my boot. I spun around to glare at the perpetrator when my mouth dried up and I had no words to say at all.

Carson Baker leaned in, smelling of sea air and amber. Of course, he would smell the same as he did when I was sixteen. He probably still used the same cologne on the off-chance he would run into me, just to taunt me more into madness.

As if he hadn't already blackened a piece of my soul.

"Hey, baby," he crooned in my ear. The intimate motion invaded my senses and sent biological survival impulses to my brain.

If I were a puffer fish, I would have puffed out by now and stabbed him with all of my spiky bits.

I hated he had this effect on me after all of these years, like I hadn't healed one rip in my heart since he had left. He was the truest form of parasite that ate your organs alive from the inside out.

I came to my senses; the evolutionary urge to flee outweighed my desperate need to freeze. "Go fuck yourself, Carson."

A presence on my other side made my hackles rise even further. Despite the roar of the surrounding partiers, I could sense Logan more than I could see him. For reasons I couldn't explain, I felt tethered to the ingratiating asshole since we had been trapped together, and it was becoming more noticeable at each run-in. Was he a friend or a foe at this moment?

I spun on my heel and used the momentum to shift my whole body, hoping to catch Carson by surprise so he'd let me go. No such luck. I could feel the sharp sting of fingernails carving indents into my skin.

I stared pleadingly into Logan's deep brown eyes, though they looked as black as the devil's in the careening spiral of disjointed flashes from the dance floor. He looked better now, a lot better than the last time I had seen him in his apartment. Or maybe it was the lighting.

I took in a breath, hoping against all hope my voice didn't waver. "Logan, please get him off of me."

His eyes met mine for a long moment. He gave an almost imperceptible nod before he shifted his body away from me and put a hand on Carson's shoulder. "Come on, we've got a night ahead of us." He disappeared into the throng of bodies toward the bar.

Carson's evil smile was amplified by the purples and blues now spinning through the club, but he let me go and turned to follow Logan.

I shook with relief, collecting myself as best I could in the surrounding bedlam before heading back to our booth.

Did Logan just do me a kindness, or was I misconstruing the whole situation? My heart still pounded in my chest as I came down from my hind-brain high. I didn't know what Carson was doing in town, but I couldn't keep running into him like this. My damage couldn't take it.

I made it back to the booth with my cocktail half spilled but Drew's beer intact. I took the time to watch them before they noticed me; Shane was regaling them with one of his elaborate stories, his hands waving wildly in the air. Cam was grinning widely, Travis was laughing into his hands, and Drew had his arms raised behind his head, mimicking whatever motion Quick had been doing. The scene was straight out of a bromance movie, like *Friday Night Lights* or something, and my pounding heart instantly settled.

I was safe here with these men. *My* men.

"There you are!" Drew reached out and pulled me to his side of the round booth, tucking me up tightly next to him. "We thought you had gotten lost."

His voice was teasing, but his face was somber. None of us could forget our last few months, even though we were celebrating tonight.

"Sorry," I said brightly, determined not to let the last few minutes ruin this moment. "Got caught up with a friend from school on the dance floor." I lightly pecked Drew on the lips and squeezed his thigh. "I'm safe and sound, Hardy Boy."

"Come here, beautiful." Travis reached over Drew and grabbed me by the hips, lifting me deftly and placing me snugly between the two of them. Drew gave him a sour look, but he said nothing as Travis kissed me thoroughly before moving to put his arm around me, playing with the ends of my ponytail. "That's better."

Drew laced his arm around my waist and tucked me back into his side. I grinned at all the attention. Whoever said they were a one-man woman was clearly missing out.

I looked up to see a mischievous expression flash across Quick's features. "Sandwich," he mouthed and nodded his head toward the dance floor with a wink.

I giggled, my anxiety from minutes before all but evaporated.

"I'd like to propose a toast," Quick, the shit-stirring instigator, announced as he handed me the cocktail I'd left at the edge of the table.

The guys all held up their glasses, and I raised mine too.

"To my Snowflake. She's one hell of a woman, and it's about time everyone noticed it. Happy Birthday, Winter."

I blushed at his praise and my heart filled with so much love for him and for this instant in time. For a woman who hated her birthday, this night was pretty damn spectacular.

I downed what was left of my cocktail in one solid swig, and the pretty highball glass landed on the table in front of me with a thud.

"Whoa there, little violet." Cam's pouty lips turned up in a rather-enticing smirk. "If anyone needs the alcohol to dance, it's me."

"I don't believe that for a second, Big Guy," I challenged him with one cocked eyebrow. "Remember last fall when you came out with us? I got a front row seat to your dancing abilities, and they did not disappoint."

Travis burst out laughing as he tugged me closer. "I forgot about that. Cam, you made her the ham in our sandwich."

"I'd prefer to not be the lunch meat." I giggled as Drew's snicker rumbled through my body. "Can I be the cheese? Like a thick cut, buttery cheese, grilled between two pieces of sourdough."

"Snow wants to be hot and bothered in her sandwich." Quick wiggled his eyebrows at me, his eyes full of dangerous glee. "Do we know anybody who can help her out with that?"

I was about to say something witty, but the words died in my throat. My head felt like a thousand pounds, barely held up by my tiny neck and shoulders. I tried to shake it, but I could only move in slow-motion. My body felt sluggishly stoned, like that terrible lapse in judgment when I let Quick convince me to eat a gummy with him in first year.

Travis' smile turned into a whirlpool of distorted facial features as all sound faded around me. Before I could be encased in silence, I caught the last of Drew's panicked voice.

"Winter!"

CHAPTER 21

LOGAN

Fuck, I felt good. No, more than fucking good. I felt better than the day Stanley had nearly died of food poisoning on my sixteenth birthday. Fucking amazing.

Carson had really done right by me tonight. Quitting cold turkey had put me in a tailspin of a clusterfuck of withdrawals, and the sweet, sweet relief of the gram I just took had skyrocketed my endorphins; I was riding the literal high.

I was a weak man, but who the fuck cared? I could count on ten fingers the number of ace businessmen who killed it in the boardroom and then enjoyed their weekend to the fullest. I could be that guy. I *was* that guy.

Georgio could go fuck himself. He wasn't getting another dime out of me, and thanks to Carson's connection upstate, I wouldn't have to rely on him again. Carson had introduced me to the party lifestyle; it was some sick twist of fate the cocky fucker would keep me in it.

The simpering idiot acted like we were best friends who had shared our darkest secrets at a slumber party. We weren't.

I didn't like the guy; never had, but we had been allies in high school. Two rich guys with shitty parents and an appetite for chaos and destruction. Mine was internal; I had a master's degree in self-sabotage in riling up Stan-the-man. Carson's was external; he brought down everyone around him, fuck the consequences. He was an even bigger asshole than me, and he relished in it.

He was my ticket out of here and someone to blow off some steam with. We had just completed the paperwork for our new business venture and decided to hit up Après for a drink. With the promise of some good blow and the potential for a mindless hookup, I was in it to win it.

We had formed an offshore shell corporation with our companies as the shareholders, and combined some of our real estate assets under its umbrella. It was a legal rollercoaster of red tape that wouldn't allow me to sell any of my properties to Georgio, even if he continued to blackmail me. The only way he would get them is if Carson agreed — and Carson would *never* agree.

I was grateful 17-year-old me had the foresight to make copies of all the evidence against Carson for almost every single crime he'd committed. Lady Luck knew I'd need it one day. She had earned one hell of a fuck.

I focused in on another Lady Luck; even only seeing her from behind, I knew the curves of that ass anywhere.

Winter Wallace stood at the bar with her slobbering loyal sidekick. The red tight dress she was wearing could make grown men come in their pants. My cock rose to attention as she turned around with her drinks and disappeared into the crowd.

"Come on." Carson nodded his head in her direction, trailing behind the flashes of crimson through the packed club.

I lingered behind, not in the mood to be his wingman or fuck-boy or whatever it was he thought he was getting out of me tonight. The lady in red wouldn't be in my bed tonight, so I was scanning the crowd for someone who could be. My eyes landed on a hot brunette in a tight white sheer dress, assessing me with interest. Bingo.

Before I could take the lead on my next conquest, I noticed the flash of crimson caught in the crowd, Carson right behind her.

Fuck's sake. I was my breed of depraved asshole, but Carson had done enough damage to the girl in high school. Enough was enough.

I pushed through the crowd until I stood right behind her; Carson had her arm in a death grip. I shot him a 'knock it off' glare before she turned to me with pleading eyes.

Fuck, those eyes. I had tried to forget every feeling I ever had for this woman, before Stanley's belt and after, but lately that had been fucking impossible. Especially when she acted like she fucking cared about my existence. Especially when she had been curled up on *my* couch, wrapped up in *my* blanket, looking so fucking vulnerable and peaceful. I wanted to rough her up and put the fight back into her. I liked her feisty.

These territorial feelings were a waste of fucking time; I needed to get my tongue between the legs of that hot brunette to forget these annoying as fuck thoughts.

"Logan, please get him off of me."

Her plea lacked her usual snark, and I saw the very real pulse of fear behind her eyes. I recognized that fear down to my very soul.

Lightly, I push Carson's shoulder away from her.

"Come on, we've got a night ahead of us." I spun on my heel and headed back to the sexy woman in the white dress, only turning back once to make sure Carson had followed.

I was the least likely White Knight in this place, but somehow, I had saved Winter from her demons tonight. It made me feel far more valiant than it should have.

I sidled up to my target and firmly wrapped a hand around her waist from behind.

"Have you been waiting for me?" I breathed into her ear, lightly nipping the top of her earlobe as she melted into me.

She looked familiar. I had probably fucked her before, but I could give two shits about that tonight; I felt good; I was hard as fuck, and I needed to forget all about Winter Wallace.

"Hey baby," she said with a breathy moan as I traced my fingers along the pointed nipples of her barely there dress. "I was hoping you'd come find me."

She wriggled her ass into me and I pulled her hips tight to mine, rolling her body to the music. We dance-fucked for a few songs before I was fully ready to take her from behind in the back hallway or a bathroom stall. I didn't care where as long as my dick was deep inside her in the next three minutes.

She tugged my hand and led me toward the back of the bar, where I caught a glimpse of the Motley Crew of Misfits crowded around little Red Riding Hood herself. Despite my raging hard on, I needed to know what the hell caused the panicked look on Goody-Two-Shoes Drew's face. I moved closer to the booth.

Winter was limp as a dick in church, her eyes glassy and face deathly pale. I wrenched my hand away from whatever-her-name-was and rushed to the table.

"What the fuck happened?" I demanded, pushing Drew out of the way as he tried to move her out of the seat.

"Fuck off, Logan." Shane shoved me aside and lifted her gingerly in his arms, bridal style. Her head bobbed like a rag doll. "We think she's been drugged."

"The fuck!?" I roared, my mind racing through the last ten minutes. The only one who I saw near her drink was …

Mother fucker. I'll kill him for this later. I needed to get her out of here and away from him.

"My place is around the corner." I grabbed her coat hanging off the hook at the end of the booth. "We're taking her there."

No one argued with me as I charged out the rear exit of the bar. Shane and Winter's harem crew of men followed behind me. I kept looking back to check on her as I led the way to my condo building and unlocked the front doors.

"We'll take the stairwell." I directed everyone into the foyer. "The elevator has cameras, and I'm not up for explaining this to anyone."

"We should take her to the hospital," Drew argued. "What if she stops breathing? Can you save lives too?"

"If it's a roofie, she won't stop breathing. Not at a drink's dose. But she's going to need a safe space to sleep it off and lots of water," I said matter-of-factly as I opened the stairwell door.

"Oh, so you're a roofie expert? A memory from your frat days?" Cam's comment would have made me chuckle, if he hadn't just accused me of attempted rape.

"Fuck you, Chase. I'm a lot of things, but the women in my life willingly sleep with me," I shot back, taking the stairs two at a time to our third-floor view.

Hillary wasn't home this weekend, so we'd have the place to ourselves. Thank fuck. She was getting attached to her new little bestie, and I wouldn't have time to see her at all if Hill were here to fret and hover.

"Here." I exited the stairwell and walked the three steps to our door. Unlocking it, I ushered them in.

"She can have my bed. It's the last door to your right." I motioned in that direction. "Take off her clothes and tuck her into the blankets. I'll get her some water."

Shane headed to the bedroom with Winter still bobbing in his arms, barely coherent. Some drugs were incredible and made the doldrums of life worth living. Other drugs were unadulterated evil, used by weak men with tiny dicks. Rohypnol was the latter.

I went to the kitchen and pulled two water bottles out of the fridge. I glared at the men who stared at me when I turned around.

"The rest of you fuckers who *weren't* invited..." I pointed the water bottle in their direction. "...can sit on the couch and stay put. I'd make you leave, but I'm not in the mood for a brawl and Hill will kill me if your blood stains the rug."

I didn't have time to listen to their muttering. I grabbed a bucket from the laundry room and knocked on the bedroom door before cracking it open.

"I have water and a puke bucket." I marched into the space like I owned it, because I did, and took in the scene. Shane had propped Winter up between my pillows and tucked her underneath my feather duvet, her hair splayed all around her. She looked like she was sleeping, appearing so fucking peaceful that my heart felt —

"She's going to be okay, right?" Shane paced the space in front of my walk-in closet with shining eyes. "Tell me she's going to be okay."

The stupid fucker was so in love with her and he had no clue. Or maybe it was straight denial. I didn't know what their polyamory friends-who-fuck dynamic was.

"She's going to be okay," I said firmly, placing the bucket and water bottles beside her on the end table.

"One of you can keep an eye on her until she comes out of it. Be prepared for a long night."

I closed the door behind me and started stripping down the hall, pulling my tie over my head and unbuttoning my dress shirt. I was in my house, and if I wanted to walk around in my boxers, my unwelcome house guests would just have to deal.

Travis stopped me before I got to the living room. He leaned against the wall like this was his place and stared at me like he was trying to see through me.

"Are you using again?" He murmured quietly, as if he had a right to know my secrets. I knew my stash had gone missing after we had gotten out of the Bourbon & Blues dungeon. I didn't expect Travis to be the narcotic klepto. Pretty Boy had secrets too.

"Fuck you, Pretty Boy. I'm not the one drugged tonight. Pull your accusations out of your ass and go help your girlfriend." I pushed past him back into the kitchen.

The uninvited guests hadn't moved from their positions on my couch.

"Okay, fuckers," I called out into the open space. "Looks like none of us are getting laid, and we're stuck with each other tonight."

Drew looked like he would strangle me, Cam said nothing, and Travis hung in the doorway looking torn.

"I'm putting in a pizza. Who's hungry?"

CHAPTER 22

WINTER

I was deep underwater, peaceful ebbs of a light current moving around me. With no difference in temperature, it was impossible to tell where my body ended and the water began. There was no sound; the only light coming from a pocket of stray sunlight penetrating through these depths the size of a flashlight head.

A strand of seaweed bobbled in the current in front of my face. I tried to move my arm to grab it but was surprised to find myself frozen; my body weighted down by some invisible force that leadened the blood in my veins. I thrashed; at least, I attempted to, but I was made of cement.

Muffled voices interrupted my panic. Slowly, the ambient temperature got warmer. A wall of heat scorched my left side and the water surrounding me evaporated in layers until my whole body was engulfed in unbearable fire.

I tried to move again. This time my head could shift, although the movement caused bile to flood the back of my throat and a nauseating wave crashed into me.

"Here." A clearer voice rang out among the rest of the jumble, and a hard, jarring surface hit my chin just before I emptied my stomach contents.

My vision cleared; the room around me came into focus with only blurred edges. Quick's familiar massive body hovered over me. He was holding the bucket to my chin, his gray eyes filled with concern and regret.

A minor tug of my hair made me realize someone else was holding it back for me as I exorcised my demons into the plastic pail. I tried to shift my body upright, but another rolling wave of queasiness was threatening enough to keep me lying down.

I closed my eyes and took in a single slow, lung-bursting breath.

"It's okay, baby girl."

Drew's soft words soothed me as he rubbed soothing circles into my tender scalp. My Hardy Boy was holding my hair for me.

Everything hurt; a deep-seated ache resonated into the core of my bone marrow.

Aside from the pain, I was wrestling with my confusion.

Where was I? Despite the throb thudding behind my eyelids, I tried to think through my last memories. It was my birthday; the guys and I were at Après, celebrating my birthday. I couldn't remember anything past getting through the VIP line and getting out of the cold.

"Winter?" Travis' soft voice was tentative and close. I slowly curved my head in its direction and was gifted with a soft kiss to my forehead.

So, the guys were here with me. Was Cam here? He had been meeting us at the bar with Travis — maybe he didn't come, after all?

I needed to sit up.

"Can someone help me up?"

I didn't recognize my voice; its distorted tone was garbled and weak. Had I gotten that wasted last night? I had never been drunk enough to black out; I would never allow myself to lose that level of control. Is this what I did now that I was safe and had men readily available to take care of me?

No. That didn't make sense. That wasn't me.

Two powerful sets of arms gently hoisted me up from my den of pillows, but the motion of the movement made me puke the last of my stomach contents into Shane's arms.

"Fuck," I rasped, my throat stripped raw from acid.

A large palm stroked up and down my spine at the same time another hand took mine and squeezed. Another few deep breaths allowed me to open my eyes to get some answers.

I was in a huge sleigh bed. It had to be a California King, my body cocooned in a thick white feather duvet with equally luxurious pillows. The room was unfamiliar. Stark white, oversized white fur lined chairs nestled in one corner with an elaborate set of bookshelves lined with multicolored spines, and black and white old Hollywood portraits lined one wall. Dark blinds covered an entire wall of floor to ceiling windows, but sunlight peaked through the slivers on either side of each shade.

Shane stood in front of me holding the bucket, still dressed in his bar clothes. Travis lay next to me on my right, Drew to my left.

My eyes settled on Cam's beautiful boxer body wearing only a tight white tank top and boxer shorts, seated on the far edge of the mattress. He met my eyes in earnest; piercing blues filled with surprising sorrow. Sorrow overlayed with unbridled rage. I hadn't seen him wear that look since the night of the fight.

I shook my cotton-filled head to straighten out my jumbled thoughts.

"Can someone explain, please?"

Quick opened his mouth to speak, but before the words exited his lips into the surrounding air, Logan strolled through the bedroom door, looking out of place in a white fitted t-shirt and gray sweatpants.

My brows knit in confusion. What was Logan doing here? Unless …

"Listen you fuckers, I —" He stopped mid-sentence, his warm brown eyes flickering up from his phone and surveying the room as four sets of eyes glared back at him.

I only gaped, though, attempting in vain to put two and two together between the folds of my blended brain. We were at Logan's place. But why? How? Nothing was making sense.

Cam's level baritone cut through the air, breaking the spell that had fallen over all of us. "Someone drugged you, little violet." His face crumpled into a serious frown. "At least, we think they did."

"We know they did." Logan stated with authority, tucking his phone into his pocket and folding his arms across his chest, leaning against the wall casually, like this scenario was an everyday occurrence.

I squeezed my eyes shut, forcing my mind to sift through the hazy memories — I couldn't. For the life of me, I couldn't even summon a snippet from the evening before. Tears escaped my eyes before I had even realized they had formed. Quick's fingers wiped them away before I garnered the courage to open them again.

"It's okay, baby girl," Drew crooned soothingly. "You're safe here." He shifted his arms to wrap me tightly in a side hug, easing me gently closer into the security of his hold.

"You're safe, beautiful." Travis repeated. His nimble fingers kneaded the tense muscles through my neck and shoulders.

I wished their comforting presence was enough, but it wasn't. I needed to know who had taken my power away from me last night. The churning in my gut told me I knew the answer, even if ignorance would have sheltered my heart.

I opened my eyes and fixated on the one man who wouldn't bullshit me or try to save my feelings.

"Tell me," I demanded, although it sounded more like a plea in my broken voice. "Please," I added as an afterthought when he stared through me, a rare fleeting moment of indecision passing through his golden irises.

Logan let out a reedy sigh, stunning me when he plopped himself on the bed — his bed? — on the other side of Travis and rolled over onto his stomach, his gaze never breaking from mine. I blinked when I once again recognized the sheer size of my pillow fortress. The bed was enormous to fit all of us on it, with room for more.

"I don't have proof," he began, steepling his fingers and pressing them against his pursed lips. "But I don't need it. Carson Baker drugged you. And we're going to make him pay for it."

CHAPTER 23

SHANE

Winter folded in on herself, her eyes staring at nothing in the space beyond the bed. I took her face in my palms, stroking her cheeks in the soothing way she loved when we were teenagers, while Travis and Drew held her between them. Her eyes were glossy with tears that by sheer stubbornness alone she refused to shed.

I witnessed her slip into the familiar robot mode as she processed Logan's admission. I hated her default setting, but I had seen it enough to know it was her strongest defense mechanism. In the past, it had had lifesaving advantages.

If this night hadn't been such a clusterfuck of emotional turmoil, I might have laughed at the scene in Logan's bedroom. Our situation just continued to bring the man in question into our web and I wasn't sure how I felt about it. In this moment, though, I had nothing but gratitude for his quick thinking and willingness to put his usual asshole self aside to help us. To help *her.*

I wasn't a panicked person by nature; there was a mental steadiness that came with always filling the team captain role and training to go pro. The psychological endurance an athlete has to learn is intense and damn useful for everything else in life outside of the field or the hill.

All the training in the world couldn't have prepared me for last night; seeing Winter violently ill and out of control had rattled me to my core, and I could admit that my stomach acid had stripped more than one layer off its lining in the last twelve hours. One hour to get to here and situated; eleven hours waiting it out as she slept off the drugs in Logan's bed.

Eleven agonizing hours as she held my hand in her unconscious state and puked into my bucket every few hours.

Even now, knowing she was conscious, breathing, and relatively okay, my heart wrenched in my chest. Her completely helpless state had brought me to my knees. No one was more important to me than this woman. I could not be the man I needed to be without her. My best friend. My Snow.

The five of us had been up all night talking, any of us getting two hours sleep tops, even Logan, while Winter slept off the aftereffects of the drugs. Carson Baker was going to pay.

I didn't need evidence. If Logan was willing to throw his 'business partner' under the bus, that was good enough for me. After our altercation at the pool hall, there was no doubt in my mind the fucker would try to force himself into her world again. The man was psychopathic.

Winter shifted in front of me, her eyes not meeting mine as she attempted to sit on her knees. She was clumsy and awkward like a little baby deer. I promptly grabbed the bucket from the floor and placed it in front of her chin just before she dry-heaved what little remained in her stomach.

Travis stroked her hair and Drew squeezed her hands; both men taking care of her when she needed it most. I was so grateful for them; I had never realized the two of us needed more people in our circle until having to endure the events of the last few months. We were stronger as a unit. We weren't just solving amateur mystery hour anymore. We were our own messy version of family.

Even Cam, who I still struggle to get a clear read on the best of days, never left Winter's side all night. He held a cool washcloth to her forehead while Travis and Drew got their micro-moments of sleep. He also rinsed out the puke bucket more than once. He and Logan had their own particular brand of snipes and gripes, but neither let their beef with each other take priority. Winter had been everyone's focus.

Our Snow.

Logan disappeared from the room when it was clear she was going to be sick again, but reappeared a few minutes later with a sleeve of soup crackers and a can of ginger ale. He placed them on the end table beside Drew and stepped back, his eyes meeting mine.

"I'm going to go shower."

When he had left the room, Drew placed the crackers in Winter's lap and coaxed her to eat. She nibbled on one corner and we all watched her in complete silence.

"So, um," she began, her eyes darting back and forth warily between the four men in the room, "how did we get to Logan's?"

Travis spoke up, giving the Cliff's Notes version of the night before; her delayed appearance at the table, the toast, the drugging aftermath; Logan's attempt at being a savior, which had surprised the hell out of all of us, but no one could deny how appreciative we were for his out of character rescue. The strong conclusion we came to that Carson had drugged her when he grabbed her on the dance floor.

I had nearly left the apartment when Logan admitted to the earlier events of the night, in search of the slimy fucker who had already done enough damage to last a lifetime.

Winter bit her lip hesitantly, her face pale even in the shadows of the darkened room. "I wish I could remember that. I don't remember anything after we got in to Après."

Cam cracked his knuckles behind me; I turned around to get a good look at the last addition to our crew. His face was stone still—a perfect mask that had to be well-practiced — but his eyes were afire with fury.

"We'll kill him." His tone brokered no arguments; At that moment, I fully believed he was capable of murder.

"I hope that's unnecessary," she whispered with a weary half-smile, stopping to finish one cracker and start on another.

"Snow," I whispered, moving back in to cup her face, peering deep into those eyes I knew so well. My heart tugged at the layers of pain I saw there. "I think it's time everyone knows what happened."

"I — can't." Her spine stiffened as she drew away from me, retreating into herself.

No. I was not letting her do this again. I would have to push her, and I'd hate doing it, but she needed to let this secret free. One less lie in our tangle of lies.

"We need to, Snow," I urged her, my tone assertive rather than pleading. "I'll help you." I leaned in to place a light kiss on her forehead and moved to stand so I could see everyone in the room.

Logan chose the perfect time to enter, his hair freshly washed and looking far less douche-y than usual. After last night, we would owe him one. He already knew the story, but he would benefit from hearing her side of the story. The *right* side of the story.

I studied Winter once more, seeking final permission. All I got was the teeny version of a bro nod, but it was enough.

I steeled myself for the fallout, but right now, it was story time. I addressed the guys.

"Has Winter ever told you about Carson Baker? I'm going to assume no from our conversations last night."

Drew shook his head. Cam stared angrily ahead without comment, but Travis spoke up.

He squeezed her arm before folding his own arms across his chest. "She told me they had briefly dated, and then he and his friends bullied her through high school. What else happened?"

I whirled around to face Winter. A guilty look crossed her face before hardening into an unreadable mask. "Is that how she put it?"

"It *was bullying,*" she shot back. "I didn't think I needed to relive the entire ordeal by mapping out every little detail." Her tone was angry enough to bite despite the exhausted undertone beneath it. "It's in the past and I've done my best to forget."

I ignored the last comment, knowing full well the incident was not in the past. It would have been impossible to put that behind her without having scars, and I'd seen the ragged edges of them on Winter's soul ever since it happened.

"It was not bullying, it was assault," I said hoarsely, silently simmering now at her denial. I shouldn't be mad at her. It wasn't fair to be mad at her. She had just been drugged by the man who had nearly gotten her killed for fuck's sake, but my adrenaline from the panic was culminating into emotions I couldn't control.

"It was *not* assault." Her voice rose to match mine, equally exasperated. "The act itself was consensual. No actual sex even happened. How could we have lost our virginity together on prom night if sex had happened?"

My mouth dropped, damn right flabbergasted she would openly admit *that* in front of these men. It was the one secret we had never shared. In fact, we had never discussed it afterward, not once. She was trying to divert the conversation and downplay the effects this terrible experience had on her, and I couldn't let her have it.

"Wait — what? I thought you guys were always just friends?" Drew, poor guy, looked so confused as his eyes darted back and forth between me and Winter, although Winter was doing her absolute best not to make eye contact with anyone.

Travis hung back, seemingly unsurprised by this revelation, but he was fixated on Winter's response too. Cam was stoic as always, his gigantic frame casually laying on his side at the end of the bed, but his eyes were sharp. I knew this story mattered to him too, despite his lack of outward emotion.

Logan shoved his hands in his pockets and leaned against the wall, his expression extremely uncomfortable. Good. Had he been a better man in high school, Carson might not have gotten away with what he did.

"Yes, we are. It was nothing. Moving on please." Winter sighed, hands clenching at her sides in obvious distress.

"You brought it up," I gently reminded her, still shocked she felt that was the right topic to bring us away from her shitty high school experience. "And that wasn't just your secret to tell."

She worried her lip between her teeth, and I saw the remorse cross her face. A discussion for later, not now. Right now, we needed to talk about *this*.

"What are you hiding from, Snow? Anyone can do a simple Google search to know. These men are falling for you and you're holding yourself back from loving them too. Don't you want to tell them in your own words?"

I held my hand out to take hers as a peace offering, clasping her fingers in my own when she allowed me in.

"I think it's time you owned it, Snowflake," I leaned in and whispered softly in her ear, for only us to hear. "You don't need to carry this anymore."

She sighed heavily, tears in eyes, her mask falling and shattering into a million little pieces.

Her gaze fell on an invisible point of the duvet before speaking again.

"I-I have trust issues. Big shocker there." She gave us a weak smile as she gathered her strength before continuing. She raised her head and opened her mouth to speak, using an emotionless monotone to tell the story.

"In high school, sophomore year, I started dating Carson. He was what a teenage girl would deem 'the whole package.' His family was wealthy, he was captain of three sports teams, he did well in school; a bit of a golden boy. He was a senior in Drew's and Logan's year, and for some reason, he was interested in me.

"We had been dating for a few weeks, when he took me back to his parent's house after school. We were alone, and he led me to his bedroom to make out. We got a bit carried away, and soon I was naked on his bed, both giving and receiving head. It had been my second time doing anything like that, and he had been so sweet, making me feel comfortable and so incredibly wanted."

The grimace that smothered her features transformed from embarrassment to disgust.

"What I didn't know was that the whole shebang was being filmed, at the perfect angle, to see absolutely everything. Two days later, the video was posted anonymously and made its way around the school. Someone conveniently edited it to hide his face and most of his body, but I wasn't so lucky."

Her bitter laugh was dull and lifeless as she gripped the edge of the duvet tighter.

"They bullied me to the point of doing whatever I could to get out of school. 'Whore' and 'slut' kept being painted on my locker, despite it being repeatedly washed off. I had to avoid most routes to school because I was ridiculed so bad, I started having panic attacks. Guys from his teams would try to corner me in hallways and parking lots, and one almost assaulted me in the girl's bathroom. My grades tanked, and I became a shell of who I was. Eventually, the video made local news headlines once the administration tried to take control of the situation. It was a mess."

Winter stopped speaking, no longer able to hold back the tears from streaming down her face. Drew pulled her between his legs and enveloped her body with his own, quietly whispering encouragements into the crook of her neck.

My chest exploded with affection for the two of them.

Cam jumped off of his perch on the bed and dropped to the floor, starting a violent round of push-ups. Travis craned his neck from above, watching our friend with concern.

"He's trying not to punch a hole in the wall," he explained quietly, stroking the stray hairs out of Winter's face. "Do you think you can finish your story?"

Winter swallowed hard; the clear pain of the memories was almost too hard to bear. She grabbed another cracker and crushed it in her hands before continuing.

"My parents were furious, Mom especially — sexual freedom and all that — so they took him to court. Carson could have been charged and sent to jail for the creation and distribution of child pornography since I was under 17 and he wasn't. My name was redacted because of privacy laws, but someone leaked it at one hearing and I faced even further hell. His parents kept his name out of the press, continually being referred to as 'a wealthy son of a local businessman,' while they made me out to be a gold-digging tramp who took the videos myself to get the attention.

"I spent most of my junior year flying under the radar as best I could, but it was pretty impossible. It took two years to properly settle out of court, and there's a bank account with my name on it full of disgusting retribution money that I want no part of."

She lifted her head and locked eyes with Logan, sparks of fire returning to them as her tone transformed from anguish to accusation.

"Meanwhile, he got slapped on the wrist. There's nothing on his record. He went away for university, and is now back in town for who knows how long, and I'm just supposed to pretend like nothing happened!"

She threw up her hands and let out a strained, high-pitched laugh that made her sound mildly insane.

"And now he's drugging me? I don't get it. I don't get why I'm his target."

She took another cracker out of the sleeve, this time chewing on one corner. No one uttered a sound; I knew if I broke her out of her rhythm, she'd clam up and never speak of this again.

"After Quick took the sting away by being my first — not a story I'm willing to talk about today — I took my sexual freedom back. No one got to dictate my worth by my sexual choices anymore. I had a lot of therapy, and then a lot of sex with a lot of people, and I have no regrets about any of it."

She bit her lip hesitantly before blowing out a long exhale.

"But I struggle with vulnerability. A lot. Carson took my ability to trust away from me. And he apparently tried to do it again last night."

She stared down at her hands for six long heartbeats. I was about to break the thunderous silence when her head lifted; she made eye contact with each one of us, her courage building with each person. "The end," she said resolutely, as if giving us permission to speak.

Drew cut through the dense fog first.

"Jesus, Winter, I must have had my head up my ass. I had no idea it was that bad. I knew there were rumors, but … I am so sorry, baby girl." Drew tightened his arms around Winter, and she let go of my hand to hug him back. She let her tears fall freely now, the ache of those years finally getting a release.

"How did you move on?" Travis asked gently, shifting in to pull her toward him.

"He left. He had to; it was a condition of his sentence. When he left, everyone seemed to forget it too. I could breathe again. I could rebuild my reputation and just try to live without the drama of just attending my high school. And I did, mostly. With Quick's help." She flashed me a genuine, soul-deep, appreciative smile that I felt through every layer of my skin.

Drew and Travis each took turns squeezing her tight and muttering softly into her ear. I patiently waited as her boyfriends gave her the love they needed. I had lived this story with her; they were hearing it for the first time. I could only imagine how desperately they would need the reassurance.

Cam had finished his lengthy round of push-ups and sprung up from the floor, surprising us all by tugging Winter out of Drew's and Travis' hold and pulling her off of the bed and into his own arms, tucking her tightly beneath his chin.

"I'm so sorry, little violet. Thank you for being brave and opening your heart."

He shocked the hell out of me by leaning down and kissing her — not a peck of friendly solace, either. A solid touch of lips, a claiming in front of everyone in the room. Winter's stunned expression morphed into calm submission as he plundered her mouth before halting mid-kiss and stepping away — his own look of dismay matching the rest of the room.

Winter touched her fingers to her lips with a rare shyness, blushing a bright pink. I moved in to wrap my arms around her from behind, concerned she might fall over from the drugs aftereffects.

A throat cleared uncomfortably in the dead quiet of the kiss aftermath. I turned our bodies to see Logan standing awkwardly still; he hadn't moved an inch from his perch by the wall.

"The Baker family has a history with Darren, Winter. It's why he went after you. I wouldn't be surprised if Wyatt had directed his son to do it. I wasn't any help to you then, because I was living in my version of hell and had my agenda. But I'll help you now, even if you won't let me."

He pushed himself off the wall and filled the space in front of us, his eyes never leaving Winter's. The air around us took on an electric supercharge, and it magnetized me in place still holding Winter to my chest.

He reached for her, cupping his hand around the back of her neck. He pressed his forehead to hers. I leaned back slightly, waiting for her to clock him in the nuts or punch him in the face.

She drew in a shaky breath and surprised the hell out of me when she mimicked the motion, cupping him back, their heads bowed together in a mute conversation.

How full circle we had come. One date in high school, but it had been Winter's first. He had pushed her buttons and had acted as a solid 'World's Greatest Dick' contender ever since. But tonight, he had saved her from someone far worse.

She pulled away first, but it was enough. The tides were turning for our little group. I assessed the man in front of me with discerning eyes.

His face lacked any smug arrogance or superiority. He actually looked kind, earnest even. It was confusing as hell, but oddly reassuring. Logan had resources we didn't have. Maybe this meant he could help us on all fronts. He was just as fucked over by Georgio as we were, wasn't he? My spirits soared at the opportunities bringing him into the group might bring, even if he was an irritating dickwad on the best of days.

Winter stared at Logan for what felt like years before dipping her head in acknowledgment.

"Thank you."

Logan returned her nod and walked out of the room, leaving the rest of us to grapple with the rest of the day's plans.

Winter turned in my arms, peering through me with her red-rimmed blue eyes I knew as well as my own. "I'd like to go home now."

Now wasn't the time to address that she intentionally spilled a shared secret without my permission, or to explore the fact that it was bringing up all kinds of confusing emotions for me.

"We'll take you home, Snow." I buried my face in her hair and held her as tight as I could, syncing our heartbeats. "I'm so proud of you."

CHAPTER 24

TRAVIS

Another day, another dollar.

I loosened the skinny black tie Georgio had insisted we wear as part of the uniform and threw it on the bench beside me before I unbuttoned the collar of my black dress shirt.

I rubbed my palms down my face, decompressing after one of the busiest nights I had ever worked. I have served over 200 drinks to drunken strangers. Two hundred drinks to wayward party-goers who didn't know their town had so many secrets.

I filled my lungs with the damp, stale air of the staff locker room and blew it all out in a rush. Life had never been necessarily kind to the Balcom family, but this month had been a particular doozy.

Mom was home, but she was frailer than I had ever seen her. She was practically immobile; every move she made exhausted her, a result of her body constantly fighting to breathe. Her lungs were failing — just another debilitating result of the disease. I was now paying for a home-care nurse to come in to check on her twice a day while I was at work since I couldn't give her around the clock care, and Devon wasn't a reliable caregiver.

I had to give him a bit of credit; in the few weeks he had been home, there had been no sign of drug use whatsoever. Of course, that was because he had a new vice of choice: Jesus, Lord and Savior.

I nearly spit out my drink when he gifted me a bible last week.

Apparently, he was now a born-again Christian, which to me just meant he had tricked himself into believing his previous actions didn't have consequences. It must be nice to dip in some holy water and have every transgression you've ever committed erased like it never happened. Too bad the skeletons he left behind didn't wash away with his sins. We'd have been all the better for it.

I handed it back and asked him to put in a good word to Jesus, in case he gave our mother a break. He only stared at me for a moment before retreating to his room.

Good. I spent most of my life protecting Devon, and would as long as I was living, but I wasn't interested in saving him from yet another failed obsession when the church inevitably let him down too. I couldn't call an ambulance to fix that problem.

I shrugged off the dress shirt and pulled on a gray hoodie before grabbing the thick wool coat stuffed at the bottom of my locker. I was staying the night at Winter's place and I wasn't going to miss it for the world.

The terrible birthday incident had been over a week ago. She had insisted she was fine after Shane brought her home to rest up, but I was worried. Her past had blindsided me, but bit by bit, all of her little quirks fell into place like the little shapes in Tetris. I felt a deep pain through my chest for hours after, picturing the teenage version of her going through that nightmare. High school was hard enough without additional trauma on top of it.

A stupid, entitled teenager who got away with a crime because of who his parents were was one thing. A stupid man who continued to believe Winter was somehow his to torture was another thing entirely. I didn't know how we were going to do it, but Carson Baker would pay for what he did to our girl.

I walked out to my black rust bucket Dodge Daytona — held together with duct tape and poster glue at this point — and noticed Logan's silver Audi striking a stark contrast beside it. The poor man and the rich man; somehow, we were both caught in Winter's web.

His windows were fogged up so I couldn't see inside, but I assumed he was in there — why else would they be condensing?

I wrapped on the glass, using the opportunity to thank him myself. His quick thinking had ensured Winter was safe when the situation could have been so much worse, and I was grateful that even assholes could change their stripes, however briefly.

The car wasn't running, which should have been my first clue when he didn't open his door or put down his window. He didn't seem to have the same issues with me as he did the other men — probably because we didn't have the same history — but he had been pretty pissed at me when I brought up his little habit, so maybe he was ignoring me.

Still, something was off. It was 10:30 pm on a Wednesday night. His windows wouldn't be fogging if someone wasn't in there ...

Oh.

Logan was getting laid or getting off. I immediately regretted my decision to reach out when a palm hit the window with such force I almost jumped out of my skin.

I don't know what drove me to do it, but I wrenched on the handle to open the door. Maybe subconsciously I registered the hindbrain indicators of someone in distress, a result of years of honing in on other people's needs.

Logan had his arms held tight to his chest, his face a sallow blue in the dim overhead light. His breaths were rapid and shallow, like he was fighting for what little air his lungs could grasp. A deep, low groan resonated from his chest.

The white powder sprinkling on the dashboard was my last clue.

"Fuck!"

I sprang into action, lifting him out of the car and laying him on the freezing cold asphalt. From what little I knew, cocaine was Logan's drug of choice. I could guess he was in the middle of a heart attack.

"Siri, call 9-1-1." I shouted into my phone as I held my fingers to Logan's pulse point. It was weak, but it existed, so that was a point in our favor. I unzipped his jacket to loosen the space around his chest.

"No." He grasped my wrist as his face contorted into agony. "I'm not" — his voice faded on a gasp — "gonna die. Call Hill."

"Logan," I warned, not willing to let the man die in the parking lot, no matter how irritating he had been in the past. I had been tapping on the window to thank him, hadn't I?

"Call Hill," he insisted, somehow being domineering even in this clusterfuck of a situation.

He limply touched his right pocket with his other hand and I took out his cell phone, waving it in front of his face to unlock it. I quickly scrolled through for Hillary's number and pressed 'call.'

"If you die, I'll make sure everyone knows you wouldn't let me call an ambulance, you arrogant fucker," I muttered darkly, my fingers still pressed against his jugular to feel for a pulse. So far, so good, but I had seen enough overdoses in my lifetime not to take my chances.

"Hello?" a melodic feminine voice filled the tinny line.

"Hi, Hillary, this is Travis Balcom. You don't know me, but I just found Logan in the parking lot of Bourbon & Blues. I think he's having a drug-induced heart attack. He won't let me call an ambulance and insisted I call you, but I'm two seconds away from bringing him to the hospital myself."

To her credit, she didn't hesitate, not for a second. "I'm on my way. I'll be there in twelve minutes if I hit all green lights. Lay him on his back and do chest compressions if you have to."

She hung up. I continued to monitor Logan's breathing, my thumb never leaving his pulse point.

"You're going to be okay, man." I kept rubbing his arm in a soothing pattern — not because we were on that level, but it's what I would have done for Devon. It's what I *had* done for Devon too many times, too many raw memories to count.

Logan just barked out a reedy laugh in response, but he didn't shirk away from me or throw out a cutting comment, so I continued what I was doing in the disquiet of the near-empty parking lot.

Hillary arrived just a few minutes later; I didn't know where she had been, but she must have broken the sound barrier to get here.

My mouth dropped when I saw her car, a Jaguar F-type coupe. It was no wonder she made it here in record time. I knew little about cars, but this had featured in a *The Fast and the Furious* movie.

The wealth of these people was nauseating.

She knelt by my side and clasped Logan's hand in her own.

"Drug?" she asked pointedly, her gaze briefly landing on me.

"Cocaine, I think," I wondered how in the world she was going to replace a doctor in this situation. Heart attacks were more common than you would think, but not for men in their twenties.

"Okay," she declared, tossing her purse to the pavement and pulling out a water bottle and a handful of white pills. "Take these. It's aspirin," she added when she noticed my dubious expression.

Her delicate brow scrunched into a frown. Her voice lowered as she smoothed her hand over his clammy brow. "What have you been up to, Loggie? How did I not see the signs?"

"Stupid," Logan grunted through his pain. "So stupid. Need to keep this quiet, 'k? No hospitals."

She tsked and pursed her lips in disapproval. "How can you think about your reputation right now? Is it worth dying for?"

"Not gonna die." Logan grimaced, but managed a shadow of his usual smirk. "Haven't married you yet. Need your money first."

Hillary giggled; actually giggled at some apparent inside joke they were sharing. These two were fucked.

"I'm going to help you through this and then make some calls to get you some private scans. But then, Loggie, you are going to get clean. Totally clean. I may not be there next time. You're lucky that" — she turned to me again — "Travis, was it? — was here to even call me in the first place."

She stared at him with a resolute fire in her eyes I had only witnessed in one other woman. "Swear to me, Logan."

He swallowed hard and nodded once. "Fuck, Hill, yes. Swear. Can I sit up now? It's fucking cold."

Hillary stood and the two of us brought him back to his feet, moving him into the passenger seat of her beautiful car.

"Thanks, Travis. I trust you can be discreet about this?" Hillary leaned over the driver's side door with a commanding presence that drove through me.

I scratched the back of my neck uncomfortably. Lies had already gotten me in scalding water with Winter, and I promised her there would be no more.

"This won't get out to anyone important. But I'm not going to keep this from Winter."

Her facial features softened and her eyes lit up. "You're Winter's Travis? Nice to meet you. I wish it were under better circumstances." She tapped the roof of her car twice and stepped in.

"He'll be okay, but I'll keep Winter posted," she hollered before slamming her door and ripping out of the parking lot, down the street.

I stared dumbly after the car disappearing into the distance, unable to move the lead in my shoes.

What in the fuck just happened?

And how was I going to tell Winter?

"To your left," I called out, struggling underneath the weight of the large leather sofa, barely in my grasp. "No, your *other* left."

"This thing is heavy, man," Devon complained as he wrestled with the other side.

He had bought Mom a new couch as a homecoming gift. He could have used the money to do something practical like pay for a medical bill, but that wasn't my little brother. I had no idea where he had gotten the money to pay for a couch anyway, but I was relieved he hadn't spent the money on drugs, so I hadn't said much.

The problem was he drove a tiny ancient Nissan Sentra, and I drove my shitbox of a Daytona. Neither of us had vehicles that could transport it, and Devon couldn't afford to pay for the delivery.

Shane's booming laughter came from behind me.

"Here." He gently shifted Devon out of the way and lifted his end of the couch with ease. Strong fucker.

Thank God for the man with his old truck with a beautifully large truck bed. He hadn't hesitated when I called him and asked for help.

"Okay, Travis, I'm going to bring this through the front door on an angle. It's gonna be tight, but this couch has got some cushion. She can take it."

He winked suggestively and effortlessly carried his end of the couch up the rickety wooden steps to our crappy trailer front door. Devon watched from below with his hands in his pockets, shivering in the cold.

I wasn't cold. Every muscle was straining underneath the weight of this cowhide behemoth and I was sweating bullets. I swear Devon saw the largest couch in the store he could find and bought it, no questions asked. I wasn't even sure it would fit in our living room.

I wasn't jacked like Shane and I didn't have a build like Drew. I had strength from lean muscles and years of hard work attached to them, but that wasn't enough to lug a thousand-pound couch a hundred yards.

Okay — 400 pounds and 60 yards. It was enough. Shane's penchant for exaggeration was wearing off on me.

I could see why Winter loved him so much. He had a big heart and enjoyed taking care of people. He drew you in with his wide smile and loud jokes and he made sure everyone felt included. If engineering didn't work out, he'd be a great elementary school teacher.

I grinned as I pictured Shane at the front of a kindergarten classroom, his size engulfing the little kids as he sang them their ABCs.

"Turn it sideways," Shane instructed from the front, snapping me back to attention.

I grunted and shifted my shoulder underneath the furniture, tilting the couch at an angle. I shuffled my feet forward in time with Shane as he pulled it through the door like he barely felt the weight of the damn thing.

We fumbled around the tight space, though thankfully we had already removed the old eighties floral couch the hour before, and settled it into the room with a thud.

There was only two feet on the one side to make it through to the bedroom hallway, but it was passable at least. With how little I was home these days other than to take care of Mom, and how little Mom actually came out of her bedroom, I doubted this couch would get much use. Maybe Devon would be inviting his church friends over or something.

"Thanks, man!" I shook Shane's hand and pulled him in for a shoulder-tap man hug, but he squeezed me tight instead. I laughed into his shoulder and gave him a light squeeze in return.

The guy loved with abandon. His complete lack of embarrassment or discomfort at just being who he was made me want to hide myself less. My natural charm had been a blessing and a curse in that regard.

"I don't keep any alcohol here," I said apologetically as I made my way to the fridge, "but I have some delicious sparkling grapefruit drinks and I make one hell of a mocktail."

"Sure!" Shane grinned and climbed over the couch to settle into a seat. "Winter says you're a drink wizard. I will happily consume your elixir."

I snorted at his outright nerdiness and turned to Devon, who lingered in the doorway looking uncomfortable.

"Would you like one, Dev?" I asked, motioning for him to take a seat and join us.

"No, that's okay," he said carefully, looking back and forth between Shane and I. "I'm going to head out. I have a meeting tonight."

I smiled softly, proud of him for sticking to his NA meetings. He had to drive to Kensington for them, but he had already gone to two since he had come home.

"Okay, man. Text me if you need anything."

His lips quirked up tentatively before thanking Shane and leaving us to our manly mocktails and the massive leather couch.

"That's fucking delicious!" Shane exclaimed as I handed him the pale pink cocktail a few minutes later.

We turned on the basketball game and relaxed in the living room. Other than Winter and Cam, I had had no one come hang out in my trailer in years — probably before Dad left, if memory served.

I had surprised myself by not even considering the fact Shane would have to see my childhood home and be exposed to my living situation when I had asked him for help today. Winter had made me realize I needed to stop hiding from those I cared about, and these men — they were becoming my people too.

"Right?" I winked and popped the sugared cranberry garnish into my mouth, relishing the tart burst of juice on my tongue. "I've been doing this a long time — you pick up some tricks along the way."

"So, you love it? Bartending, I mean?" Shane's face was curious and genuinely interested. I considered my words before responding.

"I do. I can't see much of a future with it, though." I laughed cynically. "I can't see much of a future with anything right now, though, man. I'm just taking it day by day."

Shane nodded seriously and inspected the drink in his hand. "There's a business here, but I'm not sure what at the moment. I think you have more talent than you realize." He drained his glass and set it down on the floor beside his feet, smacking his lips in appreciation.

"What about you? You're going to join your dad's firm and engineer things?" I asked teasingly, knowing full well Shane wanted to design bridges for a living. His passion came through every time he talked about it.

"I don't know anymore, to be honest." He blew out a breath and stared at the TV, his brows creased into a frown. "I don't know who my parents are anymore. I don't know what I'm walking into if I take that route. And I don't think Winter wants to stick around town after graduation, and I don't want to live my day to day without her, you know?"

I knew. I knew very well. We hadn't spoken about what was going to happen "after" but I couldn't see a future for any of us here, either. I didn't have just me to think about; I had Mom and Devon to consider.

"Yeah, I love her too," I said simply in response. I had said the words to her, and she hadn't said them back, but after her birthday revelation I could understand why. I knew when she said them, they would be a big deal, and I knew in my heart she *would* say them to me. A piece of me hoped she would say them to me first, before Drew, but it resigned me to the fact she could love us both.

I knew she loved Shane too. They orbited each other, like earth and the moon, each switching sides depending on what their needs were in the moment. I don't think either of them realized the depth of it — especially now it had come to light they had actually had sex at one point in time.

"You're all in?" he asked, his gaze no longer on the game but fixated on me.

"All in," I confirmed, drinking the last of the fizzy juice and spinning the glass between my palms. "Just like you are."

"Oh?" He cocked his head in feigned confusion.

"Yeah, man. Forgive me for saying it if this isn't what you want to hear, but you and Winter are in a full-scale, committed relationship. You have every single aspect of one, except for sex, and now we all know that that's happened at one point too."

I held up my hands as he opened his mouth to speak. "No judgments, just an observation. You snuggle, you have sleepovers where you sleep in the same bed, you can finish each other's sentences and read each other's thoughts." I let that thought trail off. "I know you love her, but maybe there's more to it than that."

He drummed his fingers erratically against the back of the couch, his body now tight as a bowstring. "She's my best friend, man. I'd do anything for her."

It was as if he was talking to himself, not to me. It was no surprise he was in outright denial; they both were. If I turned around tomorrow and Winter said they had reconnected that sexual flame, I wouldn't bat an eye. And oddly, I didn't feel the same sense of jealousy at that thought as I had with Drew.

Shane had been here first. He had taken care of her all of her life. And he would continue to, whether or not a sexual element entered their relationship. Knowing she had another person in her life who loved her at that kind of level was a comfort.

"Me too, man. Me too." I grabbed my glass and climbed over the couch—this was going to be a pain in the ass—to get to the kitchen. "Want another round?"

He dipped his chin in a quick nod, staring through the TV and into his thoughts beyond.

Looks like I gave him something to think about.

This dynamic was about to get interesting.

224

CHAPTER 25

DREW

"Thanks for agreeing to meet with me."

Mom sat at the sparse table for two in my eat-in kitchen, her hands wrapped around a mug of peppermint tea as she looked anywhere but at me.

Dad had been home recovering for a few weeks now. They had made the deal with Camden and the diner would be his by mid-April.

The kicker? He would only buy it if all current staff stayed on and the diner continued to operate 'business-as-usual,' something called a 'staff staying clause.' The clause stipulated that staff had to continue with the operation for 'six months to ensure a smooth transition under new ownership.' I'm sure if Janice quit tomorrow, Camden wouldn't give a damn, but that clause kept me there and kept me quiet.

Dad nearly pulled the plug on the whole thing and I thought his heart was going to give out. Winter, Shane, and I talked about the issue to death, but in the end, I agreed to stay. I would not be any safer from Georgio and his threats if I took on another job in Cascade Falls. I also hadn't come up with any sort of plan for the future. Six months gave me time to work out an escape route — not just for me, but for them. We all needed to get out of here.

Winter's revelations on her birthday had made me realize just how much of my life I had lived for my parents. My high school years had been a blur of long hours at school, trying out for the myriad of sports teams to carry on Dad's legacy, and working after hours in the evenings and on weekends to save for college. That I hadn't known how bad things were for Winter, despite us living in the same small town, was a wake-up call. I had lived my whole life for someone else, meeting someone else's expectations. My next steps were going to be for me. I just hadn't figured out what they were yet.

Mom was beside herself about my decision, but it wasn't hers to make. I had asked her to come over for tea to have a private chat to discuss what the next steps were for her and Dad; that, and I was going to use the opportunity to get some information out of her. Shane and I thought if she was alone, she might open up more about her relationship with Georgio and the Shambala Society.

"Mom?" I whispered, reaching for her hand across the table. "I need to ask you a few questions, okay? I know you don't agree with my decision, but I have my reasons. I need you to trust me. But I also can't continue to do this blind. You and Dad did that to me once — I can't do it again."

A single tear fell down her cheek as she looked up at me.

My mother had aged beautifully; her brown hair was streaked with silver and her temples were creased from years of laughter. Whereas Dad carried the weight of the world on his shoulders, Mom had such a zest for life and projected it onto everyone she met. The relationships that cemented Johnson's as Cascade Falls central hub of dining were because of her.

The last few months had taken their toll, though. Her hazel eyes lacked any sparkle. Her lips had been stuck in a permanent grimace since she'd found Dad on the hallway floor. I couldn't blame her, but the time for secrets was over. I knew they hadn't told me the complete story, and I would not dance around it anymore.

I stroked her hand gently with my thumb, a motion she used to do for me when I was a scared little boy.

"I need to know about the Shambala Society."

Her body snapped to attention, eyes widening in surprise. "How did you hear that name?"

"The buried secrets in this town are being dug up," I told her truthfully. "When I found out about Georgio's involvement here, I started digging. I'm being careful, but I can't sit on this anymore. I saw the photo in a high school yearbook. What does it have to do with Georgio and our situation today?"

Mom blew out a shaky breath and peered out my front window where the sun was setting over the mountainside. Twinkling lights from town were coming on as the sky darkened to an inky blue.

"We were just kids who thought that they had a clue about the world."

Her tone was sad, mournful even. She stared into the depths of her tea as if it could tell the story for her.

"At first it was just Darren, Emmett, and Georgio. They were best friends."

My eyebrows hit my hairline.

"Georgio was not always who he is now. He grew up in a family that didn't leave him much choice in his career path. Kind of what your father did to you, unwittingly." She smiled sadly, her eyes still downcast.

"Darren and Emmett had always been friends, at least for as long as I knew them. Darren didn't talk about this, but he was a foster child. Emmett's family took him in most of the time, since Darren bounced around a lot. There aren't a lot of supports for foster kids in small towns and he had little stability."

Holy shit. Winter definitely didn't know this. She had told me that her grandparents died before she was born and both her parents were only children.

"Georgio came into the picture in middle school when his family moved to the county from the south. No one knew much about them, other than the Carlos family were effective businessmen with international ties. Antonio bought up a lot of the land in the area and started a few construction companies.

"Darren and Emmett took him under their wing, and soon it became apparent that Georgio was the ringleader. Camden and Stan took notice, since the two of them were the rich kids in town naturally drawn to anyone with influence. I think their fathers were involved with some of Antonio's businesses. Darren and Emmett didn't like them all that much, but Georgio did, so they ended up becoming a group of sorts."

"Georgio's family pressures escalated in high school. That's when we started dating. He wouldn't take me back to his place because he was worried about my exposure to them. We ended up hanging out at Emmett's a lot. My family life wasn't great either, so we were each other's replacements."

Mom's parents had been dirt poor and locked in the cycle of alcoholism. Aunt Charlene and Mom had left and never looked back. I only knew part of that story, but also knew well enough not to ask. The look of pain on Mom's face every time it came up was enough to know she didn't need to relive her childhood.

"Shambala refers to a mythical peaceful society somewhere in Asia. Darren read about it in a book and started calling us that. He said it was the dream for all of us, to get out of our circumstances and build the life we wanted for ourselves. Since our group was so tight-knit no one questioned it, and it was an inside joke. Darren was beside himself when they labeled us in the yearbook."

Mom stopped speaking abruptly, swallowing hard. I waited for her to continue her story, taking small sips of my own tepid tea and willing myself to keep my mouth shut. When seconds turned into minutes, I prodded her, gently.

"I need to know the whole story, Mom. I'm fully in this now. I need your help, okay?"

Her gaze met mine and she attempted a small smile that was more of a wince. She nodded twice, almost to herself rather than to me, before finally continuing.

"Something happened at the beginning of senior year. Georgio broke up with me, telling me it wasn't safe to be around me anymore." She swallowed thickly, tears forming in her eyes again. "I loved him and I couldn't understand why he would choose to end it then, but everything else changed too.

"Darren and Emmett both accelerated their courses so they could graduate early and left town, only returning six years later to open up their firm. Stanley and Camden acted like nothing was wrong, but they withdrew as a twosome. I knew something had happened, but no one would say what.

"After graduation, everyone split up anyway. Your father had been chasing me for years and I finally relented, trying to move on from my broken heart. Georgio and his brothers all disappeared, and Georgio came back just after Emmett and Darren had set up shop in Carlisle. Your father and I had already started the diner by then."

"Georgio had brothers?" So many questions raced through my mind, least of which was my mom had settled for my father, but that fact stood out.

Mom nodded slowly, as if trying to remember the details. She tapped her fingers against her mug and hummed.

"Four. Antonio wasn't known to be faithful, even around here. Matteo was his stepson and the rest were half-brothers, I think. He was the oldest and had left before Georgio and I broke up. Rumor had it he had a drug problem. Kellan was the youngest; he would have only been in elementary school when we graduated, but he disappeared too. Jonah and Mical, the twins, were two years behind us. I haven't seen any of them since we walked across that stage and got our diplomas."

I was reeling from information overload. Finally, *finally*, some pieces were falling into place. Shane was going to hit the ceiling when he found out. I wished I had the foresight to record the conversation so I wouldn't forget anything. That man took methodical to a whole new level, but I was grateful for it.

"Why would he ask you to money-launder if he cared about you?"

Mom sighed; a heavy sigh, weighted with the years of secrets she was finally releasing in my tiny kitchen.

"He wasn't the same man when I asked him for help. He never liked Joe in the first place, but I had thought his history with me would offset that. We were desperate and took the deal anyway."

A steely resolve entered my mother's gaze. "We were victims of our own stupidity, Drew. Don't pity us. Georgio is who he is, but we agreed to the deal, not caring about the consequences of the future. *Your* future. I don't want you to continue to live with the burden of our choices."

"This is now my choice, Mom," I said gently, taking her hands in mine. "This is bigger than me. I have other people to care about now too."

She smiled wistfully, her delicate hands squeezing mine lightly. "You love her?"

I dipped my head solemnly, my ribcage filling with tingling warmth. "I do."

I cared about all of them more than I would have thought. Travis had grown on me and he took good care of our girl. Cam was a bit of a lost soul who seemed to complement the group with his stoic silence. And Shane — Shane brought up feelings in me that were growing more complicated by the day.

"Make sure you tell her then," Mom said, letting go of me and moving to stand.

I stood with her, leading her to the door. Before she could leave, I had one last question still on the tip of my tongue, needing answers.

"Who was Brenda Simpson?" This question was for Shane, who hadn't admitted it outright but was agonizing over the fact the woman who died in the accident that had permanently disfigured his mother was in the photo.

Mom pulled on her coat before answering. "A very troubled woman. It was a tragedy when she died, but an even bigger tragedy that Amelia paid her price too."

I waited for her to finish, but she opened the door and stepped out onto the top landing of my deck.

"I love you, sweetie. I hope you forgive us some day."

She took off down the stairs before I could reach out to her. I watched her quickly crossed the icy driveway towards my childhood home, a few less secrets held within its walls today.

Her advice was not lost on me. I would relay all the information I had just learned as soon as I could, but I needed to see the woman I loved.

"Hey."

"Hey!" Winter's blue eyes filled with warmth and she reached out to pull me into her arms. I stepped in to her hug and wrapped her tightly into my own, inhaling the comforting scent of body wash.

"Do you have time for a walk?" I pulled away from her and shoved my hands in my pockets, suddenly nervous.

She smiled brightly and reached for her coat on the hook by the door. "Yeah! I just finished practicing for our set on Thursday night. The fresh air will do me good."

We walked down the dim light of the hallway hand in hand. The night was beautiful. Snow was softly falling, and the moonlight reflected off of every white surface, lighting up the streets with almost perfect clarity. Sounds were muffled by the blankets of fresh snow and the world was peacefully still.

I wanted this moment to be special. I knew she had feelings for Travis; she may even love him too. Cam had kissed her in front of all of us in Logan's apartment — I had noticed something brewing between them, but she seemed oblivious, or at the very least, in denial. And I couldn't make heads or tails of her moment with Logan. Whether I liked it or not, there were other men in Winter's life she would share her heart with.

But this moment, this moment, was for us.

I led her to the park just around the block, guiding her through the snow-laden trees lining the paths. We were the only ones here, and I was glad someone somewhere was looking out for me.

I stopped at a snow-covered park bench and used my arm to clear the bench of snow, directing her to sit. She giggled and did as I asked, her face lighting up with interest.

I leaned over the bench and produced a thermos of hot chocolate and a little mickey of Bailey's from the bag I had hidden there. I waved them in front of her with a grin.

"Sneaky!" She squealed with delight, leaning in to give me a kiss.

She tried to make it a quick peck, but I needed more than that. I pressed my lips on hers, coaxing her to open up to me, for me. I leisurely explored her mouth, like we had all the time in the world, deepening the pressure with each pass of my tongue. By the time I came up for air, my dick was rock hard and her eyes were glassy and heated with lust.

I nipped her lips gently and set the drinks on the bench beside her, kneeling into her lap and cupping her cheeks. When our faces were at the same level, I used the opportunity to peer into her soul.

She was guarded, sarcastic, vivacious, and beautiful. She was headstrong and independent, and loyal and loving. And I loved her. Fuck, I loved her.

"I love you," I whispered into the night air, pouring my heart into the words.

Her blue eyes widened, but the warmth never left them. "Drew, I —"

I moved to place a gloved finger to her lips. "No, baby, you don't need to feel you have to say it back. Say it when you're ready. I just needed you to know."

I stood and pulled her to me, holding her tightly in my embrace. I kissed the top of her hat and spun us around, landing on the bench with her seated in my lap.

She turned to face me and kissed me with such a ferocity that showed she loved me too. She said so with her teasing licks and playful tongue, and that was enough.

She leaned back, a mischievous grin taking over her face.

"Let's get a buzz on and make snow angels, Hardy Boy." She bit her lip suggestively and grabbed the mickey and thermos. Opening the tiny bottle, she dumped its contents into the hot chocolate.

"What do you think two snow angels fucking look like?" She winked before taking a long drink and handing the thermos to me.

I took my gulp of the sweet liquid and then jumped up from the bench, catching her up in my arms. She shrieked and wrapped her legs around my hips, clinging for dear life as I rolled us into the snowbank.

I settled on top of her and ran a hand down her body to cup between her legs. She shivered beneath me, and it wasn't from the cold.

This woman made me want to live dangerously. She took my safe, secure, predictable world and blew it out of the water. She made me want to *live.* And tonight, I was going to show her.

"Let's find out."

I kissed her deeply and thoroughly with the taste of chocolate and Bailey's on our tongues before rolling her over in the freshly fallen snow.

CHAPTER 26

LOGAN

I fucking hated detox. I'd give anything to snort my troubles away into oblivion and hope I lived the last few moments of my life riding a massive high and sticking it to Stanley Eccles.

At least, the last part was true. If I didn't have the will to live right now, I wouldn't be suffering in fucking misery in my apartment with Hillary standing guard.

Three days. Three fucking days of being held prisoner. That woman was always true to her word, and once I was fully checked over from her trusted doctor in Carlisle and he had properly assessed the heart damage, I had been chained to my bedroom as I rode out the withdrawal.

I lived in nightmares and the need to break things. Hill, to her credit, rode it out with me. Whether it was our longstanding history, or she actually found it somewhere in her heart to give a fuck about me, I wasn't sure, but I wasn't stupid enough to say I could do this on my own.

I had tried that, and it fucking failed. Failed to the point of an overdose in my car and Travis-Fucking-Fuckface, of all people, found me.

The man obviously had experience with drug addicts. Whether it was for himself or someone else, I didn't know. I supposed I should be grateful, but all I could feel was rage. Rage, rage, rage.

Rage, and a little fear. I didn't actually want to die.

Doc had said I was on the road to killing myself, and I probably could have that night, which was the only reason I was sitting in my bed in two-day-old pajama pants sweating bullets and tossing books at the wall.

"Fuck off, Logan!" Hillary called from somewhere beyond the locked door, scolding me like a child. "If you keep destroying our wall, I'm admitting you into a treatment program, pronto."

Over my fucking dead body. I was not going into some second-rate rehab facility with the likes of trailer trash and certified cokeheads. I could admit I had a problem. I didn't have *that* kind of problem.

I bit back a furious retort, knowing it wouldn't do me any favors. Hill had a spine made of steel; she had already wrestled me into bed using some weird-ass Krav Maga move I was still sore from.

Maybe if she had let me see this side of her in the bedroom, I could have fucked her into submission.

The image of my sexy auburn-haired blue-eyed princess flooded my brain. I desperately wanted to fuck *her* into submission, and those thoughts, along with the plaguing nightmares, was karma deciding now was the time to unleash its vengeance.

It was just my luck that while stuck recovering in my Guantanamo condo, it also struck me with a fucking crisis of conscience.

Something broke in me while I watched her sleep off the drugs in my bed. Carson Baker had always been a bastard, but he was *my* bastard that *I* had control over. He went off script when he roofied Winter. And I was going to destroy him for it.

I threw a hardback at the door as the violent urge to kill the man overtook me. The loud thump gave me a small sense of satisfaction when Hillary stormed through our doorway, her face contorted in anger.

"What the fuck, Logan!"

I jumped up from the bed and glared at her, never one to cower at her demands. I was playing ball right now so I could get my fucking life back on track, but she would not play power trip on me today.

"Fuck. Off. Hill." I said slowly, breathing deeply to control the fire burning in my gut. She'd incapacitate me again in that sneaky move I'd have to learn a counterattack to, and my shins didn't need any more bruises.

"No, *you* fuck off." She shoved my chest lightly and picked up the book I had just thrown at the door. Her face softened as she sat on the bed, crossing her arms and staring me down.

"What is this about?" She nodded her head towards the pile of books in misshapen heaps in the corner. "I mean, besides the obvious. More nightmares?"

I scrubbed my hands over the stubble on my cheeks and let out a frustrated growl. "Fucking Carson."

Her eyes flashed viciously. I had confessed when she had come home just as Winter and her Merry Men of

Misfits were leaving. Hill didn't know about Georgio or the Fight Night incident, but since Carson was now in the picture with our business arrangement and her inheritance being issued in a few months, I had tried to appeal to her inner-feminist or whatever.

So far, it wasn't clear if it had been the right move or not. I was biding my time and banking on the fact Hill had hated Carson since high school. Since she and Winter had become 'sister besties' all of a sudden, Hill might spend some of that Grandmother Grinch money to help.

At the very least, I needed her to bail me out. But I was holding my cards on that one.

"Have you heard from her? Is she okay?"

"We're not *friends*, Hill." I sneered the word. "We don't text about our day or the cute pair of shoes we saw in the window."

I folded my arms and mimicked her stance as we continued to scowl at each other in a good old-fashioned domestic stand-off.

I hadn't heard from Winter. I had debated texting her a few times but thought better of it. We may be on neutral ground now, given my White Knight savior move, but I doubted she'd want to hear from me. And I had been busy trying not to fucking die of a heart attack and trying not to kill Hill in my home-rehab situation.

"She's not really answering my texts, either." Hill exhaled loudly and dropped her arms, flopping back on the bed behind her. "I'm worried about her. I don't think you understand how terrifying that is for a woman ..." She cut herself off as her face changed from worry to sadness. I waited for her to finish, but she didn't.

"Yeah, it was fucking scary for us too, Hill." I moved to sit beside her on the bed, my anger forgotten for the moment. "The boys were like deer in headlights; fucking useless. I've never seen her so" — I searched for the word — "helpless."

"I'm glad you took care of her," Hill whispered to the ceiling as she squeezed my arm. "I knew you had some good in you."

I snorted, but sat up and turned to grin at her, the throbbing ache between my temples subsiding temporarily. "I'm still only marrying you for your money."

She snickered and poked me in the bare chest. "One month until D-Day." Her face sobered as she searched my eyes for the truth.

"Are you going to stay clean, Logan? We need this to go through, for both of our sakes. And I don't want to marry you, but I don't want to find you dead until you're at least 75 and have taken Stanley for all he's worth."

After a moment, she continued. "You have my permission to go after Dad too. I'm only worth this trust fund to him. That's becoming all too clear."

"I'm staying clean," I answered honestly. I'd work on the other parts of that plan later.

Satisfied, she sat up and stretched her arms upward, her tight little body arching like a cat. Hill was always hot; the blond, blue-eyed Barbie of men's wet dreams, but I wasn't attracted to her, not anymore. Fucking figured.

"Want some eggs? I'm going to make some breakfast." She walked out the door without another glance.

I moved to grab a shirt from the drawer to follow her.

She called out. "And clean up the fucking books!"

I shoved my hands into my pockets as I stared at the apartment complex in front of me.

Fuck me, I did not want to be here.

I didn't know how the fuck Shane Quicksilver, of all people, had gotten my number, but I had taken the call, thinking it was a business associate I had been trying to reach over a real estate transaction.

When Shane's irritating boom came through the speaker, I almost hung up, but the sneaky fucker only had to say the three magic words to get me to listen.

"It's for Winter."

Of course, it was for fucking Winter and, for some reason, I was becoming more consumed by the woman by the day. I didn't like this hold she had on me. I was trying to detox, not find another obsession.

So here I was, standing in the fucking cold, debating whether I was actually going into the hillbilly's apartment.

"Are you just going to stand there like a scared plucked chicken, or are you going to join us?"

I turned to see Cam and Travis standing behind me, carrying boxes of pizza and beer. Cam cocked his head to the side in challenge, and I instantly hated the fucker.

"Go fuck a chicken, Chase, or whatever the fuck it is you Southern gentlemen like to do," I mocked, grabbing a box of pizza and yanking open the glass door into the building. The door immediately buzzed, and I wondered how long Shane had been watching me just standing there like an idiot.

I hated all of them.

I marched through the steel door to the stairwell and stomped up the three floors to his place, not wanting to stand in the fucking elevator with Tweedledee and Tweedledum.

My stomach growled at the smell of sausage coming from the box in my arms, and I realized I was starving. I stopped in front of the number he had texted me and knocked hard.

The door swung open. I had been expecting Shane's goofy annoying face, but it was Winter who answered, her tentative smile disarming me.

"Hey." She hesitantly reached for the pizza box and took it out of my arms, a softness on her features that had never been shown to me. My chest squeezed involuntarily, and I couldn't tell if it was from the detox, or from her.

Probably the detox.

I entered the room and immediately regretted coming. Shane lived in one small open box, and there definitely wasn't enough room for us all to sit in the living room. Shane and Drew were already seated on the sofa, and there were two chairs opposite the coffee table. We'd all be on top of each other like one little cozy family.

Gross.

Winter tossed the pizza on the coffee table as I took a seat in the recliner by the wall. I left my coat on and eyed the rugby jerseys on the wall.

"I'd say this is a nice place, but it isn't."

Drew opened his mouth to speak, but Shane stood; he folded his arms and loomed over me in my seated position.

Well fucking played, Quicksilver.

"Ground rules, Logan. We're all grateful you helped us out with Winter's incident. That does *not* mean you get to come in here and be a jackass all night. Shut up for a minute and hear us out. We've figured out some things since you've come out of Georgio's basement, and they may help us take Georgio down and make Carson pay."

"To be clear," Drew spoke this time, growing a backbone in the time he had fucked Winter. Good on him. "We asked you here to help. You said you would help Winter in front of all of us. Now's your chance."

Travis and Cam had come in while Shane was doing his overprotective dad speech, and Travis was the next to offer his two cents. I still hadn't thanked him for his 'right place, right time' lifesaving action, and I felt a little guilty over that. I should probably say something.

"And, it's only fair to tell you," Drew added, "we all know about the other night. We know you're in recovery, and we're going to give you some leeway for being an asshole when right now you might not be able to help it. But do your best, all right?"

"You've got to be fucking kidding me!" I jumped up from the poor-man's La-Z-Boy and barely held back from punching Travis in the face. I had almost thanked him, only to find he was spewing my secrets to these fucking assholes like they had any right to know my business.

Winter stepped into my personal space, placing a calming palm on my chest.

"Hey." She spoke softly, staring up into my eyes. "This room is a safe zone. You're about to hear some of our secrets, and we'll keep yours, okay? I know you don't trust us, and I can't say that I have a lot of faith in you either, but you took care of me, and Travis helped save your life, so we're all kind of in this together."

I willed my anger and the cocaine-withdrawal emotional spiral to fade as I quickly considered my options. M was holding me by the balls, and Shane could be my ticket to getting an in with WAQ. If I turned on my elusive winning personality, I could get the information he needed to finally cut me loose.

I looked around the room; five desperate men were better than one. I liked those odds.

And I was about to learn information I could hold over their heads too. If I was vulnerable, so were they.

I reached up to squeeze Winter's hand at my chest, pushing her away from me and spinning her around, her back to my front. I wrapped my arms around her and fell back into the chair behind me, her ass dropping into the chair on top of my dick.

"What the fuck, man!"

Drew jumped up from the couch and Travis dropped the pizza to move into my — our, personal space.

I held up a hand. Winter was unexpectedly compliant in my arms, not fighting me like I expected. "You wanted to talk, talk. Princess is fine right where she is." I nuzzled my face into the crook of her neck and shot Travis a devious smirk.

"I am right here and can speak for myself, asshole," Winter muttered and pushed away from me, but she didn't move to get out of my lap completely.

She looked around the room at the panting idiots watching her. "It's fine, guys. If this shuts him up so we can get through this as painlessly as possible, it's a sacrifice I'm willing to make."

She turned towards me, a stern, but impossibly cute, expression crossing her features. "This is as close as you get to me, Pretty Boy. One false move and I will destroy your dick faster than Adam Skinner's gonorrhea."

My grin grew at the joke she'd remembered from our one and only date. I wasn't as repulsive to the Princess as she made me believe, not one fucking bit. I didn't even care that she had adopted Cameron Chase's irritating nickname. I liked it when it came from her lips.

"I mean it," she muttered softly. "I'm the only thing stopping them from killing you right now." She turned to me with fire in her eyes. I liked it when she burned for me.

"Wouldn't dream of it." I winked at her, a smug grin on my face and a little extra blood running to my cock.

I was still getting glares from all sides, but I didn't fucking care. Winter Wallace was sitting in my lap, on my dick, and her harem band of horny men couldn't do a thing about it. Winning.

She reached over to grab two slices of pizza, but she hesitated over the case of beer.

"Can you have alcohol? Will that hurt your recovery?"

My brows rose at her thoughtfulness. Other than Hillary, I didn't have anyone to care about what was best for me, and that had been a recent development.

"I shouldn't have anything," I said simply. "But alcohol isn't my temptation, so you go ahead."

She took a bottle of water instead and handed me the slice of pizza and a napkin, avoiding the open stares from her boyfriends. That would be one fun discussion later. To be a fly on that fucking wall.

I gloated internally. Apparently, Winter really responded to men who took care of her. Classic Daddy issues.

I'd keep that under my cap to use later.

Shane started talking and didn't stop. The yearbook came out with the photos to start. I stared dumbly at the picture of our fathers, looking like they enjoyed life instead of the miserable fucks they were now.

The Johnson family as a bunch of money-laundering criminals took the cake. I didn't know pussy-footing Drew had it in him, but the man had "family expectations" written all over him, just like I did.

Winter having no idea her family was even from here or that Darren was a foster kid, was an interesting nugget. I just thought he was an ignorant fuck who didn't like me; history with Dad shouldn't come as a surprise. The only person I knew who could tolerate him fully was Camden, and that was probably because their businesses were so entwined he had no choice. More likely, they were trying to marry their kids off to line their pockets; the greedy fuckers deserved each other.

That Georgio had been friends with them even back then wasn't any sort of epiphany for me. It surprised me Emmett had been friends with them, though. Of everyone in this little circle of friendship and trust, Emmett was probably the most straitlaced. At least Shane came by his annoying pleasantness honestly.

Cam wouldn't share his story, only that Georgio had offered to get him out of some legal trouble and now owned his soul for it. He was smarter than he let on, that fucker.

Travis was in debt to Georgio for a deadbeat brother and a sick mom. It wasn't surprising he sacrificed himself for his family; the man screamed Daddy issues too.

I wondered if Winter called him 'Daddy' in the bedroom? My cock stirred beneath her ass still tucked into my lap, and I took a deep breath to bring the blood back into my body.

She had slowly let down her guard and settled into my arms, contentedly resting against my chest. Barely, but she was. My still-teenage hormones were not willing to let her go yet.

When Drew mentioned Georgio's half-brothers, Winter froze so still in my arms, I could have snapped her in half with one push.

So, the little minx hadn't told them about that rendezvous a few years ago. She certainly wasn't speaking up now. I squeezed her inconspicuously in my arms, just like the fucking Cheshire cat in satisfaction I was the only one who knew that story. Another little secret Princess and I would share. Maybe another little secret I could use to my advantage.

Everyone's damage was being served to me on a platter, and I would have devoured it with glee if this situation wasn't so fucked.

I snapped to attention when Shane told us he had hired Blaise to hack into the files. That was my ticket right there. All I had to do was play nice with the kids at the playground, then I could get what I needed to move on with my life.

Fuck yes.

"Why are you telling me this now?" I asked suspiciously, always wary of the trap behind the door. Too many people wanted to fuck me over and even Boy Scouts could go bad.

"You've got money and influence." Shane stuck his chin out in challenge. "You're coming into an inheritance, right? You're loaded now. You've got an in with Eccles. You help us, you're helping *her*" — he dipped his head toward Winter — "and maybe we can find something you can use against Carson too. We're all too tied together to not work together on this."

Drew steepled his fingers in front of his face and scowled at me through them. "Are you planning on telling us anything? You haven't reciprocated this entire conversation."

"I didn't say I would talk." I arched my eyebrows defiantly and returned his gaze. "You know I'm in business with Carson, that I'm now going to use that to destroy him, and that I'm a recovering addict. What more do you want?"

"What's your real link to Georgio?" Winter shifted in my arms, her blue eyes staring right fucking through me. "Why were you desperate to pay Cam to win the fight? What does he hold over you?"

"We all owe Georgio, Princess. I took a loan to save face a few years ago. He wants it back, and I don't have it." I wasn't willing to divulge anything about Hillary's inheritance or M today, if ever. I owed these fuckers nothing, and they needed my help more than I needed theirs.

There would be no quid pro quo here, unless we counted Travis, and I'd send him a fruit basket or something.

I stood carefully, still holding Winter to me before placing her back into the seat.

"I'll do what I can. 'Safe zone of secrets'." I mimed air quotes sarcastically. "But that's all you fuckers are getting from me today. Thanks for the pizza."

I couldn't seem too eager, and I wasn't in the mood to take on a boy band group of new friends, either. This was the slow play, and I would play it. Not too slow, though; my time was running short, and I knew I'd need those answers soon.

I left the walk-in closet Shane called an apartment with five pairs of dumbfounded eyes gaping after me.

Letting myself get out of the building, I got into the car before I let the excitement take over me. This gullible group of Winter's groupies would set me free. Things were coming up aces for Logan Eccles.

But fuck, I could use a hit. I tapped the speed dial on my phone before peeling out of the parking lot. She picked up before the second ring went through.

"Hey, Hill, just doing the standard 'I've got a craving' call …"

This was going to be fucking annoying.

CHAPTER 27

WINTER

"Well, this is a pleasant surprise."

My mother greeted us at the door, wineglass in hand, as if this wasn't a pre-planned dinner about to be more awkward than a stripper at Grandma's tea.

The five of us had driven together in Quick's truck. It was the only vehicle large enough to hold us, and it had been a hilarious drive of banter and joking from the men who filled my life. When we pulled into the circular driveway of my parent's massive modern home, all chatter stopped.

True to his word, Dad had invited me and my boyfriends to dinner. Travis had invited Cam because he didn't want him left out and I had invited Quick for moral support. Dinner with my parents was an exercise in restraint on a good day, and tonight was going to test me to my limits.

"Hi, Mom!"

My over-exaggerated exclamation sounded false even to my own ears, and I winced. We hadn't spoken much since Christmas, and the text I had received on my birthday at 9 pm was a last-ditch effort at best. Miranda Wallace had never possessed the maternal gene, but there had been a particular strain on our relationship lately.

"Hi, Shane," my mother gushed and pulled Shane into her arms for an awkward looking, wine glass holding hug. Mom had always loved Shane. She preferred men to women anyway. I had often wondered if my relationship with Mom would have been better if I had been born a son.

Drew and Travis followed in behind us, both standing in stunned silence as their eyes wandered the large open space.

Cam strolled in behind them, visibly impressed. I forgot sometimes that his day job is construction and, from Travis' endorsement, Cam had a natural talent for it.

This house had that effect on people. The floor to ceiling windows with the mountain view, the three-story modern open wood tread staircase in the center of the home, and the slate tile and hardwood accents throughout were impressive. The stone tile two story fireplace in the middle of the great room with the white bear skinned rug in front of it looked like it belonged as the feature of a magazine.

About ten years ago, Dad completed the build. This house was a Scandinavian design, and one of the first built like it in North America. It was beautiful to look at, but barren of any heart or soul. It was hard to call it a home when Nanny Jacobs wasn't here.

"Hi, Drew." Mom gushed again as she pulled him into another weird one-armed hug and I cringed.

I don't know if she realized she was fawning over my men, or if she just couldn't turn off her primal cougar magnetism. Either way, it was grossing me out.

Was this normal behavior when daughters brought their boyfriends home to dinner? I doubted it, but I wouldn't know. This was the first time I had done it.

I unzipped my jacket and put it on a hanger in the closet, knowing Mom wouldn't want any evidence of people actually living here. Shane grabbed a couple more hangers and put his and Drew's coat beside mine. He knew the drill too.

"You must be Travis!" Mom's high pitch giggle let me know this was not her first glass of wine, or the second. As she rubbed her hands down Travis' shoulder, he handed me his coat too.

I was grateful for Travis' charm when his face broke out into its signature heart-stopping grin, snow-dusted curls falling over his eyebrow. "I am, Miranda. It's lovely to meet you."

"And who is this?" Mom just couldn't help herself. Her eyes roamed lasciviously over the GQ model of a man that was Cameron Chase. I rolled my eyes, willing the universe to open up the floor beneath us and swallow us whole. I didn't believe in a heaven or hell per se, but I'd be willing to take the risk right now.

"Cameron Chase, ma'am." The combination of his smooth baritone and Southern hospitality turned the woman to putty in his work-worn hands.

"Miranda, please." Mom winked at me once she removed her jaw from the floor and motioned us all into the kitchen to the left of the foyer. "Darren's just finishing up the last few touches of our dinner."

"Dad's cooking?" My spirits immediately brightened. Dad rarely cooked, but when he did, he applied his engineering skills to whatever he was making and crafted a masterpiece. It was one skill I had so wished was genetically passed down, instead of the stupid ability to roll my tongue.

Although... I snuck a glance at Travis; that had its advantages. I remembered what rolling my tongue over his piercing always did to him. He caught me looking at him and cocked an eyebrow at my amused expression. I giggled despite my nerves, then turned to see Dad in an apron chopping herbs into fine dustings of greenery on the large wooden cutting board.

He looked up from his task and grinned. "Hey, honey!"

He looked genuinely thrilled to see me and it warmed the ice in my heart just a smidge.

"I'm just finishing up the sauce. I don't want to burn the rosemary."

Dad was talking to at least three people who didn't cook. Shane and I burned rice. I couldn't be sure about Cam's talents in the kitchen, and I know Drew always ate at the diner. Maybe Travis? Something to ask him later. Either way, Dad's cooking skills were going to knock ours out of the park.

I took a moment to stare through this man who'd raised me; a man who wasn't a perfect father, but who loved me in the ways he knew how. Was it his lack of a home life growing up that made him keep me at a loving distance? Was it because my whole lineage had been a lie, down to the fake dead grandparents, and a history in this town that had never been acknowledged?

I hoped to get the actual answers one day.

Mom directed us to the large harvest table in the open dining room off of the great room. The table was set like we were about to have Christmas dinner; fancy gold linens and multiple utensil settings, like we were in Hillary's house instead of my childhood home where I usually ate at the kitchen island with Nanny Jacobs in an otherwise empty house.

I guess we were trying to impress people tonight.

Mom shifted the place settings and added two more, since I hadn't told her we'd be having additional guests — oops — and we all sat down. I sat in the middle of Drew and Travis on one side, Shane and Cam on the other. Mom and Dad took their places like palace royalty on the ends.

Soft jazz music played in the background — a playlist I had heard hundreds of times growing up. Mom liked to write to music, and Frank Sinatra and Etta James had played on repeat for days at a time. It was how I had come to love jazz in the first place.

Dad placed two large salad bowls in the center of the table and Mom poured wine for everyone, filling her glass as close to the brim as possible.

"The main course is just about ready," Dad announced as he looked around the table at my eclectic group of men. "Dig in to the salad while I finish up. I've been experimenting with a new fig dressing!" He clapped his hands enthusiastically before leaving us to our own devices … and Mom.

Dad was relaxed and content, taking the time out of his busy work schedule to cook my boyfriends' dinner, and Mom was nearly drunk, fawning over each one in turn.

I felt like someone had trapped us in the paradoxical time warp of a bad 90s sci-fi show; I had definitely entered an alternate reality.

The conversation was surprisingly effortless. Travis and Shane could talk easily with anyone, and Drew was quick to offer anecdotes that complemented their stories. Cam brought his thousand-watt smile to life every time the group laughed, and I found the evening actually enjoyable.

Mom and Dad were openly endearing to each other, as always; so much so I questioned my sanity. Had I imagined seeing my father with another woman? Despite their busy lives and conflicting schedules, the love these two had for each other was real, or at least appeared so real they could be Oscar-winning actors.

Mom was an open flirt, but that was her normal. She never seemed to understand boundaries, and I had always chalked that up to the daily world of sexual exploration she was immersed in for her research.

I was missing something here, but I had no idea what.

Dad served his confit chicken with potato galette on heated plates like a true professional, and it was probably one of the most delicious meals I had ever put into my mouth.

After dinner, I took the men on a tour of the house, walking them through the modern rooms and stopping to admire the view of the sun setting beyond the horizon.

"This is a beautiful space," Cam said, his voice touched with awe as we entered Dad's study.

It had a full view of the mountainside through floor to ceiling glass windows, but both walls of the room were lined with 12-foot-tall, espresso-lacquered, wooden bookshelves. A gold and cream shag rug added a touch of feminine luxury and two cream wingback chairs faced the windows, with a practical, well-organized, dark-stained wooden desk behind them.

The room belonged on a Pinterest board, and it was my favorite place in the house.

"It is," I agreed, lovingly stroking the velvet of my preferred reading chair as the last of the sun crested in the distance. The only light was now coming from the twilight reflection of the dusky sky. "I used to do all of my studying in here."

I had midterms coming up I hadn't studied for; life kept getting in the way of my second-rate education. I made a mental note to put in some time overthe coming week. Drew could quiz me and reward me for every right answer. I squeezed my thighs at the thought.

"Think your dad has any files in here? Something else we could use as evidence? Maybe another hidden flash drive in his books?" Shane spoke softly. He was examining the set of encyclopedias on one of the lower shelves.

I startled, having not considered that fact until this moment.

"Yeah, it's a possibility. I just don't know how we're going to be able to check."

Shane clucked his tongue and nodded, lost in thought.

Travis stepped in front of me and stroked his hands up my arms. The swirling designs of his tattooed forearms peaked out from underneath the sleeves of his button up sweater.

"I'd like to see your bedroom, beautiful." He bit his lip, tantalizingly playing with his lip ring with his tongue before leaning in to nip the tip of my nose.

"You've seen my bedroom." I raised an eyebrow at him teasingly. "You've slept in it half of this week."

The warm presence of a large body settled behind me as Drew's arms slid around my belly, pulling me tight to him. Faint scents of cinnamon and bergamot tickled my senses, and my body flooded with comfort endorphins. This man loved me.

These men loved me.

How lucky I was.

"He means he'd like to see your pretty pink bedroom, baby girl." Drew's stubbled lips brushed the side of my neck and I shivered at the contact. "Every man wants to see his girlfriend's childhood bedroom."

Travis' fingers trailed up the side of my neck as he stepped even closer, sandwiching me between the two of them. He cupped my chin in his palm. "Drew's right, beautiful. I'd like to see your bed, personally. Did you touch yourself for the first time in there? How many times did you make yourself come in that pretty pink bed of yours?"

Drew's hands slid past my hips setting my skin on fire. Then he cupped my hot pussy and stroked one finger along the seam of my jeans. My innocent Hardy Boy was taking control, and I loved it. The slight touch over my clit made me arch into the rock-hard evidence of his erection.

"It's purple, actually," I managed to get out between panting breaths. "I'm not really a pretty pink — kind of — girl."

"Even better," Travis whispered wickedly, as he nipped my bottom lip between his teeth.

Drew placed a slow trail of kisses underneath my earlobe as Travis leaned in to lick up the other side of my exposed neck. A set of hands — Drew's? No, Travis' — unbuttoned the top of my pants and slid down beneath the satin fabric of my panties, his long fingers reaching the apex of my thighs and softly stroking through my wetness.

Drew's hands moved up to gently squeeze my breasts, his thumbs circling my nipples and sharpening them into aching points.

It was a heady feeling, Travis' fingers slowly dipping into me as Drew worked me above, and my mind raced with images of our first moment coming together as a threesome. As a foursome?

I was going to need new panties.

I couldn't help the squeak that escaped me as Travis nipped the tender flesh just beneath my ear, or the release of the moan as Drew's cock gently thrust into the crest of my ass. The press of both of their bodies against me was too much, too—

An awkward cough behind me brought me back to reality. All three of us froze like we had been encased in ice. Regardless, my panties gushed with heat.

Drew reluctantly stepped away from me and I immediately mourned the strength and heat of his body. He sheepishly rubbed the back of his neck, his eyes landing on Quick behind us in apology.

"Sorry, man."

Travis removed his hand from my pants, but not before slowly bringing two fingers to his lips and sucking them into his mouth with a feral wink. He shifted backwards and moved to grab my hand instead. We spun around to see Quick still leaning against the bookshelf. I met Quick's stare and winced, but it wasn't the indignant expression of ire I had been expecting.

Was that ... envy in his eyes? As quickly as I had seen it, it was gone, and I questioned my sanity for the second time that night.

I snuck a glance at Cam in my periphery, but I couldn't make out a readable expression in the room's darkness. Not that Cam was overly readable, anyway.

I cleared my throat. "That was ... inappropriate, and I'm sorry you guys had to see that."

I straightened my now-soaked jeans and ran a hand through the tangles in my hair. "Let's go back down for dessert!" I exclaimed with fake brightness, then turned to lead the way back down the stairs, but not before noticing the discreet adjustments of cocks in pants.

From all four of them.

Rather than focusing any energy on that, I entered the kitchen and grabbed the first plate I saw.

Mom and Dad had already seated themselves in the great room in the brown matching armchairs next to a roaring fire, wineglasses in hand, and were idly chatting.

I sat down on the cream leather couch opposite them and looked down at my stolen plate with layered chocolate cake nestled in cherry sauce. Dad cooked titillating meals for the taste buds, but he couldn't bake a premade cherry pie without incinerating it to a crisp.

My heart panged knowing Mom had made my beloved birthday treat. I knew without tasting it that it was Nanny Jacobs' recipe.

Travis and Cam sat beside me while Drew and Quick settled into the opposite side of the enormous sectional, their own plates in hand.

We devoured the delicious food in silence, enjoying the peace of the space and the crackle of the fire. This house had been so lonely growing up; the space felt anything but, though, with my men beside me.

"So, given your situation, we thought now would be the perfect time to tell you."

Mom's abrupt interruption of the tranquil moment brought on a wave of trepidation. Their "announcements" always ended up in my disappointment from the consistency of good intentions and broken promises.

Dad set down his wineglass and interlaced his fingers with Mom's. They were giving off very positive vibes for parents about to drop a bomb.

"Honey, we have been waiting to tell you this. When you told me you were seeing a few different men, we figured now was the perfect time. I realize that having an audience isn't the norm, but you're obviously very connected to these men and it makes sense that they're all a part of this too."

I waited for the punchline. Everyone in the room was stone still; Travis had his charming mask back in place, looking as comfortable as could be. Cam looked indifferent, but to the trained eye — *my* trained eye — I could tell he was fighting the urge to leave the room.

Quick couldn't hide the open curiosity eating away his eyebrows; they were so close to his hairline, and Drew looked deeply uncomfortable to be a part of an intimate family conversation.

Amazing timing, as always, Wallaces.

"Okaaaaaaay," I said slowly, looking back and forth between them. "Are you going to make me guess, or ...?"

"Winter, your father and I are very happy in an open marriage. We think it's time to introduce you to our partners."

Bomb dropped.

CHAPTER 28

CAMERON

My fist tore a hole through Zimmerman's cheek, the fleshy skin spraying me with a fresh batch of blood. It was the third one tonight.

Drake had no rules. No rules and no rigging. A good old-fashioned bloodbath to cleanse the cobwebs from my mind and the demons from the dark reaches of my soul.

We had taken off the gloves long ago, just bare knuckles and bone crunching on bone in the dim light of a cold warehouse in the industrial part of Kensington. I wished I were a better man, but this — these moments — were my glory.

Pop had taken me to my first fight at twelve. I had broken the arm of the class bully — I couldn't even remember his name, but he had torn Sarah Evanson's shirt in trying to see her bra. I could only remember the fiery heat of fury flooding through my body and the satisfying snap when he screamed in pain.

Momma had made Pop take me, I'm sure of it. They spoke in hushed tones for hours while I watched TV in the living room, waiting for them to hand me back to the adoption agency where they had gotten me.

When Pop led me to the Chevelle and told me to "buckle in," I was near tears and willing to beg they keep me. When we pulled up to a warehouse in an older part of town, I had thought they'd given up on me altogether and Pop was just going to kill me and bury me dead.

Twelve-year-old boys think a lot of things, most of them foolish. All I could smell was fresh sweat, salt, and stale vinyl mats when we entered the cavernous room, and my ears had filled with the dull thwacks of pounding fists on rawhide.

The sound was still sweet music to my ears.

Barry Lester gave me my first lesson that night. And a hundred more after, breathing new life into the angry little boy I had been. The anger never left, but the outlet saved me from expulsion more times than I had fingers, and I'd always be grateful for Momma and Pop believing there was some goodness in me.

There was no goodness in me right now. I was channeling a spirit from hell; its force guided my body to destroy.

I didn't want Zimmerman to die. He was a decent man, fighting his own demons with the track marks on his arms and the few teeth he had left in his head. But I wanted him to hurt. Better him than me at this moment.

Darlene Knightly had sent me away, the mirrored reflection of Daisy Knight with a face matching mine. No call since, no attempt of contact of any kind.

Months — years — of sacrifice in this tiny town of terrors, only to be outright rejected again.

"Chase, stop! *Stop!*"

Drake's man bellowed as I continued to punch Zimmerman into unconsciousness on the dingy mat. I was on top of his limp form, his nose drowning in its own blood before someone even larger than me pulled me off of his ragged body.

I swung blindly, needing the contact and the pain that came with it. A burst of agony exploded behind my eye socket as someone punched me hard in the face.

"*Fuck!*" I bellowed and collapsed to the concrete in a heap.

Adrenaline and dopamine flooded my body, and I was high on the cocktail.

"Get him to the hospital," Drake barked to someone in the background as I counted my breaths one by one.

He wasn't talking about me. I was concussed and had split my eyebrow open, but nothing that required a medical visit. Zimmerman must be down and out.

It was the risk we took in fights like this. Any man who fought at this level was willing for death if it took him in the ring. I didn't consider myself suicidal, but I wasn't living for much either.

I got my bearings after a few minutes of calm, men moving around me like I wasn't even there. A cold bottle of water had been handed to me along with a compress, but they otherwise ignored me. I'd receive an envelope of cash after I had cleaned up and was ready to leave.

I had bet on myself tonight, and I'd won.

I winced and picked myself off of the floor, my muscles burning from lactic acid build-up and overuse.

Zimmerman's fight had been my last of the night; I had been fighting men with their own death wishes for over two hours.

I tried to get a good look at the gash over my eye in the cracked mirror of the dim locker room that was straight out of a bad horror movie. It was worse than I thought; it would need to be stitched at the very least.

Fuck.

Travis had known I was here tonight, but I hadn't wanted to involve him in my exorcism. The man had a heart too big for this way of life, and he already took care of too many people. I could do my own stitches, but I was going to need his steady hands to help me, or I'd risk infection. I knew I had a pretty face, but I couldn't care less about the scarring.

Let the physical match my mental state.

Still, it was him or the hospital, and I wasn't going to the hospital. Nothing was going to tie me to this warehouse and Zimmerman's plight tonight.

I picked up the phone and dialed the only man in this world I would kill for.

"Hey brother, can you meet me at my place? And bring a medical kit?"

Travis knocked twice on the thin wooden door and strode into my apartment with three uninvited guests in tow.

He grimaced when he saw the state of me, sitting shirtless on my couch wearing an old pair of gray sweatpants with a bag of frozen peas held to my forehead. I had washed off most of the blood.

"Sorry, man. I was with present company" — he nodded to Shane, Drew, and Winter standing behind him — "when you called, and they all insisted on coming." He shrugged his shoulders halfheartedly. "We're all family now though, right?"

I let out a deep sigh, not impressed by the invasion of privacy, but too spent to tell them to go home.

Winter had seen me fight before, but I hadn't wanted her to see me in this state. She didn't need to witness me licking my wounds. The drive home from the initial rejection had been enough wallowing in her presence.

Other than the information session at Shane's and the invitation to her family home that I was sure was a pity invite, I had seen little of her since I'd succumbed to my urges and kissed her with abandon in front of everyone in Billionaire Boys Club's luxury apartment. I had overstepped and had been afraid she wouldn't speak to me again. Her presence tonight brought hope to my heart.

I peeked through the bleary haze of my left eye and caught Shane's typical curious expression. He reminded me of an overeager puppy, but with the temperament of a wise old dog.

Drew wore a look of concern, his brows frowning like an overprotective brother.

I wasn't used to this kind of attention.

Winter marched over to me, gently grabbed my chin, and turned my damaged face toward her.

"Oh, Cam." Her whisper was soft and sad as she placing a lighter-than-air kiss on my ragged skin. "Why do you torture yourself?"

She stared into my soul. Her eyes held a melancholy that wrenched on a small piece of my heart, and an unfamiliar feeling of guilt snuck in its place.

I didn't dignify the question with a response, choosing to place my hand over hers as she still held onto my chin, peering back into the pools of blue and green. There was no judgment or pity reflecting back; tender care and kindness was all I saw, and I swallowed hard at the grace she was granting me.

"Quick's going to do your stitches," Winter stated quietly, her hand leaving mine to step away from the couch. "He's the only one with proper training, and he's pretty good at it."

She smiled at him with pride and my heart took another squeeze.

I wanted her to look at me that way.

Shane stepped in and grinned wide. "You're in luck. I was teaching at the hill tonight and had my kit with me. Decided tonight was the night you were going to die, huh?"

He said it jokingly, but there was no laughter in his eyes. "I'll bet we should 'see the other guy'."

He used air quotes and his booming voice filled my small living room, but I couldn't joke along with him.

"He's in the hospital," I admitted, cringing at the nerve-tingling zing from the iodine as Shane cleaned the wound out thoroughly.

The room went quiet as a church mouse and I knew what they were all thinking. We didn't need to say the words aloud.

Shane grabbed the suture kit from the medical pack he had brought up from his car. It was a professional grade kit, probably something he had used on the ski hill. He had heard I was hurt and apparently forced his way into coming with Travis. I wasn't used to friends with that level of dedication.

"How much did you win?" Travis asked finally, as the first thread of the needle poked through my skin.

"Just over a grand," I said dismissively, not at all concerned about the money. The cash I earned at fights helped pay off my parent's debt load and nothing more. It was a means to an end, but not something I ever cared to speak about.

I fought to release my burden; the raw pain held within my humanity. I was repaid in bruises and twenty-dollar bills.

Shane let out a low whistle and I focused on staying as still as possible beneath his steady hands. The needle stung, but pleasantly so. True to Winter's word, he was a professional.

"Ever consider going pro?" Drew asked carefully, having not said two words since he settled into the single chair at my tiny kitchen table. "You're obviously good enough and professionally trained."

I shook my head and Shane grunted, turning my face back into position.

"Sorry," I muttered. I tried to eye Drew in my periphery. "This isn't my future." The words came out more vehemently than I intended, but they were the truth.

"Do you know your future?" Winter questioned thoughtfully as she sat next to my legs on the shitty, stained blue carpet. She grabbed my hand and interlocked our fingers, turning my palm over and stroking it in a soothing rhythm.

"Does anybody?" I countered, doing my best not to move this time. "Fighting isn't my career of choice. It's a... hobby." The word felt false in my mouth, but it fit.

"The only one here with a future at the moment is Quick." Winter smiled forlornly, but it held happiness for her best friend. "The rest of us will have to stumble along together."

Shane clucked his tongue in response, tying off an intricate and tight knot at the end of his stitch. "Don't count on that yet. Blaise said he'll have something for me this week. I may jump ship from WAQ soon enough."

"I hope for your sake that isn't the case."

"I hope for *our* sakes it isn't the case. But I could probably do it in an equally awkward-as-fuck announcement like your parents the other night."

Travis shook with laughter behind Shane, and soon the entire room was knee-deep in tear-streaming chuckling.

After Winter's parents had announced their open marriage, the conversation had died a painful death and Winter had asked Shane to take us all home.

She wouldn't talk about it on the drive, asking Shane to blast some eighties pop music. The only words Travis could coax out of her were "I'm not against open marriages. It would have been nice to have been in the loop."

Now we were *all* in the loop.

Her parents were odd, telling complete strangers their hidden secrets, but I didn't know them from Adam, so that could have been their normal. Their beautiful house and life of professional luxury was a far cry from the woman I knew in front of me.

Winter sighed dramatically and squeezed my hand before letting go and standing. "Thanks for the reminder, *Quick.*" She stuck her tongue out in his direction, and I smothered a snort. Her brattiness was cute, and their dynamic even cuter. It made me long for a sibling of my own.

"Before I'm done, I'm going to do a quick concussion test, okay?" Shane said as he wrapped up his kit. Travis threw the bloody gauze in the trash can under the sink.

"I'm going to stop you right there." I held up a hand and clasped him on the shoulder in thanks. "I have one. But it ain't my first one, and I'll be fine."

"You really shouldn't be left alone after a head knock, Big Guy." Winter bent down in front of me to stare into my eyes, as if she'd see secrets in them. "Why don't you come stay with one of us for the night?"

"I'm tired and I'm sore, little violet." I reached out and cupped her warm cheek, smiling at her thoughtful care over me. "I just want to crawl into my bed and sleep this night away."

"Travis, can you —" Winter looked at him imploringly, but he shook his head regretfully.

"Sorry, beautiful. I'm the only one who can look after Mom tonight."

"I would," Shane piped up, "but I've got to get that assignment finished for tomorrow morning and I left all of my stuff at home," He folded his arms, looking regretful. "I could go grab it and come back …"

I waved a hand dismissively. "I appreciate the sentiment, but I don't need anybody to —"

"Cam," Winter said sharply, her eyes flashing in warning. "You look like a tractor hit you and you're openly admitting to a concussion. Like hell we're leaving you home alone tonight."

"I can do it." Drew stuffed his hands in his pockets and looked at me. I knew him the least of all of them, but he seemed a nice enough guy who took care of the people around him. I was grateful for the offer; I was. I just didn't have space in my tiny apartment for another man only slightly smaller than me to sleep.

"Drew, you've got that paperwork signing first thing tomorrow, and Cam's is over half hour away." Winter nodded in my direction, as if we weren't sitting in my place to begin with. "Ryker's is only ten minutes from here. If it's okay with you guys, I'll stay."

I blinked at her slowly, thinking the concussion was worse than I had gauged. Winter was volunteering to watch over me while I nursed my self-induced concussion back to good health.

Travis tilted his head like he could see the world better sideways. Then he fixed himself right-side up and smirked slightly, leaning over to give her a light kiss. "You don't need my permission, but I'm comfortable with you staying the night here to take care of our boy."

Drew didn't look at me when answering. He stood from the tiny creaky plastic folding chair and gravitated to Winter's pull, wrapping his arms around her. It wasn't the possessive touch of a man exerting dominance, it was the caress of a man exerting trust. He murmured some private words into her ear and pulled back, sealing the deal with a brief kiss of his own.

"Can you grab my backpack from your truck, Quick? I'll need my homework for class, and I have an extra set of underwear in there for emergencies."

Travis cocked an eyebrow. "Seriously? Like, orgasm emergencies?"

"No." Winter's face shone with exasperation, and it brought a smile to my lips. "That was one of Nanny Jacobs' biggest lessons. She put the fear of God into me that we'd get into an accident one day and I'd need a pair of clean underwear. It's a thing."

"Do you need me to pick you up for class tomorrow?" Travis asked as Shane went out to grab Winter's things.

"I can walk." Winter smiled sunnily, as if this wasn't a big inconvenience for her. "Or Cam can let me drop him off to work in his pretty car, and I can have that beautiful rig for the day."

Travis scoffed. "Not a chance in hell, beautiful. No one is allowed to drive Cam's car."

"Challenge accepted." Winter winked at me playfully and moved to kiss them both goodbye. These kisses were real heartfelt promises of love and devotion.

I never knew the sin of jealousy until now.

After Shane had brought Winter's bag back up the rickety steps and took the men home, Winter ordered takeout delivery from the little mom and pop Chinese restaurant around the corner from the laundromat. She brought me a large glass of water and two aspirin, then she cuddled in beside me on the couch. I sat in the dim light with my eyes closed while she worked on her homework.

She lightly shook me awake some time later.

"Hey, Big Guy. Time for bed."

She refilled my glass of water and followed me to the bedroom. I groggily made my way to the double bed pushed tight into the corner of the room. My dark sheets were still messy from the night before, but the bedroom was stark in contrast to her bright and colorful home.

"I'll tuck you in." A trace of a smirk flickered across her lips as she pulled the covers back to push me in.

I complied, too tired and achy from my punishment to argue. When she turned to leave, my mind jostled into gear.

"Where are you going?"

She stared down at me, the first look of hesitation since she'd decided to babysit me tonight, crossing her features.

"I'll sleep on the couch and check on you throughout the —"

"Like hell you'll sleep on my couch." I struggled to sit up in the bed, my bruises on bruises taking hold. "You take the bed, I'll take the —"

"You're injured, Cam. You're not taking the couch."

"I'm not letting a woman who gave up her night to take care of me sleep on my couch." I glared at her. The intense heat of a southern man challenged for his hospitality, or lack thereof. She was not winning this one.

"Compromise?" She held up two fingers in an attempt at a 'Scout's honor' symbol. "I sleep next to you, but I can have my own blanket so I don't disturb your sleep and —"

I laughed. "This is the one duvet I have, little violet. I'm a bachelor."

I nodded to the dresser in front of her. "Grab a pair of sweatpants and a t-shirt from the top drawer. It'll hang on you, but you'll be comfortable. Then crawl in here with me. No more compromising your time or sleep for me tonight."

She bit her lip, the crease in its pink flesh taunting me with visions I had no right to have. Finally, she nodded acquiescence.

"Okay," she said, more to herself than to me. "Okay."

I turned to face the wall while she changed, then felt the bed shift under her weight as she crawled in beside me. Her body was warm and soft and the sweet smell of lavender and vanilla dusted my sheets. She was careful not to touch me, and I rolled over to face her before she shut off the light of the lamp beside her.

"Thank you."

"I like taking care of you, Big Guy." She spoke the words into the dark. "Someone has to."

The even sighs of her breathing lulled me into a deep place of peace and calm in a matter of minutes.

Hours later, I awoke with a start to the wispy streams of daylight peeking through my curtains.

A beautiful woman lay encircled in my arms, her auburn head nestled on my right pec, her legs entwined with mine. Somehow, through the night, our hands even interlaced in our sleep. We were snuggled within my only blanket like a continuous human pretzel.

There was no hope for me now.

CHAPTER 29

SHANE

I stood under the blistering hot spray of the shower willfully burning every part of my dreams away.

It had been a weird week. Between Winter's drugging and the ensuing bonding in Logan's apartment, Drew's discoveries with Eileen, and the alternate reality dinner party at Winter's parents, my mind was on overdrive.

No amount of distractions had taken the edge off like I'd hoped. Instead, I was now plagued with even more confusing thoughts, and my dick was constantly at full-mast.

Like now.

My cock bobbed against my abs, as ready for action as it had been when I woke up just an hour before. I grabbed my shower gel from the shelf.

Those dreams. Faceless bodies of familiar silhouettes, naked and tending to my every need. Freud would have a fucking field day.

I squeezed the soap into my palm and lathered it over my shoulders and down my chest, scrubbing away the sweat and my dirty thoughts. I loved dirty thoughts; these were just... forbidden.

I stood under the spray again, allowing the water to rinse me clean. Another unbidden picture entered my mind and my cock turned to granite.

Fuck. Me.

An accidental walk-in was now controlling my dick in the worst ways possible. And that little display in the study the other night ...

I reached down, glided my hand over the head and squeezed slowly.

Fuck, that felt good. I took hold of my shaft and held tighter, tugging in the familiar rhythm that would get me off the fastest. I braced one hand on the wall and increased my pace, jerking my hips towards the tiles.

Her naked body was the first thing I saw when I closed my eyes. Her long hair cascading down her back as he fucked her from behind, her breasts bouncing to the beat of him thrusting inside of her. The sharp tingle rocketed up my spine as I thrust harder into my hand, matching his pace in my mind.

The image shifted; I was now the one doing the fucking. The sweet tang of her wetness was all I could smell. The hot vise grip of her pussy held me so tight. The need to come was pure agony.

My breathing became shallow and fast. My balls drew up, preparing for release.

Fuck yes, fuck y—

The image behind my eyelids changed to the muscled back of my friend now under me, my cock pounding deep between his ass cheeks. The masculine groan of pleasure coming from him was—

"Arrrrrghh." I growled as hot ropes of my cum painted the shower tile, the blissful release flooding my limbs and turning my whole body to Jell-O.

I braced myself against the wall reminding myself to breathe.

I was in some serious trouble.

I couldn't remember a time even as a teenager when I had been perpetually horny. Maybe when I had finally admitted to myself and the world I was attracted to men *and* women but—

My phone buzzed on the other side of the glass shower door. I fumbled to grab it without slipping to my death in the soapy semen spray on the shower floor.

Blaise's name flashed on the screen. "Hello?" I answered quickly. I had been waiting for this call all week.

"Oh, hey, Shane. I was expecting to leave a voicemail." Blaise let out an awkward cough, and I grimaced.

This was definitely not an ideal scenario. Just seeing him at the diner weeks ago had been challenging. But he really was my only hope at cracking those files, outside of hiring someone on the black market, which I had absolutely no idea how to do.

This wasn't some spy movie where we all had secret useful skills for the mission. We were bumbling idiots with a hope and a prayer.

I liked the Buried Alive crew better than the Scooby Doo Crew, but we hadn't really elevated our status with the name change.

Yet.

"I think I've found what you're looking for." Blaise's voice broke my reverie. "Can we meet tomorrow after the joint project panel? I don't want to have these files in my hands any longer."

Huh. He must have found something big. Blaise wasn't prone to exaggeration, so whatever it was, he really didn't want it on his conscience.

I swallowed hard and nodded, before remembering he actually couldn't see me in my naked, half-showered glory.

"That sounds good," I croaked out, my mind whirling with the potential possibilities.

I hung up the phone after managing to utter a few pleasantries and stepped back into the shower to finish.

What are you involved in, Dad? Do we have any hope in hell of getting you out?

It was weird to be in the WAQ offices now. The building that had felt like another home ever since I was a little boy was now a den of inequity.

I was nervous to be in here ever since we realized our fathers could be involved in something darker than anything I could have imagined in our sleepy little town. My co-op would be over in a few weeks, and then I could wash my hands of this place.

Temporarily.

I missed the lightheartedness of living an ignorant life. The more we found out, the more depressed I became.

I was still taking my pills, though. I wasn't willingly jumping out in front of this train wreck unmedicated.

Blaise, three other co-op students, and I finished our review meeting of a support structure design that would loop into the entire project should we get the go ahead for the tender. Everyone was on pins and needles waiting for the verdict; it would mean several hundred million dollars worth of work over the next ten years and had the potential to break some engineering world records.

Too bad it was tainted by illegal activity.

I was speculating, having not seen any of the files from Blaise yet, but it was a pretty obvious conclusion by now. Darren's comment to Winter had cinched it for me; Eccles was publicly traded, but WAQ was not. If they secured this deal, WAQ intended to go public. As a private stakeholder in WAQ, Eccles would have the potential to buy the stock and make a fortune.

I didn't know the legalities behind what they were doing and if that could be considered insider trading or not. Stock market jargon bored the ever-loving crap out of me and despite my need to research, I just couldn't bring myself to care.

Logan was the man for that job. He wasn't exactly warm and receptive the other night, but I wasn't expecting that kind of response from our dear, self-absorbed jackal. We needed his skills, and it looked like he needed us, too.

An eye for an eye and all that.

It was a good start, and I knew we'd whittle him down. His soft spot for Winter would be our biggest advantage. She could handle him even if I didn't love the sacrifice she was making to do it.

My cock twinged uncomfortably in my pants. The unwelcome dreams of my two *friends* were turning into living nightmares, haunting me during my waking hours.

I followed Blaise to an empty conference room and closed the door behind me. My eyes swept the room for hidden cameras, but then I supposed if they were hidden, I wouldn't be able to see them. I was going to have to read a few more *Jack Reacher* novels to be any good at this spy stuff.

This room was the only one without windows facing the interior office space. I turned to him, satisfied with my very basic knowledge of potential camera locations.

He shifted from foot to foot, clearly uncomfortable. I had offered to pay him to do this for me, but he'd brushed it off, muttering something about "closing this chapter." Seeing as how *he* broke up with *me*, I could only guess he had some unresolved feelings of his own.

I assessed my old lover. He was most definitely attractive, with a boyishly handsome face and curly red hair that fell haphazardly over depthless green eyes, but he no longer held the same appeal. I was relieved by that recognition; this man had held me in his metaphorical grasp for so long, but I had finally let myself free.

Into the clutches of another, but that was another story.

He thrust the flash drive into my palm and shoved his hands into his pockets.

"I could crack it. I wish I hadn't, but I did." He looked everywhere in the room before his eyes finally landed on mine.

"How long have you known about this?" He nodded his chin towards the tiny metal block in my hand as if it were a poisonous spider.

"About what?" I asked carefully, unsure of what he'd found or if he had taken the time to sift through it.

It was a risk we had taken, but it had been a risk well worth it. I just hoped it didn't get him into any sort of trouble. I didn't need yet another thing weighing heavily on my conscience.

He glanced at the door before stepping closer. "The embezzlement. That flash drive holds accounting records from every year since the company was formed. Someone had siphoned millions of company dollars into a shell corporation that's owned by another shell corporation. It's like a fucking Russian doll in there."

He gestured at the flash drive again, his eyes darkening in frustration. "Three shell corporations down the line, I was able to uncover Eccles as one shareholder, under a pseudonym. And someone, a company with CCH as the label, is dumping serious sums of cash into the company from another account for work I can't find records for at all. What the fuck is going on, Shane?"

"I don't know," I answered honestly, sitting my ass down on the boardroom table and running a hand through my hair. "It was really by accident, and now" — I released a waspy snort through my nose — "I don't know what the fuck to do with this information, Blaise. Like, involve the feds or something? Does a person just call the FBI's 1-800 line and leave a message that their father's company is committing fraud on an astronomical scale and is probably money laundering, too?"

I nearly choked on the last words, knowing in my heart they were true. I'd bet my spleen WAQ had been money laundering for Georgio ever since they started the company; the same arrangement as the diner, but on a grander, more elegant, more *hidden* scale.

I pushed past Blaise to open the door. I turned to him and forced a smile on my face like my faith in my father hadn't just been destroyed like the Death Star in Star Wars.

"Please, don't say anything about this to anyone. This is my responsibility and I'll figure it out."

I spun on my heel, tucking the flash drive of doom deep into my jeans pocket, not even bothering to grab my coat before I left the WAQ offices.

Drowning in the possibilities, I suffocated from lack of hope with this newfound information.

Were the embezzled funds going back to Eccles somehow? Camden had an ownership stake in Eccles and in Carlos Construction. Was this just a massive IRS evading tax loop? Why would our fathers agree to this in the first place?

I had no idea what it all meant or how to even look for it. I wasn't the man for this job.

I had to get the files to Logan.

CHAPTER 30

WINTER

"I'm sorry. Could you say that again?" I coughed hard after nearly choking on the bit of burrito I had been mid-chew when Hillary had asked me her question.

It was a Wednesday afternoon; my classes had been canceled, and I didn't have to work at either job tonight, so I had taken her up on her offer of shopping for the afternoon.

We sat in the Carlisle Mall food court after a long afternoon of errands for last-minute items for her wedding to Logan. I knew Hillary had people who could do this for her, but she had insisted on picking up the items herself. The woman loved control.

"I asked you to be at my wedding, Winter. God, you'd think I'd invited you to a torture chamber or something." She side-eyed me mischievously. "Unless you're into that sort of thing."

I took a sip of water and drew in a deep breath to gain some composure. "Ha, hilarious. Two boyfriends do not make me some sort of kink queen, Hill."

"Just two? Logan told me your harem was a lot bigger than that." My beautiful blonde and blue-eyed heiress friend winked at me and took a long draw from her green smoothie, not seeming to care the drink looked — and smelled — like dirt.

I snorted into my rice and bean consortium of deliciousness. The audacity of that man. "Since when does Logan make it a point to talk about me?"

Her face softened a degree, and I realized in that moment she genuinely cared for his Royal Asshole-ness, despite all the reasons not to. It was getting harder for me to ignore the human side of Logan too.

"I think he'd talk about you a lot more if he realized his own feelings. He's the kind of man that when he makes a decision, he's all in, obsessed ev—"

I held up a hand to stop that thought from escaping her pink painted lips. "Please don't, Hill. I don't need my delicate brain space taken up with thoughts of Logan. That man gives me whiplash on the best of days."

"He's complicated," she stated, tapping her fingers on the polymer plastic of the food-court table. "But I wouldn't call him a lost cause."

"Is that why you're going through with the wedding?" I asked curiously, still ignoring the apparent 'I'm invited' part.

Their dynamic confused me, especially with the added bits and pieces I had collected from my conversations with Hillary since we'd started this... hoemance?

What a terrible expression.

"No." Hillary looked at me discerningly before glancing around us as if she were about to spill the nuclear codes or something. She leaned across the table and dropped her voice so only I could hear. "I'm marrying him because it's the only way to get the money. And then we'll divorce shortly after."

My jaw unhinged at that information. I took my time to pick it off the floor before asking the inevitable question.

"So, this wedding is all a ruse? Like, 'No Way, Jose' this marriage actually has a hope in hell of working out?"

Was that why Logan was so casual about the upcoming nuptials and acting way too handsy with me lately? As much as he was slowly worming his way under my skin like a parasite, I couldn't shake the fact that he was engaged; that, and that 94 percent of the time he was a slimeball. Six percent of the time, though, six percent was okay.

Not great odds, really.

"Yup." She sucked on her straw so aggressively only one tiny drop of nutrient soup remained in the cup. "All a ruse. And aside from our fathers and our lawyer, you are now the only one who knows."

Wow. I hadn't known why Hillary latched onto me so hard since our bonding moment at the diner, but I had to admit I enjoyed having her trust. And this?

This was a trust moment.

I wanted to ask one thousand and one questions, but we weren't there yet. That she'd tell me this alone was brain bending, so I wouldn't push my luck.

"So, to be clear," I repeated slowly, "you just invited me to your real wedding, that's actually a fake wedding, that's less than two weeks away. And in one year's time you're going to walk away with millions and Logan will get" — I searched for the right word — "a house for his trouble?"

"Try three months, and it'll probably be a building for his business or something, but yes. Total sham of a wedding."

She grinned at me like we were sharing a big inside joke.

"My aunt was a crafty old bird who made sure no one could access the money but me, and that I'd have to be married by the time I was 25 to do it. Our fathers are furious and are trying to save face, Logan is fucked and won't tell me why or how, but he's willing to go along with it, and I've got to figure out a way to take the money and run for the hills."

I blinked rapidly, trying to imagine being in her situation. All Hillary had in her life in Cascade Falls were people trying to use her for a situation she had no control over. Our newfound friendship was making a lot more sense.

"Huh." I was dumbfounded. My heart actually squeezed for Logan in this situation. Hill had told me they didn't have a choice in their relationship, and now, though Logan was about to lose everything, he was going through with it, anyway.

It was a snowy day in hell to be feeling empathy for Logan Eccles.

"How much is it a plate again?" I teased sarcastically, knowing full well it would be my cost of groceries for the month.

"$325." Her blue eyes brightened, a sly smile forming. "It's going to be insatiably exorbitant and downright scandalous the amount of money I'm blowing on this fake wedding. So come, won't you? You can even bring a date." She winked and snagged one of the lone tortilla chips still sitting in its cardboard container.

"Well, I have two boyfriends, so can I bring two dates?"

I was pushing my luck and I knew it, but I wasn't going to choose between Drew and Travis. As it was, Quick was going to be off his rocker jealous I'd been invited to the most talked about event in Cascade Falls in years, and Cam … another heart squeeze when I thought of Cam.

Cam only had us.

"I'll do you one better." She crunched her chip and snagged another. "Daddy's *dearest* friends are going yachting in Panama and can't make the wedding. That frees up another two spaces I've already paid for. You can bring all *four* of your harem."

I was grateful I had already finished my burrito because I would have surely died a Darwinian death by choking in a mall food court.

"They're not my harem," I managed to get out between dry coughs. "But I will absolutely take them to stick it to your dad."

She wiped her hands on my crumpled napkin and stood, adjusting her Prada purse and grabbing her tray. "Great. And no gifts, please. I need nothing to 'wish us well' for the three months we'll be stuck wearing wedding bands."

She marched through the mall like she owned the place — and, well, she kinda did. Partly, anyway. The Lanes had an ownership stake in most of the commercial shopping districts in this town.

The wealth of this woman was mind-blowing.

"And," she smiled in triumph when we got to her car in the parking lot, her gaze looking me up and down. "I know the perfect dress you can wear! That dark purple one with the white trim. That'll look smashing on you."

Oh, right. The one Quick had stuffed at the back of my closet. I shrugged, not caring what I wore. "Sure. Might as well dress me up and make me look pretty while we're at it."

I had meant it as a joke, but her eyes widened; she grabbed me by the shoulder and spun me towards her. "You're not my doll, Winter. I just loved that dress. Don't think that I —"

"I was joking, Hill. I know you're an overbearing know-it-all and I happen to like you that way." I smiled appreciatively at her. "I'll wear the dress. I'll bring my boyfriends, and my two *not-boyfriends*. It'll be fun. I've never been to a wedding like this before."

"Your parents are going. Didn't they tell you?" She cocked her head in thought. "I think Shane's parents were invited as well — Daddy's insistence, I'm sure."

Nope, another thing they forgot to mention. I shook that thought and moved on — I wasn't spending a single second thinking about them today.

"Great." I swallowed and attempted a genuine smile. "The whole family will be there."

We had left the parking lot and headed toward the freeway to head back to Cascade Falls when I had a thought.

Well, I had been thinking about it for a week and hadn't settled on what I was going to do. Now though, now I was being presented with the perfect opportunity.

"Do you mind if we make a quick detour?"

I checked the clock display on the window — we'd still have time.

"Sure, I don't have to be back until seven. What's the detour?"

"I just have to grab some information from an insurance company," I said, though it was a lie since I was not willing to give up secrets not my own.

It took twenty minutes to cross to the other side of town, to the run-down insurance company of Darlene Knightly, mother-extraordinaire.

I asked Hill to wait for me in the car, then I channeled her energy and confidently walked in like I, too, owned the place.

The dingy furniture and stale air weren't much to brag about owning.

"May I help you?"

Cam's familiar face in female blinked back at me. The woman was like a worn Persian rug; previously brilliant and beautiful, now faded and worn from years of overuse.

Her tired brown eyes didn't match Cam's icy blues; they followed my every move.

"Darlene?" I asked hesitantly, losing a bit of my bravado.

"Yes," she said expectantly, and I realized she didn't recognize me. That would either be a blessing or a curse for this conversation.

"My name is Winter Wallace. I'm a friend of Cameron Chase."

She didn't startle or shrink away. The name meant nothing to her; my eyes prickled with tears at the sadness of it all.

"Cameron Chase," I repeated slowly, "the man who has been looking for you."

"I don't know what you're talking —"

An anger I never expected burst from my gut and through my body, its heat devouring my limbs.

"No," I spat angrily, "You don't get to deny him like that." I stepped toward her with intention. "You don't get to pretend he doesn't exist when he has spent the last year of *his* life looking for *you*."

Her head swept side to side, glancing toward the hallway in anxious anticipation.

"I can't talk about this. Especially not here. Please go."

She stared at me imploringly, begging me with her eyes to leave.

I couldn't leave. Not yet. I lowered my voice to a whisper on a hiss.

"Did you know his parents are dead? Drowned, just last year. He packed up his bags and searched the country for you. He has a Master's degree, he's kind and hardworking, and he's so damn sweet and you *rejected* him."

Her eyes filled with tears though she sat mute before me. She brought a trembling hand to her lips before uttering, "Please, go."

I tossed a small piece of paper on her desk — with Cam's name and phone number should she choose to make a move.

"I'll leave," I said, finally moving toward the dirty glass door. "But if you choose to reject him again" — I nodded at the paper sitting innocently on her keyboard — "you definitely weren't worth his sacrifice."

I stalked across the parking lot and tore open the car door, slamming it behind me in a silent rage; Hill just looked at me from the driver's seat, the picture of bemusement.

I shook my head and folded my arms across my chest and huffed angrily.

"I hate insurance people." I muttered in half-assed explanation. "Let's go home."

CHAPTER 31

TRAVIS

"I'm just going to run to the washroom," I told Colin, though my gaze never left Winter's luscious body as she sang on stage at Bourbon & Blues.

"Heard that before," Colin mused. "Be back in ten, or I'm cuffing your ass. And if you can get it done in ten minutes, I need your secrets, man."

I chuckled, knowing I had left Colin to his own devices a handful of times to 'get it done' with my beautiful stage girlfriend, but that wasn't what I was up to tonight. Besides, she still had five more songs to go.

"You just need the right woman." I winked conspiratorially, leaving him to fend for himself. It was a smaller crowd tonight, likely because of the treacherous weather and mid-winter blues — no pun intended. I would use it to my advantage for my mini-mission, though.

Drew's unveiling of Georgio's half-brothers hadn't sat right with me. Something about the names of the brothers had jogged a distant memory, and I needed to uncover it before letting everyone else know. If it was nothing, I didn't want to bother worrying anybody, but if it was something ...

I warily watched for any sign of Georgio as I left the bar area. Our money pick-ups were always from scheduled drops through Angelo, so I hadn't actually seen much of the man since the night in his office; only at a distance, and he never acknowledged me. Winter and Cam had said the same. I supposed it was a good thing that with Mom out of the hospital and Devon off of the drugs, I hadn't needed to beg for any more of his blood money. I couldn't help feeling like he was a sitting cobra, waiting to strike at the moment any of us made a wrong move.

I didn't like being prey.

I made my way through the back corridors to the staff locker room and took my phone out of my locker; the saved article still on my main Safari page that I had flagged to read when I had time. It had taken me hours of searching, but I finally found it in an old digital archive from the Cascade Chronicles online edition. The anxious anticipation had been melting away my insides, and I had only made it halfway through my shift before caving.

I sat on the bench and loosened my tie, just for the second it took for the article to load.

It had been a reprint of a national news article featuring the Carlos Cartel crime family. Georgio's name was surprisingly absent, save for a summary of Antonio Carlos's sons. Three different photos featured the five men; I scrutinized the photos closely to see if I recognized any of them.

A large blond man who belonged on a professional football field looked familiar, and I was sure I had seen him at the club before, although it hadn't been for at least a year. There wasn't anything memorable about the twins, two brown-skinned, dark-featured men who could pass for each other's reflections, even in adulthood.

My gaze stuck to a very familiar man wearing a black suit and dark sunglasses. His hair had been longer when I knew him, and he hadn't worn a short beard like the picture showed, but it was him all right.

I searched for the name in the caption, now feeling like I was about to puke up my melting insides; my heart, my brain—everything.

'Matteo Banderas was the label beneath the photo, but when I knew him, when *we* knew him, he was Matthew Balcom.

Dad.

My hands trembled worse than a patient with Parkinson's as I read through the rest of the article. Matteo Banderas, son of Antonio Carlos, suspected accomplice to multiple killings and rumored to be Antonio's right hand on the weapons side of the operation along the American West Coast.

The article was only a few years old. Dad had walked away thirteen years ago and hadn't been in touch since. The live wires buzzing in my belly turned from anxious tremors to vicious vibrations.

Dad had abandoned us, two little boys and our mother, yet there he was, in living color on my cracked phone screen, looking like he hadn't a care in the world.

That meant ...

Georgio. Georgio wasn't just some stranger to me. Georgio was some fucked up version of family.

The vibrations caused my stomach contents to explode like butter in a microwave; I ran to the bathroom to vomit.

The expulsion did nothing to calm down my rioting body. I was a sweating, shaking mess; I needed to get out of here. I couldn't be working in the club my apparent *uncle* owned tonight.

I sent Colin a text letting him know I was sick and would have to leave, but he could have my tips for the night. It was a shitty sacrifice to make, given my current circumstances, but I liked the guy and would never have left him in the lurch otherwise.

I had grabbed my jacket and turned to leave when a soft female voice on the other side of the locker bank caught my attention.

"You know you can't be calling me while I'm working here," the voice whispered hoarsely, sounding fearful.

My nerves had dialed down from 250 percent to 120 percent with the distraction I so desperately needed. I strained to hear over the hum of the ventilation system.

"We're almost there," she hissed, "but it won't get any faster with you checking in like this. I've got another witness, and the evidence is —"

A loud thump came from outside the hall.

She cut herself off. "I'll call you later. Don't call again."

I waited until I heard the metallic door click before closing my locker door as quietly as I could, waiting a minute before leaving the premises myself.

Was there a mole on the inside?

The last ten minutes of my life had led to information tilting my universe on its axis, and now this place may have a spy.

Shit.

Did that mean they knew we were at the fight nights? Did that mean they could jail us as accomplices after the fact?

Shit. Shit. *Fuck.*

I walked down the hallway as nonchalantly as I could, bumping into Georgio's petite brunette assistant.

"Travis?" She blinked like an owl behind large round glasses. "Shouldn't you be at the bar?"

"Heading home sick." I grimaced, not needing to exaggerate my waxy facade. I probably looked deathly ill if my mental state was reflected in my skin.

"Oh." She gave me a critical once-over before nodding dismissively. "Okay, then. Feel better."

She passed me as I walked out into the freezing fresh air. I took desperate gulping breaths and willed the oxygen to cleanse my soul as I grappled with my ancestry and all that came with it.

I unlocked my car and sat in it for minutes, numbly staring out the window at the brick and metal building in front of me. Georgio's building. The Carlos Cartel's building. My *family's* building.

I had to watch over Mom tonight. I'd be a few hours early, but I didn't have the time to head to Drew's or Shane's to hash this out. I wasn't sure I even wanted to. How could I share a secret I wasn't even sure I understood myself?

I revved up my shitbox and drove home, relieving Devon of his home care duties. Despite Jesus being his best friend now, he still complained about the minimal work he had to do to make sure our mother stayed alive. I would give my brother my last kidney if he needed it, but "Love thy neighbor" was selective, apparently.

I wrestled with my need to come to terms with this revelation and the need to share the burden with someone. Winter would still be working for another hour, and she had early classes in the morning. Cam was also working a private function at the club that evening, and Shane was going through all of the files with a fine-tooth comb after

Blaise had shattered any hope of finding their parents innocent in this whole mess.

I dialed the number of the last man standing as I drove the last few minutes home. If he could come to me, I could get this off my chest.

"Hey man, can you come over? There's something I need to talk about."

"Shit." Drew blew out the word between his teeth like it was four syllables instead of one. "So, you're Georgio's ..."

"Nephew," I finished for him. "I think. Unless Dad has an evil twin somewhere, but I'd call him the evil one." I laughed caustically, the acidic bite burning my insides once again.

We were sitting on my front deck in the darkness of the night in two mangled metal folding chairs from the nineties. A sole spotlight on the property lit up the icy driveway.

Mom and Devon were still inside, but I didn't want to risk them overhearing, and I hadn't had the foresight at the time to sit in the warmth of Drew's Corolla.

Drew shoved his hands in his pockets, his breath visible in the chilly night air. "So, really," he mused aloud as he stared up into the night sky, "you've been 'bailed out' by your uncle this whole time ... as what, a control mechanism? He's got to know that you're family."

I shrugged my shoulders, at a complete loss for what game Georgio was playing. Was this just an intricate game of chess to him, and we were little pawns scurrying around the board while he sacrificed the queen?

I'd wondered if he even gave us a second thought since his intentional display of power after the staff meeting all those weeks ago. Who were we to someone who couldn't even get jail time for a very obvious illegal gambling, fighting, and drug ring, where local authorities swept everything under the rug?

Nobody. We were truly nobody.

Still, I couldn't be a complete nobody to Georgio. He had consistently provided me financial aid when I needed it, and I knew through my channels he had laid down the law with his dealers selling drugs to Devon.

I didn't have any family outside of our threesome. Mom's brother had died before I was born, and Dad had mentioned nobody at all in the twelve years we had lived under the same roof.

Now I knew why.

"I guess so. I've never had an extended family, so I don't know how they're supposed to act. Is it normal for uncles to hold debts over your head by blackmailing you into doing illegal jobs for him?"

Another acerbic laugh, this time from Drew. "My uncle is an alcoholic; my aunt married a man that had all the same fantastic traits as my grandfather. She divorced him two years ago and has a court-ordered restraining order against him. Our uncles just suck."

I held out my can of non-alcoholic beer to tap his in an ironic "cheers" motion.

"I'll not-drink to that." I snickered at the parody of the two of us sitting on my deck bitching about wayward uncles.

I was grateful he'd answered my call and even more relieved he had come over within twenty minutes. How far we had come. If only Winter could see this—

"Shit!" I cursed, digging into my pocket to grab my cell phone.

I had two missed messages from her and one phone call. I was supposed to drive her back to her place after work before heading home for my caregiver shift. The stress of the evening made me completely forget.

I was an asshole.

Drew eyed me quizzically as I failed to explain. I hit redial on my phone screen and put the phone on speakerphone.

"Hey, beautiful, I am so sorry, I—" The words came out in a rush before she cut me off.

"It's okay!" Her calm and, better still, cheerful voice came through the canned speaker, clear as a bell in the quiet night. "Colin let me know you went home sick. Cam's going to drive me home. What happened? Is it your mom?"

My heart was in my throat at the complete faith she had in me. We were well past the lies and distrust of months before, and I would never take this second chance with her for granted. Never.

"Not my mom," I answered truthfully. "I figured out something about Georgio that really threw me. I'd rather tell you in person, but Drew's already here, so —"

"Drew's there? Okay, this must be bad. Please don't make me wait until I see you this weekend. Spill."

I recapped the last few hours of my night, every gut-wrenching up-chucking detail. It was two minutes of dialogue at most, but the words took up agonizing space in the universe. A simple news article had changed the way I viewed my entire life.

"Oh Travis, I'm so sorry." I could feel the empathy in her tone, wrapping around me like a warm blanket. "Want us to come over? We can be there within the hour…" she trailed off, but I didn't doubt that she would drag Cam here after midnight if she thought that was what I would want.

Fuck, I loved this woman.

"No, that's okay, beautiful. Drew's got to head out here soon, and I've got to check on Mom. You go with Cam and I'll see you on Friday. I love you."

"All my kisses and hugs to you too," she sang, and I laughed.

It was the phrase she'd used since I had first told her I loved her. She hadn't said those three specifically back to me yet, but it was in every touch, every glance, every one of our interactions.

When I got the words, they would mean so much more.

I hung up the phone and Drew raised an eyebrow. "She hasn't said them back to you either, huh?"

I shrugged like I was indifferent, but it gave me a small sense of satisfaction knowing she hadn't told Drew she loved him yet, either. I knew she did — how she felt about him was in every one of their exchanges too.

Still, I liked that we were on even ground.

"Speaking of that..." Drew let the words hang in the air, his tone changing to intense seriousness. "What do we do when she falls for Cam?"

I pursed my lips, having considered the very thought a lot over the past few weeks watching the two of them grow closer. She might not admit it yet, but Cam was getting in deeper by the day. He just hadn't fully considered that sharing her was a real possibility. One that was working.

"I don't think there's anything we *can* do. I don't even know if she knows it yet. But there's definitely something there, for both of them."

Drew sighed dramatically, downing the rest of his near-beer and crushing the can between his fingers. "I know. This is never the dynamic I would have considered for my life, but here we are."

"Here we are," I repeated. "You're not so bad, man." I grinned with a shake of my head. "If I had to choose a husband-brother, you're at the top of the list."

He snorted. "We need a better title than that. Husband-brother sucks."

He left a few minutes later, promising to share the information with Shane tomorrow. I knew Winter would tell

Cam, and Logan would probably find out at our next rag-tag meet-and-greet.

I knew he was important to what we were trying to achieve, but I didn't trust him. He was erratic, entitled, and completely self-involved. And I *definitely* didn't like the way he kept looking at my girlfriend.

Our girlfriend.

I opened the screeching screen door and kicked the snow off of my boots before entering my tiny abode. Devon was sitting at our kitchen table, his body facing me as if lying in wait with his arms crossed.

He looked like he was about to stage an intervention and I would have chuckled at the irony if I hadn't had to stage three with him already.

"So, *the* Georgio Carlos is our uncle now? Dad is alive? And your girlfriend sleeps with other men and you're okay with it? What the hell is going on, Trav?"

Curse this trailer and its paper-thin walls. I scrutinized my brother, the tormented soul whose abandonment issues had led to everything else in our lives. He had been deeply affected by our father's choice too.

I grabbed the other chair, spinning it around to sit on it backwards and faced the man who looked so much like Matteo Banderas it hurt to admit.

I wouldn't be able to tell him all of it. It wasn't my story to tell. But I was going to have to tell him something. And Georgio was his uncle — *apparently* — too.

"Okay, so this is going to sound a little crazy, but ..."

CHAPTER 32

CAMERON

"Hi, um — it's — uh — Darlene Knightly calling. I was wondering if you'd be willing to meet for coffee. I — er, ah — if you'd still consider seeing me."

"How did you get this number?"

"Your friend — Winter, was it? She gave it to me when she came back. I'd — I'd like to meet you. I have some — there are some things you should know."

I had been steamrolled by the phone call, so blindsided by the unknown number and the voice behind it, I would have fallen out of my chair if I hadn't been safely buckled into my Chevelle.

My little violet had given her my number? I was so confused by the admission I dumbfoundedly agreed to meet Daisy — Darlene — at a dingy café in Carlisle, a few blocks over from the crappy insurance building the next afternoon.

I arrived early; Momma's cardinal rule so ingrained in me I couldn't have been ten minutes later if I tried. My mind smiled at the memory of her scolding me for the one and only time I was late to pick her up from a church meeting as a teenager. She had hit me with her purse and refused to make my favorite biscuits for the rest of the month. It was one lecture I was prone to never forget.

I seated myself in a small booth that made the diner in Cascade Falls look fancy and faced the door. I wanted to see her when she came in. If she didn't show up today, I was closing this chapter on my life and locking the book up tight. I'd pack up my things and leave town and beg Travis and Winter for their forgiveness later.

My mind wasn't ready to consider that thought just yet, but it was waiting in the eaves for when the disappointment inevitably came.

She didn't see me when she first arrived. I watched her as she hovered in the doorway like a lost hummingbird.

I waved a large palm in her direction. The movement caught her attention as she hurried toward me like she was evading prying eyes. There was no one else here. No prying eyes to be had.

She slid into the bench across from me as the only waitress pounced on us with her order pad in hand; we were likely her only opportunity for tips this hour. I ordered a coffee and Daisy—Darlene quickly ordered a tea.

"Would you mind giving us some time, sugar?" I asked the strawberry-blonde server with a practiced smile. "We haven't seen each other in a long while and would like a bit of privacy."

The braces-clad twenty-something bobbed her head in acknowledgment before scurrying back to the counter to put in our orders. We waited in awkward silence for her to come back, neither of us willing to start the conversation with potential eavesdroppers nearby.

"You said Winter came to see you," I said bluntly, after we'd received our order in chipped ceramic mugs.

I stirred three of the little creamers and two sugars into my coffee to make it drinkable. "Explain."

The older female version of me licked her chapped lips and stared me in the eyes; she looked nervous, but resolute.

"She came by a few days ago with your name and number on a piece of paper." Daisy winced. "She, ah — was not kind about how I treated you."

A warmth I had never known bloomed like a wild rose across my chest and settled into my center.

"And why are you here now?" I asked, just as bluntly, no longer willing to give this woman a shattered shard of my heart until she'd given me a piece of her own to glue it back together.

"I —" She paused, and tears snuck into the corners of her eyes. "I'd dreamt of that moment for years. The impossible day when I'd get a chance to see you again. To know that you were safe and whole and the man I had hoped you would grow into, as far away from my life as possible."

"And when the day came" — she swallowed hard, tears falling freely down her cheeks and dropping into her tea — "I panicked. You used my real name. A name I haven't heard in years. I've tried to bury that name and you dug it up again and I panicked."

She silently sobbed into the tissue paper napkin. I reached into my pocket and handed her a packet of Kleenex. I didn't speak. It wasn't my time to talk.

"You weren't Cameron Chase when you were born." She drew in a shaky breath and held it before releasing it slowly through her teeth. "You were Theodore Knight. I called you Teddy."

I gripped the underside of the table and willed my hammering heart into soft submission. This was going to be a hard story to hear.

It was. It could have been a movie. She spaced it out through quiet sniffles and sips of her slowly cooling tea. I listened stoically, trying to read between the lines for the truth and the lies we tell ourselves.

She had grown up poor in Alabama and ran away from home at seventeen with an older boyfriend with bad intentions. She got stranded in Sequoia County when he left her for another woman. She had no education and no job prospects and leveraged her beauty as an escort to support herself.

She had worked for the same company for years when the business changed hands. The owner took an interest in her and requested her for all of his events, usually only for appearances. She fell for him and they took on a more personal relationship. He wasn't a good man, but he was good to her.

I snorted at that explanation. Good men could do bad things and wicked men could do good things, but that didn't forgive the sins of the damned.

I didn't know which version of man I was.

She'd seen some things she shouldn't have. She'd gotten pregnant, and she'd been terrified what he would want out of the deal. She didn't want her baby in his world, so she left.

She left, had me in her hometown, and then decided I wasn't worth the trouble, only to go back into the arms of the man she had been so afraid of.

She never said that part, but that was all I heard as she tried to explain why she put me up for adoption and fled the state to return to a life she had never wanted.

An hour passed as she shared her pain and sorrow. I barely breathed a word, other than to offer more Kleenex and accept a poorly timed refill of coffee.

Her agony wasn't enough to crack my hardened shell, despite all my hopes it would. Maybe one day it could, but that day wasn't today. I wrestled with my demons and the insidious craving for a cigarette.

"I think I've heard all I can for today."

The one-sided conversation had stilted my inability to ask the deeper questions taunting me in the stagnant silence.

I reached for the jacket hanging off the dangling hook at the end of the booth; I had taken it off in the middle of her story. I turned to stare into her watery eyes, the only portion of her face that didn't match mine.

"Thank you for meeting me, Daisy. You're welcome to reach out again, but for now, I'm going to need to process. I had a good life with Momma and Pop. I never wanted for nothing. I also don't want to live the rest of my days without family in my life, and I've got no one left to fill that space in my heart. You can decide if that's a place you want to be. And I can decide if that's a place I want to put you."

I tossed a twenty-dollar bill on the table and nodded to the waitress as I walked out the door.

It went against my southern boy indoctrination to leave her sitting in the café without another glance of acknowledgment, but the need to tighten the reins on my control outweighed the need to take care of this woman.

I needed to take care of another woman. The woman who had already shown that she would take care of me.

The shadows of doubt and deliverance hovering over me momentarily disappeared while I drove out of the parking lot in the car Pop had left me. The photo of him and Momma smiled down on me in the cheap photo keychain hanging from the rearview mirror.

There was a stop I needed to make that couldn't wait.

I buzzed her number at the door and waited for her to respond, the need to see her had fueled a fire in my belly. I needed to repay her for this kindness.

The conversation with Daisy Knight had been nothing like I had pictured. It wasn't a reuniting of open arms of kindred lost souls, but it had given me a few answers, and most of all, a portion of closure I had been seeking since the day I had found out I was the adopted son of Landon and Octavia Chase.

I saw her cute little green car in the parking lot, layered with a fine dusting of snow. By sheer luck and circumstance, she was here.

Dusk was setting in and the darkening night sky was a blend of blues and purples, the coloring similar to a fresh bruise on pale skin. It was prettier in the sky than on a man's skin, but both were beautiful in their own right. I shivered in the cold as I waited for her to respond to the buzzer.

"Hello?" Her groggy voice finally answered just when I was about to turn around and head back to my car.

I fought to keep my voice steady and even.

"Hey, little violet. Sorry to drop in on you like this. May I come up to see y'all?" The southern drawl always came out most when I was nervous.

The door immediately buzzed to show it was open, and I stepped inside the tight lobby and bypassed the elevator to the stairwell beside it.

I took the stairs two at a time, anxious energy overpowering my senses. There weren't enough steps in the building to dull the burn. I knocked twice on her door before she opened it, with glassy eyes and bedhead from sleep.

Wearing an oversized t-shirt and another man's boxer shorts, she let me in and closed the door behind me.

"Hey, sorry, Big Guy. I was taking a nap after studying for my midterms and I—whoa!" she exclaimed when I lifted her by her hips and swung her around in the air, mimicking the move I'd seen her and Shane do.

Unlike Shane's spin, she wrapped her legs around my waist and entwined her arms around my neck, giggling like an excited little girl. The sound crept into the deepest crevices of my heart and broke something open in me.

I kissed the tip of her nose and stared into the deepest recesses of her soul through the spyglasses of her blue-green eyes.

"I just saw my m — Daisy," I corrected myself, not willing to call her 'Mom'. She'd have to earn that right.

Apologies filled her face. "I'm sorry, Cam, I overstepped and I shouldn't have, I was just so mad and —"

I didn't let her finish the thought. I couldn't. She was trying to apologize for one of the kindest acts anyone had ever done for me. I needed her to know what it meant to have someone who'd care enough to defend me.

I kissed her, fiercely, pressing my lips to hers to stop the flurry of unnecessary requests for forgiveness. The warmth of her skin and the sweetness of her breath made me hunger for her — a starving man needing satiation. I had only allowed myself the indulgence once until now, and that had been under extenuating circumstances.

She was as delicious as I had remembered.

She froze in my arms, not pulling away but not responding to my plea, either.

Instant regret washed over me; I had kissed my best friend's girl without her permission, in a heated moment where I had convinced myself I had the right to do so.

I moved to pull away when she tightened around me, pressing her breasts and pussy into the hardness of my body, and kissed me back.

It was a desperate kiss of passion and pain. I kissed her to show her my appreciation of her mind, her soul, her body. I plied her lips with my own, forcing her to open up to me to explore every part of her with my tongue.

The steel of my erection grew between us, and she moaned into my mouth as she rubbed herself against me and the sensation shot sparks off into my cock and my brain.

It took all the willpower I could summon and the reliance on my gentlemanly upbringing to pull myself back from the kiss and look at her.

"Sugar," I whispered breathlessly, basking in the flushed cheeks and glazed eyes that were only for me. "If I don't stop now, I won't be able to. And I don't want to get in trouble with any of our friends."

She nodded, a small smile playing on her lips. "Thank you for caring about that." She traced a finger down the side of my jaw before kissing it lightly. "Now may be a good time to mention that Travis and Drew called me out on my crush on you a few days ago."

I blinked rapidly through my haze of hormones and lust. I didn't pretend to understand their group dynamic, but it intrigued me they'd had that conversation openly. That they had that conversation at all meant Travis had seen the writing on the wall even when I couldn't — or wouldn't.

"This will not get us in trouble, Cam. Only if you don't want it or mean it. We can stop right now."

Could I kiss her and walk away? I didn't think I could, but I didn't know how to be in a group relationship.

"I care about you, little violet. I want—... more." I swallowed hard at the confession, relieved to admit it to her and to myself. "But I don't know how to fit into" — I searched for the word, but it was escaping me — "this."

I lowered her to the ground and cupped her cheeks in my palms, stroking them gently with my thumbs. "I want you." I took her hand in mine and placed it over the tight seam of my jeans, rubbing it over my granite-hard cock.

"I need you. But I wouldn't feel right if I took you on this floor like an animal when I don't know how to commit to this kind of... thing."

"We don't have to have sex, Cam. It's okay." She smiled at me softly with nothing but care in her eyes.

She teasingly squeezed the bulge in my pants before bringing my hand up to her lips and kissing my fingertips one by one. "I'm just glad to know you're interested and that this isn't fully one-sided. I've been wrestling with my feelings for you for a little while."

She stopped speaking and slowly trailed kisses up my middle finger before slipping it into her mouth. The wet heat sucked me down to the knuckle before slowly releasing with a pop.

My body was absent of blood as it all went southward to service the needs of my cock.

Her sultry grin had me questioning my first statement. I could strip those boxers off her in the middle of this living room and sink so deep into her we would fuse together, welded and beautiful.

Abandoning all thought so I wouldn't change my mind, I picked her up and carried her into her bedroom, a room I had only viewed as an outsider from the hallway on friendly visits.

"No sex," I repeated, sticking to my vow until I could wrap my head around where I could fit into her world. "But

I need to thank you. A gentleman always gives his proper thanks.”

I laid her on the bed and dragged down the black boxers, giving her ample time to say no and push me away. She didn't, her eyes never leaving mine, as I removed the boxers fully and spread her legs wide to get a good look at my feast.

Thick droplets of her arousal coated her pussy and my mouth watered. Her plump clit was swollen and ready to be devoured. I needed to taste her. I wanted to inhale only her until I couldn't breathe, smothered by her pussy and her cum.

“New plan.” I growled, pulling her up from the bed and laying down where she had been seconds before. “Sit on my face.”

She willingly complied, only hesitating for a second before shifting her body to hover over me, giving me the full view of the goddess she was.

She didn't face the headboard as I had intended. Instead, she faced the rest of my body, her full ass cheeks in my face to knead while I drenched myself in her juices.

It was better than I had intended.

I speared my tongue into her, her sweet taste overpowering my senses, and I used my lips to open her up, nipping and sucking on her tender skin and lapping up everything I could savor. I shifted her forward to get better access to her clit, swirling my tongue over and over, increasing my pressure with each pass. She cried out in pleasure when I inserted my thumb into her pussy, pressing along her walls in a clockwise motion until I hit the spongy bullseye of her G spot.

“Fuck!” she cried out, her groan bringing my cock to the point of pain as a burst of flavor hit my tongue. She was gushing wet, her cum dripping down my chin and clinging to my fingers.

I wasn't done. The masochist in me needed to hear that sound again without the hope of coming in her pussy tonight.

I continued to lick her clean, adding my other thumb to her pussy and massaging along her walls. She arched into me, suffocating me as I made it my mission for a second orgasm.

Scream for me, little violet.

Her mewls of pleasure were going to make me come in my pants, but I couldn't find it in me to care as she rode my face so hard she was going to have stubble burn across her thighs.

I was close to my goal when she halted my progress. Pitching herself forward and unzipping my jeans, she reached into my boxers and pulled my cock free.

Her warm hand stroked up my shaft, my body convulsing at the touch. The heat of her mouth wrapped around me, taking me so deep I could feel the back of her throat bump against my head. She swallowed and the tightness around my cock brought stars to the back of my eyelids. I was so tense, so coiled from her responsive body. It was going to take seconds of this treatment to make me explode.

I pulsed into her with my thumbs and lapped at her clit with forceful licks while she sucked my cock in the same rhythm. The frenzy made me a desperate, needy man.

I pressed my lips against her clit and vibrated them against her tender flesh. A deep muffled groan shuddered around my cock at the same time. The final straw. Her second gush of cum covered my tongue the same time my own coated the back of her throat. Our joint release collapsed on the bed together.

I sat up, reaching to turn her around to tuck her body into mine. I held her to me with my pants still undone and her t-shirt rolled up, baring the evidence of my invasion of her to the world.

"That was one hell of a thank you." She yawned into my chest, the shadow of a smile dancing on her lips. "I hope I didn't push you too far, Cam, I —"

"I don't have a single regret," I assured her, my arms flexing around her to hold her closer. "I'm a grown man, Winter. I'm in control of my body."

"Of mine too, apparently." She giggled, the high-pitch titter sweet music to my ears.

"I'll figure this out," I murmured, stroking her hair as I closed my eyes, sinking into the comfort of the feather pillows and duvet beneath us. "Just give me time."

Words I had said for the second time that day.

"I want this, little violet."

"Me too."

If she said more, I didn't hear it. The softness of her body, her bed, and her breathing lulled me into the elusive place of tranquility I had been seeking for over a year.

CHAPTER 33

DREW

"What do you mean, I'm fired?"

I blinked slowly, not comprehending Camden's words as he sat in the office seat — *my* office seat — as I stood in front of my father's beaten-up old desk.

"You're being let go, Drew. Johnson's is under new management, or haven't you heard?"

Camden cocked a smug eyebrow at me, and a lesser man would have punched him in the face by now. I was trying very hard not to be the lesser man.

"I'm being fired," I repeated, still in a bit of a daze at his abrupt statement.

I had been in a hurry to check on Dad and get out the door this morning — the first official morning that Johnson's was 'under new management,' as Camden was calling it — and I was being fired within the first five minutes.

"Why?" I asked finally, folding my arms across my chest and spreading my athletic form out as far as I could spread.

Camden was thin and reedy; I was not. If I couldn't match him in attitude, I'd overpower him with stature.

"You are no longer an asset to this operation." Camden stood, matching me height for height, not taking my bait. "You'll receive a severance package for your troubles, but I'm legally requesting that you no longer frequent my new business."

"Excuse me?" My anger could no longer be held beneath the surface; it sputtered like lava from a freshly blown hole in the earth. "You're *banning* me from the diner? On what fucking grounds?"

"I don't need to discuss this with you." Camden grinned like a shark and pointed to the door. "Please pack up your things and leave the premises immediately."

It took every ounce of self-control I had to leave the room and not commit a felony in the only workplace I had ever known.

Jobless was better than jail.

The fucking nerve of that man. I had to sign page after page of legal garbage committing the next six months of my life to this place, and now I was being *fired?*

Fuck him. Fuck him and his power plays and the Shambala Society, and whatever game this was to him and Georgio.

Hillary must have some redeeming qualities, because Winter was friends with Satan's spawn.

I would look into this later. I'd pour over legal textbooks and call my old business law professors and file a formal complaint with the labor board. Not because I wanted this godforsaken job back, but to irritate the ever-living fuck out of him.

Maybe I'd sue him and take one tiny portion of his millions, use it to buy a cabin in the woods and become a hermit with my now jobless life.

For now, I would call Winter and Shane, hoping one of them could blow off the day to spend it with me, getting drunk in celebration of my only career path being torpedoed with minimal options in this town.

Cheers to my new life.

"I'm quitting too." Winter's statement hung in the frigid air as she sat tightly wedged between Shane and me on the chairlift.

We could have taken the warm gondola to the top, but Shane had his sights on a double black diamond run on the other side of the mountain.

To help 'get my frustrations out.'

Winter had finished her final midterm this morning and Shane called in sick; he only had a week left of his co-op and since the flash drive unraveling, he'd called in sick every day after. The two of them convinced me to hit up the hill for a day of 'snow therapy.'

I could admit the sunny winter day and fresh powder were lifting my spirits.

"You need the money, Winter," I admonished, wrapping my arm tightly around her and pulling her closer. "I don't need you losing your income to stand up for me." I kissed the top of her helmet. "I appreciate the sentiment, though."

She lifted her rose-tinted goggles and peered into the blue tints of my own. "I've been thinking about that, actually." She drew in a breath of the icy chilled air and blew it out noisily. "I think I'm going to tap into my settlement money. I always said I wouldn't touch a cent, but now — now, I think I can put it to good use. Maybe that's a sign of working through trauma?"

She was trying to make a joke of it, but her voice didn't match the pain in her eyes.

Shane had wrapped his arm around her from the other side, pulling her in for a helmet kiss, too.

"What do you want to use the money for?" he asked gently, looking over at me with a bemused expression. This was news to him too, I guessed.

"A fresh start," she said matter-of-factly and her gaze fell toward the winding paths of the skiers below us. "It's not a small amount of money. Maybe we can figure out a Plan B. One that doesn't require us living in Cascade Falls. I don't think" — she swallowed hard and licked her wind-burnt lips — "I don't think I want to be here anymore."

As if it was an afterthought, she added, "I'll finish school. But then ..." She let the words trail off. "Would you come with me?"

"Yes," I answered, without hesitation, squeezing her shoulder in solidarity.

I was in, all in, with this woman. Where she went, I'd follow.

"Yes," Shane echoed, just as the lift reached the top of the hill, forcing us to end the conversation and get off before one of us got hit with the revolving bench.

We skied for the rest of the afternoon, ripping down runs with reckless abandon. The day was a reminder I hadn't had fun, real fun, in a long time.

"I'm blowing off Bourbon & Blues tonight too." Winter smiled breezily as we packed up our gear to go home. "I look deathly ill, don't you think? Why don't we go to Haven's Head for the evening? Some hot steamy water for those tired, sore muscles?" She sang the words and grinned, wriggling her eyebrows at me.

"Quick," she called to Shane, who was dusting off his board to put in the back of the truck. "Are you in? You guys can crash at my place tonight if you don't mind the couch."

"Drew shows up and now I get the couch, huh?" Shane lightly jabbed her in the ribs as he teased her, but his voice held an underlying layer of ... something.

"Well, if you guys weren't so damn *big*" — she winked at me suggestively and I smirked — "you could *both* fit in the bed with me. Too bad it's just a double. I'll buy a bigger bed when I tap into my hush money."

There was still a hesitancy in her voice, but it got stronger every time she said something related to her past. Opening up to us had given her the chance to let her hope out of Pandora's box.

I was proud of myself for my mental analogy. Usually, Travis was the eloquent one.

"Sure." I shrugged my shoulders, enjoying their company and not eager to get home, anyway. I wouldn't be having the 'I'm fired' conversation with my parents tonight.

We arrived 25 minutes later, taking advantage of their swimsuit and towel rentals.

I settled into the deep pool, relishing the soothing sounds of lapping water and swooshes of wind through the pine trees. Steam hovered over the water like thick mist in a horror movie, blocking out all sense of time and space. We could have been on another planet outside of this little bubble.

It was oddly calming.

Shane joined me first, sitting across from me in the deepest pool at the farthest end of the hot springs. I had only seen two shadowy figures whom I assumed were people on the other side of the spa, but there was no one else here.

A desolate, people-free, alien planet.

Winter joined us a few minutes later, wearing a deep blue one piece with a center cutout from between her breasts to her belly button. I wanted to kiss her body everywhere there was exposed skin and then strip the suit off her and lick her clean.

A public pool was probably the wrong time for a stiff cock.

I averted my eyes to coax my cock into shrinking, but a glance in Shane's direction was doing me no favors. I didn't know how to describe another man's body in a — *sexual* — way exactly, but the bronze skin and sculpted chest on display as he spread his arms wide across the slate tiles of the pool deck was very … appealing.

Winter sank into the corner next to me and let out a relaxed sigh. The minus-20 temperatures were counterbalanced with the 90 degree water, and the contrast from water to air was its own form of therapy.

"Ugh." Shane groaned and closed his eyes, sinking deeper into the water. "My shoulders are killing me. All this detective work is destroying my body."

"Who knew that the tech-y spies need the most massages?" Winter teased, flicking a droplet of water at him.

He sprung out of his position on the bench, his face lighting up like a Christmas tree. "Excellent idea, Snow. I volunteer you!"

He glided through the water toward us and turned around, giving Winter his back.

"Start with the left one, please. It's the worst."

"Since when do I give you massages?" She rolled her eyes at me, but dug her thumbs into the firm muscles beneath his shoulder blades. I had never noticed how smooth his skin was. Despite myself, I reached out to touch it; to touch *him.*

I rubbed my palm up one shoulder and across his arm, squeezing the muscles of his biceps, and then languidly repeated the motion.

He groaned into the night air, the sinful sound carrying across the water and lighting up my cock in ways it shouldn't.

It really shouldn't.

"Yes, please don't stop," Shane urged, moving his position from in front of Winter to in front of me. "You're better at this. Snow, take a break."

She snorted with amusement and cuffed his ear. I tucked myself back into the deep seat, spreading my legs wide so he could sit on the ledge in front of me. I worked my fingers through his tight knots. His proximity caused a fire in my belly that had nothing to do with the water surrounding me.

I was actually pretty decent at massages with my extensive high school sports experience; working out knots had been a necessity to play as much as I did.

I made a mental note to give Winter more of them.

Slow moans escaped Shane every time I worked out a tough knot, and the sound was forbidden music to my ears. And my dick, if the full-mast situation I was currently sporting, was any indication.

Fuck.

I took a few pained breaths and willed my body to calm down. I would *not* make a big deal about this. We were just two guys sharing a hot pool with my beautiful girlfriend. Nothing to see here.

Shane shifted in his seat and his ass rested solidly against my stainless-steel shaft. Not only had I been fired today, but now I was going to die of miserable embarrassment.

I was hard for my best friend in front of my girlfriend.

His body stiffened against me in what had to be realization. Instead of pulling away and shrinking against the other side of the pool, he leaned into me further, pressing his ass against the head of my cock pushing at the borrowed swim trunks.

Winter shifted beside me and turned her body to face ours. Her cheeks were flushed from the heat of the water as she watched us.

"I'm not going to lie, this is kind of hot," she said breathlessly, revealing wanton interest as her eyes never left mine.

"You like this, Snowflake? Two sexy, muscled men rubbing on each other like this?" Shane turned in his seat to taunt her, but when his gaze landed on mine, something unspoken passed between us.

Understanding, maybe? Approval? I couldn't put it into words, but I hoped my interpretation was right.

He pushed off the ledge with his feet and spun in the water, standing at his full height to face us.

"Do you give me permission to touch your boyfriend?" Shane smirked and winked at me like we were sharing some practiced joke. My heart galloped in my chest at the suggestion.

He couldn't be serious.

Winter bit her lip, her blue eyes darker and harder to read in this light. Her gaze roamed over me in assessment; I had no idea what she was seeing, but I hoped it wasn't the betrayal of my unbidden feelings for our best friend.

I loved her enough to leave everything I ever knew to follow her out of this place. Whatever I was feeling for Shane didn't take away from my feelings for her.

Satisfied by whatever it was she saw, Winter turned to Shane with a mocking head shake. A meaningful look passed between them; the language spoken only by people who had known each other for a long time.

"Does my boyfriend *want* to be touched by you is the better question, Quick. We believe in consent around here."

Shane's gray eyes landed on mine; tendrils of dark, damp hair had fallen out of his ponytail and he looked … hot.

He looked hot.

"Do you give me permission to touch you, Drew?"

All flirtation had left his voice, and it was the most serious tone I had ever heard him use. This wasn't a joke anymore. He had asked an honest question and was expecting an honest answer.

My eyes darted back to Winter's; I needed to see acceptance from her before I'd ever be willing to say the words out loud. I wasn't sure what admitting my desires would bring, but I wasn't willing to lose her.

I wasn't willing to lose Shane, either.

She smiled that beautiful Audrey Hepburn smile and gave me a slight shake of her head. "It's okay, Hardy Boy. If you want this, it won't hurt what we have."

I wasn't going to lose either of them. My body sagged with relief at the same time my cock soared to attention.

I licked my lips hesitantly and finally owned up to the truth in my head and my heart. "Yes."

Shane stepped closer, his body hovering over me with less than a foot between us. "Have you ever done this before?"

The question had been a whisper, like it was a secret only the three of us would ever share.

"No."

He took another step, and I felt his hands underneath the water, prying my legs apart so he could stand between them. I shuffled forward in my seat, bringing our bodies closer.

He searched my face one last time, cupping my cheek in his hand. "Any hard limits?"

"I don't know," I said honestly, my pulse now reaching near heart-combustion levels. "Show me."

I was expecting a kiss, his full lips just hovering above mine so closely I could smell the faint scent of the Juicy Fruit he had been chewing on the drive here.

I was not expecting his other hand to run down the length of my body underneath the water to palm my aching cock.

I gasped at the touch, his hands brushing against the nylon fabric to tease me as he tilted my head up to meet his lips.

They were surprisingly soft; pillowy and pliant. He was testing me, slowly persuading my lips to open by gently licking the seam and prodding through my defenses.

I had none, though. Shane was kissing me and I didn't want it to fucking end.

I opened up to him and kissed him back in the same way I would kiss Winter; giving as good as I got. I nipped and sucked, rubbing my stubble over his smooth face as he deepened the kiss further, capturing my breath and holding it hostage.

I reached up and grasped the back of his neck, pulling him closer to me. His fingers played with the waistline of my swim shorts.

I arched my hips upward, giving him better access while his tongue explored every part of my mouth. His calloused fingers followed my hairline beneath the fabric and onto—

Oh. Fuck. Me.

The heat of his hand covered my cock like a thick glove and he stroked me upward, rolling his palm over my head and stroking back down again, tightening at my base. When he repeated the motion over again and again, a groan I couldn't contain escaped from deep within my chest.

A familiar mewl of pleasure came from beside me. I broke off the never-ending kiss with Shane to see Winter's face contorted in ecstasy, eyes closed as she writhed against her hand beneath the water.

She was touching herself while watching Shane and I. I had never been watched before, but this was a new kink unlocked. Knowing she enjoyed watching … we'd be exploring that one later.

I knew that face well; she was close to coming, so I wouldn't interrupt her. I wanted to see her mouth fall slack and the pleasure in her smile.

I wanted to taste the cum on her fingers.

Shane kept his hand steady, not stopping even as his own gaze landed on Winter. His breath quickened, and it was enough to make me realize this 'threesome' might actually *become* a throuple.

He wasn't looking at her like she was his best friend.

He wanted to have her in his bed, too.

She cried out with her orgasm, her voice soft and discreet compared to her usual screams when I made her come.

It didn't matter; combined with Shane's hand stroking me with a move I'd have to learn later and the newly formed thoughts of me between them both, I was desperate for release.

I turned my head to stare into the steel-gray of Shane's eyes as I came, my entire body collapsing back against the stone seat of the hot spring.

He drew his hand up out of the water, a few remnants of my cum still coating his fingers. He held them at my mouth with a salacious grin.

"Open," he commanded. I complied, letting him massage the cum into my tongue before swallowing the salty flavor down.

As he finished himself off in front of me, his own groan filled the air, the masculine shudder one of the sexiest sounds I had ever heard.

We sat in silence together and came down from our high. Shane settled on my right and reached for my hand, squeezing it beneath the water. Winter cuddled into my left side, resting her head on my shoulder. We enjoyed the steam and the heat and blatantly disregarded having used a very public setting for a mutual masturbation session.

I had expected it to be awkward, but it wasn't. Sitting sandwiched between the two of them, their half-naked bodies wrapped around mine, felt as natural as breathing.

"Would you want to do that again?" Shane asked quietly before we made our way back to the central building to leave for the night.

"Yes," I answered resolutely. I couldn't regret what had just happened between us. It felt right, *he* had felt right, and my soul was lighter than it had been in a long time.

Today had sucked, but I was finally free from the diner and all of its baggage, once and for all.

Then Winter and Shane had just given me the freedom to explore something I could have only ever done within their love and safety.

Shane had found us some actual answers and Logan was using his evil powers for good so that we may all be able to move on with our lives.

Maybe there was some real hope on the horizon after all.

"Fuck, yes."

CHAPTER 34

LOGAN

Halle-fucking-lujah.

Quicksilver could never have fucking realized what a gold mine he'd handed to me when he dropped off the flash drive to my office earlier this week.

I had only had to put up with one meeting with the Dimwit Parade and I already had exactly what I so desperately needed to give M and his golden handcuffs the big 'fuck off'.

I had kicked my assistant Beth out of the office with a surprise 'employee appreciation' spa day. I could review the files in the privacy and comfort of my very secure office. I wasn't risking any spyware servers or internet trolling malware touching any portion of my 'get out of jail free' card.

If I was still using, I'd have snorted a delicious line of celebratory powder. Three calls to Hillary in the same span of hours had stopped that thought in its tracks, but the insatiable urge was so, so tempting.

Years and years of embezzlement in the millions. Huge numbers for any business, let alone one about to get into bed with the highest level of government for one of the largest projects in the world. Fuck gold mine. This was platinum to its core.

M had been pushing for an insider trading angle. I didn't have it. Eccles was probably putting their ducks in a line to do so when WAQ finally went public, but I couldn't prove anything on the front.

Maybe they could start doing their fucking jobs and prove it for me.

I wasn't worried. This was enough to prove years of highly illegal activity and incarcerate the fuck out of Daddy Darren and Emmett. With any luck, Camden and Stan-the-man Eccles too, if they could figure out the shell company connection with all of their tax-funded government resources.

If they could prove any connections with the Carlos Cartel? Bingo. Georgio would get what was coming to him and fucking rot in a prison cell until he experienced death by shanking.

A part of me, a micro part, felt something for Winter, knowing this information had the power to tear apart her family. I hated Stan, Hillary hated Camden, but Winter and Shane actually had a decent home life.

Well, maybe. I really knew nothing about their home life. And I didn't care. It was time for me to leave the drugs, the baggage, and the target M had painted on my back. I could move on by burying Carson in a sealed coffin with only an hour's worth of air to breathe.

I wasn't a murderer, but it might come to that. Carson Baker would not live to terrorize my princess again. I knew a group of men who would help me with the body.

I left the office with plenty of time to spare, eagerly anticipating my moment of fucking freedom. I drummed my fingers against the soft leather of my steering wheel, waiting for M to hurry the fuck up. I had been sitting in the Kirby Park parking lot for twenty minutes, my eyes on our usual meeting spot at the gazebo in the distance.

I snagged the pack of gum laying in the center console and popped out three pieces, chewing them aggressively to curb the hunger for stronger substances clawing at my insides.

It was my fourth pack in two days. I was going to need a different distraction for my cravings.

Finally, the large shadow of a man slowly moved towards the gazebo and sat on the bench on the other side of the pathway.

The snow was melting, the first signs of spring in early March. We could finally meet without me fully freezing my ass off.

I got out of my car, shoved my hands in my pockets to thumb the flash drive, my shiny golden ticket. I had made three copies and stashed them in various safes on my properties; I wasn't taking any chances. Shane was a wimpy puppy dog, but he was smart enough to make copies too, I was sure of it.

"You're late," I barked and sat beside him on the bench, struggling not to shiver in the chilly night air. "I'm getting married in two days, you know."

"Oh, I know." M's grin was all teeth and no sincerity. "We'll be watching that little charade. What do you have for me?"

"Found proof of embezzlement. Lots of it. Not directly tied to Georgio, but indirectly tied to his companies and projects he's been working on. But I need assurances before I hand it over."

"Oh?" M quirked a brow at me condescendingly. The smirk on his face riled me up to wanting to punch him in the kidney.

"Yeah, oh," I snapped, not in the mood for this cloak and dagger blackmailing bullshit anymore. "I need assurances that my record will be erased, my 'informant' status will be revoked, and I can walk away without any of this blowing up in my face. I've done everything you've asked, *M*," I spat his name into the snow beneath my feet. "This is it; I'm done with you."

"If the information you provide is what you say it is, then yes." M folded his arms and stared me down, his face unreadable. "I don't like you, Logan, but I'm not planning on fucking you over. If this gets me what I need to take down the bad guys, you'll be free. I'm not committing to anything until I see the information."

After a moment, M added, "Georgio is the man we want. So, unless this information leads to Georgio properly, there are no guarantees that this relationship is over."

"Do your fucking job then." I glared at him through the soft light of the street lamp a few feet away. I tossed the flash drive into the snow a few feet behind him and turned on my heel to walk back to my car.

"And don't call me anymore," I called back, trudging through the snow to take care of one last item on my list before I had to go through with our stupendously stupid spectacle of a wedding.

I shoved two more pieces of gum into my mouth before peeling out of the parking lot, no longer caring about discretion or the ridiculous nature of the secret spy life I had been living.

This was my new lease on life. Time to fucking live it.

Hillary was packing her bags when I got back to our condo, the Louis Vuitton hard cases strewn all over our bedroom.

"Are you moving out?" I mused as she carried armfuls of her wardrobe from our closet to the bed, parsing through dresses and stuffing them in garment bags.

Her wardrobe cost more than my car, and Stan-the-man made sure she spent more of it each month at his stores. The new level of wealth she was about to come into with the marriage to me was the fucking dream of all dreams I'd now never be a part of.

Yet, I couldn't hate her for it.

She looked up from her task, eyeing me discerningly. She did this every time she saw me, like she was searching my aura or something for signs of drugs in my system.

"Eventually," she said airily, "and I'll probably start living in the Carlisle condo next month. Right now" — she waved her hands over the mess around our room — "I'm choosing which clothes I'm going to give to Winter."

My eyebrows shot up. Their cozy little friendship was PornHub's wet dream, and it was weird to see Hillary with any real girl friends.

I reached over the bed and grabbed a sexy one-piece lacy negligee with the tags still on.

"This one." I tossed the outfit at her and she laughed out loud, catching it and gently placing it in the garment bag, along with a dozen other outfits.

"You've got some high hopes there, Eccles. She's got four boyfriends coming to our wedding."

"What the fuck? You invited *all* of them?"

The images of Winter wearing that sexy little number dissolved when it was replaced with one of the four other men from the Dimwit Squad standing beside her.

"Yup." She tossed her hair over her shoulder and giggled, a knowing look in her eyes. "That's some tough competition. Tone down the caveman and go for a more collaborative approach."

I scoffed, not at all interested in sharing my princess with anyone. There wasn't going to be a slumber party in my bedroom with four other men fucking her body raw.

She was going to be mine, and mine only.

"Nah, thanks," I responded casually, as if the thought of her beneath me in that white little number hadn't brought the blood to my raging dick. "I don't do sloppy seconds, or thirds, or whatever number she's on now."

Hillary stiffened, clenching her jaw as she turned toward me with fire in her eyes. The familiar face held far more anger than usual.

"Watch it, Logan," she snapped as she stalked toward me and waved a red-tipped finger in my face. "She's not a toy and she's not a whore. Don't you dare treat her that way. Stop being a dick and start coming to terms with your feelings, or you're going to lose all chance with her, and trust me, she's a far better woman than I am."

"I'm getting relationship advice from my wife now, am I?" I mocked, grabbing her finger and shoving it into her chest. "Is that what we are now? Each other's besties?"

"Don't pretend I mean nothing to you either, Loggie." Her words were soft and the steely resolve in her eyes had faded into her typical over-bearing confidence. "And I won't pretend you mean nothing to me."

She blew out a breath and wrapped her arms around me. I froze, the move surprising me out of my smugness. We weren't huggers.

She didn't relent, still fucking holding me after ten seconds of extremely awkward standing. I sighed and gave in, pulling her tighter into me and pressing my chin to the top of her head.

"I'm sorry we have to go through with this," she mumbled into my sweater. "Let's get through the next few days, and I'll buy you an island in Fiji as a wedding present, okay?"

"Sure, Hill. Buy me all of Stan's buildings while we're at it. I know you're good for it."

She laughed, leaning up to kiss my cheek before turning back to her task at hand.

I left the room to grab a drink of whiskey, then I remembered Hill had removed the alcohol from our house, every drop. I grimaced, not in the mood for a sparkling water to take the edge off my long day.

Three months; in three months, this fucking charade of a love fest would be over; we'd quietly divorce, get the legal stuff sorted, and move on with our lives. And maybe she would still buy me an island in Fiji.

CHAPTER 35

WINTER

I had never experienced this level of luxury in my entire life.

Hillary's wealth was of no consequence, something we all knew. But her event planning skills? The paltry gatherings I had attended in the past were nothing compared to the lavish setting we found ourselves in now.

Spruce Acres Mountain Lodge had been decked out in the most exorbitant display of opulence this town had ever seen.

I snuck a peek into the banquet hall on our way to the ceremony area. I couldn't help myself; I dragged Travis into the cavernous hall as Shane, Cam, and Drew grabbed our seats in the next room.

The view from here was gorgeous. Vast windows looked out onto the mountainside, and Hillary had timed the wedding to coincide with the sun setting behind the ski slopes.

Large round tables decked out in creams, golds, and champagne colors featured elaborate ice sculptured centerpieces in the shapes of blooming roses. The intricate details were stunning to the eye. When I peered closer, I realized flecks of gold glitter were embedded in each one, reflecting pockets of shimmering light around the room like a disco ball.

"Think there's real gold in there?" Travis mused, stroking a finger down the stem of one. His tone held a blend of awe and disgust.

I snorted, too taken by the elegance to hold any judgment. "I wouldn't put it past her."

Each place setting had a cream linen napkin, folded into the shape of another elaborate flower I couldn't name. A tag tucked into its petals and I plucked it from its fabric resting place, reading it aloud:

"Thank you for joining us on the happiest day of our lives. Please enjoy this token of our favor in memory of such a beautiful occasion.

All our love,

Logan and Hillary"

I laughed out loud, imagining Hillary dictating the sappy lies to the poor planner who had the misfortune of being hired for this wedding. I'd bet she was working very hard for her money.

The favor was an honest-to-God crystal champagne flute. If this was the kind of money she'd shell out for a fake wedding, I couldn't imagine what Hillary would do for a real one.

The conversation we'd had in the diner where she'd admitted to wanting a small ceremony on a beach somewhere came to mind, and my heart panged. Despite all appearances, this was the last thing she would have wanted, real wedding or not.

Still, if she had gotten her way, the small wedding would be in the Maldives on a sophisticated floating dock in the middle of the ocean with imported luxurious flowers, and the small number of guests would probably get an all-expenses paid trip as the favor.

Hillary just couldn't help herself. This was her world; we were just guests in it.

"Come on." Travis interlaced his hands with mine and guided me towards the door toward the ceremony. "We don't want to miss the party."

His tone held outright disgust now, and it took me by surprise. Of everyone, he was the most resistant to being here. As predicted, Drew was curious, Shane was beside himself, and Cam was indifferent, although he'd had a few choice words to say about Logan.

"It's egregious," he'd told me flatly when I'd asked him to go with me. "My mom could barely keep a roof over our head working two jobs, and I have to sit next to people who spend money on beluga sperm for face cream."

He was only here because I'd begged him to be, and despite his moral compass, he didn't want to be left home while the rest of us scoped out how the other half lived. I'd managed to sell him on the entertainment value, but it would not be enough to keep him here.

"Hey." I squeezed his hand and placed my hand on his chest, looking up into those mesmerizing green eyes. He was wearing little black plugs in his ears today, a black studded lip barbell, and he had styled his wavy dark hair over his eyes in tousled curls. The black suit jacket and purple dress shirt he wore were tailored to all the lean curves of muscle on his body, and he was panty-melting sexy.

He stared down at me, flickers of pain and dejection cycling through his face as he tried to mask it with his charming smile. I could see through that charm now; his layers unraveling like unspooled thread as he showed me the real man beneath his amiable exterior.

"I know this is hard for you. Thank you for being here for me."

My throat gulped back the forming saliva as I prepared myself to say the words I'd been holding on to for months.

"I hope you know this, but just in case you don't, I love you." His eyes widened, his mouth opening to speak, but I pressed a finger to his lips.

"I love the man you are, Travis. I love the man you are and who you'll become. You're not impressed by any of this." I waved my hand toward the ice sculpture with emphasis. "I love that about you. I love that you take care of those you love, and that you always persevere, no matter what life has handed to you."

Travis had spoken little about Georgio being his alleged uncle. He was still processing. Uncovering the information had brought back all his unresolved feelings of abandonment from his childhood. I wished I could take away that pain and insecurity, but he'd have to settle for being smothered by my love instead.

"You're resourceful, and kind, and you stay positive even when the world is crumbling around you. You see people for who they are, and you accept them for what they are. You see *me.* Who cares what these people have? We don't need it. I don't need it. But I do need you."

I reached up on my tiptoes to kiss him. It was intended to be a soft promise, but he'd lifted me in his arms and fiercely pressed his lips to mine, taking my air away as he pushed every emotion into my mouth. Pain, sadness, longing, elation, passion; love.

"I love you, beautiful," he whispered against my lips, continuing to kiss the shit out of me and causing sparkling stars to bloom behind my eyelids.

"This is why you're taking so long." A dry, familiar timbre resounded through the empty hall somewhere to my right.

Travis withdrew his lips from mine and softly lowered me to my feet. I turned to see Cam standing in the doorway, leaning coolly against the frame with a knowing smirk dancing across his sensual lips.

He too had worn a purple dress shirt, the color more of a plum than the eggplant Travis was wearing. Black dress pants stretched across his thick thighs, leaving nothing to the imagination.

Given what we had gotten up to a few days ago, I could attest what he was packing under there was sure to be a deadly weapon.

I couldn't wait to get my license for it.

"Sorry, got sidetracked!" I sang with a sunny smile on my face, the relief at letting those words out into the universe and Travis' reciprocation had put me on top of the world.

I took a hand from each of them and entwined our fingers, urging them down the hallway to find the other two men in our har—*group.*

The ceremony hall was enormous with another stunning view of the mountainside behind the elaborate champagne and white themed flower archway at the front of the room.

Fifteen rows of linen-covered chairs with ten seats on each side filled the space, each chair embellished with a golden ribbon and a single white rose blossom. Hillary had informed me that the final guest count was sitting at a paltry 321 guests.

Quick and Drew were sitting in one of the middle rows on the far right, and I made my way past the throngs of people I didn't know to sit with them.

My sneaky men were gossiping school girls in coordinated outfits; the two of them had also chosen purple dress shirts — *who knew they all had purple dress shirts?* — Drew's more of a lilac and Quick's was on the mauve side. Quick's hair was braided in a herring-bone pattern and Drew had trimmed his beard and gelled his hair. Two gorgeous specimens in a room full of toads.

My wet dreams had become a repetitive loop of the scene at the spa. Drew and Quick together had been one of the hottest moments I had ever seen, and I had once attended an orgy.

Hillary may get married today, but I was the luckiest person in the room.

I had taken Hillary's suggestion and worn the deep purple dress with the white trim sitting in the back of my closet. It had capped sleeves with a sweetheart neckline and landed mid-thigh, accentuating my curves in all the right places. She was going to gloat in satisfaction when she saw me.

We were a cluster of grapes in a sea of penguins.

My parents were seated alongside Emmett and Amelia Quicksilver, closer to the front of the room. I hadn't spoken to them since our awkward dinner party, and tonight wouldn't be the night to reconnect. I wasn't upset about the open marriage; I was upset about the hypocrisy. Mom had made it her personal crusade to drill sexual freedom and health into my brain from a very young age, yet my parents had hidden this very important piece of their relationship from me my entire life.

That, combined with the proof Dad was a straight-up white-collar criminal, meant I wouldn't be visiting my parents any time soon. I just hoped when it did eventually happen, it wouldn't be from outside of a prison cell.

It didn't look promising.

I sat next to Drew, Travis and Cam to my left. The room was buzzing from the din of the crowd as a few members of the media hung back at the rear of the room with Canon cameras to get the best shot of the bride.

A female Justice of the Peace stood statue still beneath the archway, holding a binder thicker than my business law textbook. Another person who'd probably earned every penny from this transaction.

A live four-piece orchestra played symphonic arrangements of popular pop songs in the background. Trust Hillary to turn Billy Eilish's "Bad Guy" into a quartet masterpiece. I snorted at the irony — I'd bet my bottom dollar every single song she'd chosen was foreshadowing her and Logan's inevitable split.

That girl was far more cunning than anyone gave her credit.

I continued to scan the crowd while my men chatted among themselves. The Governor sat at the front, and most local politicians, including Ralph Sutton, Sequoia County's Sheriff. Georgio sat next to Stanley, their heads bowed in whispered conversation.

How many people were crooks at this wedding? Was there a single innocent person left in our ersatz little town?

Logan entered the room from the other side just beyond the archway, and muttered something to the officiant. I wished I could say he looked like every other man to me, just a guy in a suit waiting for his bride, but I'd be lying to the world and to myself.

He was wearing a navy-blue suit with a champagne-colored tie and crisp white dress shirt; his short hair had been styled away from his face. Logan wore a suit almost every day, so today wasn't particularly special; maybe how I saw him in that suit was different.

Our dynamic had shifted; we weren't friends, but we no longer were enemies. We were in a relationship purgatory; I didn't want him in my inner circle, but I didn't want him outside it either. He had shown me a rare piece of himself, but I couldn't decide if he could be trusted. I also couldn't count on being able to stand his attitude for longer than twenty-minute bouts at a time.

Indeterminate. Another discussion for another day.

The music abruptly changed to a soulful, melancholy tune and one by one, each row stood, shifting their weight in unison to glimpse the bride. Hillary slowly glided down the aisle. The Atelier Versace champagne gown molded to her thin frame, her golden hair had been swept into a simple up-do and a crystal tiara was tucked into the crown. She was the most beautiful woman in the room, maybe in the world, and my chest split in two for my gorgeous friend. I hoped she'd get her dream wedding one day.

Camden Lane's beaming smile was stitched in place as he murmured greetings as they walked forward. I'd guess that Hillary's happiness had never been a priority.

It struck me that Hillary or Logan had no wedding party; no best man, no bridesmaids. Hillary had told me they didn't want to bring any more people into the nuptial ruse, but the more I got to know her, the more I realized neither of them *had* close friends. It would have been a lonely existence, locked in a loveless relationship without loyal friends to lean on for support.

My heart tingled with emotion as I thought of my relationship with Quick, and the love and support I'd always had, especially through the dreaded years when Carson's lies hung around me like a noose.

I reached my arm around Drew and closed my hand around Quick's, squeezing in gratitude for this saint of a man who'd always been my sword and shield. He quirked an eyebrow in question, but blew me a kiss with a small smile before turning back to watch the procession.

We sat down in our seats once Hillary had finally made it down the aisle to stand underneath the archway. Camden passed her hand to Logan's in the most archaic demonstration of marital ownership still allowed in our society and sat down.

As predicted, Hillary intentionally made the ceremony itinerary as ridiculous and drawn out as possible. I swallowed my smiles as guests started shifting uncomfortably in their seats, the droning of the fifth poem about the sanctity of love finally boring them into fidgeting submission.

Quick had lost that battle long ago; I had to give him a pen from my purse to twirl obnoxiously between his thumbs to keep me from hitting him every time he scraped his chair across the floor in antsy anticipation.

Finally, the bride and groom shared the briefest of kisses and the relieved officiant pronounced them husband and wife, but as Mrs. Hillary Lane and Mr. Logan Eccles. I couldn't help the wide grin that stretched across my face as she bucked the archaic tradition of losing her name. Girl power.

Everyone around us clapped with vigor as Hillary and Logan waved to the crowd, their false smiles firmly held in place by family expectations and a small country's GDP.

I moved to stand, eager to leave the hall before the crowd inevitably swarmed us, when the abrupt noise of marching boots on wooden floors overtook the din of excited chattering.

I craned my neck in its direction. A group of heavily armed officers in navy jackets emblazoned with FBI took up the back of the room, standing in formation to block the exit.

An officer in his late forties stepped out of the line, marching up to a now glowering Logan with determination and satisfaction on his face.

"What the fuck do you think you're doing?" was what I think Logan said — it was mostly just lipreading since he was out of earshot. I realized whoever it was, Logan was eyeing him with the venomous contempt of familiarity.

Logan knew this man.

The officer raised his voice and spoke to the crowd more than he spoke to him. This was a display of power, and for whatever reason, he was intentionally making a spectacle.

"Logan Eccles, you're under arrest for suspected bribery of an elected official. You can come with me quietly, or I can have Officer Burnheart here," he pointed at another officer with a shaved head behind him, "can take you out in handcuffs."

I pulled my attention from the riveting and very confusing scene when an officer with blonde hair tightly held in a high ponytail and a stern face marched toward our side of the room.

My stomach seized into my throat. There was no way this was a coincidence; we were all about to get arrested for the information we'd found. Someone was on to us and —

"Winter Wallace?" the woman snapped, her voice harsh and no-nonsense. The people surrounding us had gone deathly still and just as quiet, eagerly watching the drama unfolding before their very eyes. The Cascade Falls rumor mill would churn out lumber lies in spades tomorrow.

I gasped in shock; my jumbled thoughts had expected a group arrest for our part in Georgio's empire and the illegal hacking, but I never expected to be singled out. What could they could single me out for? My body shook in panic as the icy fingers of fear wrapped around my throat, choking me into stoic silence.

I heard shouts behind me, but nothing registered as I stared into the hard green eyes of my captor.

"You're under arrest for the suspected solicitation of a minor and prostitution offenses."

That snapped my men out of their stupor.

"The fuck?" Shane roared, grabbing for me as the woman pulled my hands behind my back and cuffed them into place.

Prostitution? This had to be some kind of sick joke played by a vengeful man who hated women with sexual autonomy. Was this Carson? Some Gertrude in our tiny town who thought a woman with two boyfriends was surely a harlot?

My mind had finally snapped; none of this was real. It couldn't be real.

The bite of the cold metal trapping my wrists had nothing on the bitter cold now frosting over my insides.

The shouts from my men faded out of existence and panic overtook me. The world around me only muffled sounds as my pounding pulse filled my ears as I gasped for oxygen to breathe.

My body went limp, the terror pushing my body into my usual form of survival—to freeze.

The irony of Winter freezing was the last thought that floated through my mind before the rest of the world went dark.

CHAPTER 36

LOGAN

If looks could murder a man, I was going to fucking murder M.

After I murdered Carson.

No, before I murdered Carson, after Hillary paid my bail and I got out of this fucking place. The fucking nerve of this fucking federal asshole.

They escorted me out of my wedding like a fucking criminal and into the waiting FBI van. Winter had been carried out by two officers and laid on her side in the back of the van beside me.

Arresting a woman who wasn't coherent and placing her in police custody when she wasn't even conscious? This was more fucking illegal than anything we had ever done.

This whole scenario stunk of jail bait. M was using us for something. It was the only logical explanation. Winter as a prostitute? It would be fucking hilarious to consider if she wasn't laying at my feet in the fetal position, still unconscious.

I did a visual assessment for the hundredth time that hour. They had transported us to a nondescript gray building in the middle of nowhere, the inside lined with barred cells. Luckily, they put us in one together.

Unluckily, the officer was smart enough to cuff me to the wall.

Winter was still breathing, but her breaths were short and shallow and a light sheen of sweat coated her pale face. Her lips were a light purple, likely a result of her panic attack.

I knew all about panic attacks.

I needed to hold her in my arms and check her pulse; at least do fucking something to confirm she was fully functional. She looked worse than she had when she'd spent the night in my condo sleeping off Carson's drugs.

I didn't know how I was going to fucking do it yet, but I would kill both men who hurt my princess.

My charges were a crock of absolute shit. Bribery of an elected official was impossible, because it had never fucking happened. I had career-destroying dirt on many people in our town, but I had never taken the risk at the government level. I knew corrupt federal agents manufactured evidence all the time if it suited them, but there would be nothing legitimate to support that claim because it didn't exist.

My only actual crime had ever been drug possession, because somehow in this fucked up country, it was illegal to be an addict. Another genetic legacy Stan-the-Man Eccles had fucking left me.

Winter stirred and let out a gurgled moan, the sound stirring a monster beneath the surface of my skin.

She shot up to seated, her hands still handcuffed behind her back and her head spun around in panic. A fury boiled over in me to see her this scared.

Footsteps echoed down the concrete corridor, and I waited in eager anticipation to blast the fuck out of M, the most useless fuckface in the FBI.

"Welcome, Logan! It's great to see you, *friend*."

M's fucking cheery tone was going to get him killed even faster. I'd savor the moment the fucker died in a matching coffin in the same graveyard I would bury Carson.

He used a passcode to open the cell door and strolled in like we were about to have lunch in a fucking café.

"And welcome, Winter! It's time you and I got to know each other."

Winter shuffled her body on the floor, facing towards me. Her confusion turned to clarity as she pieced together what I'd been up to.

"You're an informant?"

"Sure is," M responded, his cheeriness melding into fucking childish glee as he continued his little power trip. "And when we got an anonymous tip from someone in the public reporting you, Winter, it was the perfect opportunity to push Darren Wallace into some challenging decisions. We've been trying to turn him for months."

The Feds were pressuring Darren to turn on Georgio and crew? How many layers of informants did the FBI have on this fucking operation? And how fucking clueless were they to not have this wrapped up with a bow by now?

Realization dawned on me.

"So, she's actually not under arrest?"

M continued to speak to Winter.

"You, my dear, were the perfect bait. I'm sorry to do that to you, I am, but it had to be in a public setting to push Darren over the edge. The Eccles highly publicized wedding was the perfect place to do it."

Winter snapped out of her fugue state as rage blazed in her eyes.

That's my girl.

"So, my reputation is just a casualty in this little game you're playing, is it? Prostitution, of all fucking things?"

"That was actually the charge you were reported on, so that wasn't a lie."

Her brows knit in confusion, and I was at a loss myself. Who the fuck would report Winter for prostitution?

M clapped his hands together, as if he was a schoolteacher addressing the fucking classroom. "Anyway, we've got lots to discuss, and I have someone I need to introduce you to."

A familiar face I hadn't seen in years walked toward us from the end of the hall. Built like a Viking with a beard to match, the last time I had seen him in Cascade Falls he'd been leading a beautiful woman at Après to his room, about to get his rocks off.

"Hi, little songbird." The brute form of Kellan fucking Carlos, Georgio's half brother and supposed Columbian Commando of the Carlos Cartel, entered the small cell.

Winter choked in disbelief, left completely speechless at the sight of her old lover.

"Welcome to our little operation."

How did Winter meet Kellan Carlos? Check out Winter's Song, Cascade of Lies Book 0.5 for a short snippet and a steamy chance encounter.

Thirsty for more Cascade Falls? Of course, you are! Winter's End, Book 3, is available for pre-order! Get your copy today!

About the author

One day, Cora Flynn decided to sit down and write a book – for funzies.

What started as a fun project on maternity leave became an entirely new adventure between the pages of her created worlds; complete with characters who've become her best friends, an abundance of book boyfriends, beautiful bromances, and story plots that keep her up at night.

When she's not writing, Cora attempts to manage the chaos of a two-toddler household with her extremely patient husband, while maintaining a job in the 'real world.' She loves reading as many books as she can fit on her Kindle, her bookshelves, and her nightstand, and doesn't discriminate against any genre, although reverse harem will always be her favorite.

Come on and join the fun on Instagram and TikTok by following @coraflynnauthor.